Outgunned

Masi looked straight ahead again, and while he still saw the group of children, something was now blocking his path to them, something that had rumbled out of the thick brush on the edge of the village.

It was a tank.

A very large tank.

With a very large gun that was pointing directly at him.

Masi saw the next few things all at the same time. The huddled children were now pointing at him and laughing. A man in the turret of the tank was looking at him too, through the goggles of his overly large battle helmet. Masi also saw a shell explode out of the tank's gun barrel and head right for him.

It didn't make sense—who would have the guts to fight them like this? But Masi could think no more about it.

The tank shell hit him a split second later. He saw only a stream of fire, then a bright flash—and then nothing but black.

Other Books by Mack Maloney

Strikemasters Series
Strikemasters
Rogue War
Fulcrum

Starhawk Series
Starhawk
Planet America
The Fourth Empire
Battle at Zero Point
Storm Over Saturn

Chopper Ops Series
Chopper Ops
Zero Red
Shuttle Down

**For more exciting
E-Books, Audiobooks and MP3 downloads visit us at
www.speakingvolumes.us**

ROGUE WAR

A STRIKEMASTERS NOVEL

SPEAKING VOLUMES, LLC
NAPLES, FLORIDA
2014

Rogue War

ISBN 978-1-62815-115-2

ROGUE WAR

MACK MALONEY

PART ONE

THE GHOST
SOLDIERS

CHAPTER ONE

THE women of the village of Aylala began crying as soon as the sun started going down.

They knew they'd all be dead by the time it came up again. Before that they would be raped. They would see their daughters raped. They would see their sons hanged and disemboweled. They would see their husbands and fathers have their skulls crushed with sledgehammers. Their ancestral village would be burned, the food they'd worked so hard to harvest would be stolen, and then their throats would be slit and their lives would finally come to an end.

Such was Darfur. Life, death in western Sudan.

The women knew all this was coming because their village had been surrounded by the notorious Janjaweed militia since early afternoon. The women could see the militia's Range Rovers and technicals dotting the crests of the shallow hills that ringed the village. They could see the Janjaweed soldiers smoking hashish, chewing qat, drinking antifreeze and working themselves into a frenzy as a prelude to their attack.

This was not a battle awaiting them. The villagers didn't have any weapons, or anyone to defend them. Not their own government, or the United Nations, or the superpowers. They were lambs, just waiting for the slaughter. Innocent but doomed.

The sun was dipping faster than usual; the sky had turned a deep bloodred. The villagers didn't understand why they were about to be massacred; they knew nothing of the politics of the thing. Or of the oil that might or might not be under their family ground, or of the people half a world away in China who wanted that oil to enrich themselves. The villagers only knew that nothing—no man or god—could save them now.

As soon as the last of the sun went away, they could hear the militia starting their vehicles. Hoots and screams rained down from the hills; the intoxicated soldiers were peaking on the stimulants they'd been ingesting all afternoon. A few started firing their weapons in the air; some of the bullets came down on the village's huts, a prelude of what was to come.

The women had stopped wailing by now. In a disturbing act of surrender, they separated their children, boys from girls, oldest from youngest, simply to allow the militia to distinguish whom to kill first, to rape first, just so the horror would go quicker. The engines up on the hill began revving faster. The sun was gone, the stars were coming out. The long, last night for the village of Aylala had begun.

THE militia approached from three sides: north, east and south. They numbered 550—there were 1,200 people in the village. Each militia member was armed with a QBZ-95 Chinese-made assault rifle, complete with a razor-sharp bayonet, and at least a couple fragmentation grenades.

This would be the sixteenth village this particular militia had attacked in the past month, and their overall commander had complained that in the previous massacres, the militia had wasted too many bullets on their innocent victims. Thus the bayonets and frag grenades. The sharp ends of their assault rifles could accomplish the same result as bullets but with less expense. And if as many as a couple dozen people could be squeezed into a hut, one frag grenade tossed in would kill them all.

The militiamen drove slowly toward the village at first, beeping their horns, yelping and hooting to further terrify their victims. The smallest group, consisting of ten pickup trucks and Range Rovers, was approaching from the east. The attack plan called for this group to come up on the backside of the village and prevent anyone from escaping.

Their pickup trucks were outfitted with machine guns— "technicals" they were called in this part of the world. Several of the Range Rovers also had machine guns mounted on their roofs. All of the vehicles had open backs and were carrying up to a dozen militia members each. Even now, just moments before the attack, the militiamen were passing around bottles of moon juice, the lethal combination of fermented dates and antifreeze. Some of the fighters were so excited at the prospect of bloodletting they were drooling. Others were sexually aroused.

This small group was about five hundred feet from the village now, traveling a bit faster than the rest of the units. They could see people running in terror inside the village, could hear their cries, their desperate prayers for mercy. This only excited the attackers further.

The man driving the lead vehicle was the field commander of this small band; his name was Ulu Masi. He pressed down on the accelerator, as he wanted to be among the first entering the village to bayonet someone—hopefully a child. That way he knew his night would be off to a good start.

A race of sorts began with the Range Rover traveling next to him. Masi laughed and accelerated even faster. The truck beside him did as well. In seconds they were traveling at very high speed across the flat, dry desert, a contest to get to the killing ground first.

Masi looked into the village again, spotting a group of children huddled near a tree on the edge of the settlement. They were watching with terror in their eyes as the trucks approached. Masi licked his lips—this was perfect for him. His first targets. It made him want to go faster, so he pushed the gas pedal to the floor then looked over at his competition and laughed wildly. The man riding in the other vehicle's passenger seat laughed back at him—and then, suddenly, was gone in a flash.

Masi thought he was hallucinating—moon juice could do that. He blinked and looked again—but yes, the truck beside him had vanished in a puff of smoke.

He heard a man on the back of his own truck cry out. Masi then looked at the man riding in his own passenger seat and saw that this man's head was gone. No noise, no flash. He was simply headless.

Masi looked straight ahead again, and while he still saw the group of children, something was now blocking his path to them, something that had rumbled out of the thick brush on the edge of the village.

It was a tank.

A very large tank.

With a very large gun that was pointing directly at him.

Masi saw the next few things all at the same time. The huddled children were now pointing at him and laughing. A man in the turret of the tank was looking at him too, through the goggles of his overly large battle helmet. Masi also saw a shell explode out of the tank's gun barrel and head right for him.

It didn't make sense—who would have the guts to fight them like this? But Masi could think no more about it.

The tank shell hit him a split second later. He saw only

a stream of fire, then a bright flash—and then nothing but black.

THE gang of militiamen attacking from the north saw the flashes off to their left—but they assumed they were vehicles in the eastern group colliding with each other. Everyone was highly intoxicated, and in previous actions, during the rush to begin the slaughter, vehicle collisions were not uncommon.

But then the northern group saw more flashes, off to their right. And then even more in front of them.

The commander of this larger force, a man named Sombu, was riding in the vanguard. He began screaming as soon as he saw the blasts going off nearby, but no one could hear him. Sombu reached over and forced the man driving his Range Rover to stop. The man hit the brakes; there was a screech of tires on the dry desert floor. The truck traveling behind them plowed into their rear end. In seconds, all of Sombu's vehicles came to a squealing halt.

There was an eerie quiet for about five seconds. Then suddenly dozens of explosions began going off around the stalled column. Their trucks were disappearing in a string of violent flashes.

The militiamen panicked. Who was shooting at them? In five years of terrorizing this part of the Sudan, no one had so much as lifted a finger to stop them, or try to protect the innocent people they were preying on.

So—what was happening here?

Sombu stuck his head up through his truck's roof and looked above him. What he saw looked like something from a nightmare: Long streams of bright white light, surrounded by fire and smoke, were coming out of the clear night sky.

This didn't make sense—hell itself was falling on them,

but the monsoon of flame was coming from nothing. Sombu could still see the stars, bright and sparkling. There were no clouds, no light reflecting from anywhere else. And certainly no aircraft were above them. Were these streams of fire coming from outer space?

As with his colleague, that was the last thought Sombu ever had.

The storm of fire swept across his stalled unit like a wave hitting the beach. It lasted just a few seconds—and then it was gone, leaving nothing but burning wreckage and bodies in its wake. The third Janjaweed force, the one coming up from the south, actually reached the outskirts of the village. They'd seen all the fire and the flashes, but were so high and so excited about what was to come, they couldn't give anything else much thought.

They dismounted their trucks and approached the hamlet to find villagers standing in their doorways looking back at them somewhat curiously. Some were smiling. Some were even waving.

This was strange.

Where was the terror? The screaming? The panic?

Twenty of the militiamen walked into the village itself, on guard because nothing was happening like it was supposed to.

That's when the ghost soldiers appeared.

They were floating down from the clear night sky, coming from nowhere as no airplanes could be seen over the village. They landed on their feet, heavily armed, wearing dark camo uniforms, their faces painted black, their helmets oversized and opaque. It was as if they were jumping down from the stars.

The militiamen never had a chance. Some started laying down their weapons, hoping for a small act of mercy, but none was coming. When one foolishly pointed his weapon toward one of the ghostly soldiers, a chorus of return fire opened up.

It was bloody and gut-wrenching, with pieces of bodies flying everywhere. Few militiamen stood and fought—they were mowed down immediately. Many ran—and the ghostly soldiers followed. Some attackers tried to get back in their vehicles to escape, but the ghosts blew up the trucks before the gang members could flee in them. Other militiamen ran off into the night. Again the phantoms coolly pursued them. Each one was caught and shot in the head twice. It took less than five minutes to kill them all.

Then suddenly, everything was quiet again. The carnage around the village was great—and yet none of the people in Aylala could understand exactly what had happened.

But one thing was for sure. Because of these ethereal soldiers, the Janjaweed militia would never bother their village again.

WATCHING all this from a hill to the north were two men in plain desert military camos.

They were agents of a Sudanese Special Forces unit known as SID, for Second Intelligence Department. Any dirty work the central government needed done, SID was usually the group called on to do it. Their job here in Darfur was helping local warlords drive the indigenous people off their land so the oil below could be pumped out and sent to China. The two agents served as advisors to the Janjaweed militia, guiding them on their genocidal rampage, keeping them supplied with weapons and ammunition and filling their leaders' pockets with money.

The agents were in total shock. Try as they might, they couldn't fathom what they'd just seen. One moment, the attack on the village had all the makings of a routine massacre; the next, their protégés were little more than either clouds of smoky ash blowing in the desert wind or a hyena's next meal. They'd seen what might have been a tank—but did not see where it came from. They'd seen a group of

shadowy soldiers too, but again, it was as if they were spec-
ters, materializing out of nowhere.

But it was the rain of fire that baffled them most. Even
as it was coming down—the flames, the explosions everywhere—the SID agents saw nothing but a typical bright
starry African night sky. There was no sound above them,
as an attacking aircraft would make. No silhouettes of war-
planes going over. No exhaust trails. Nothing.

The two agents were wired on qat as well, and this whole
thing was threatening to short-circuit their brains. There
had been rumors in the past month or so of militia gangs in
other parts of the Darfur region going out on raids and
never returning. Of their forward camps being found empty,
with just a few scattered bones about and nothing else. But
no one believed these stories were true, only because this
region was so isolated and the people here so superstitious
that at any given time there might be a half dozen or so
ghost stories making the rounds—something that had been
happening here for hundreds if not thousands of years.

But now—the two SID agents had seen it for real. The
entire Janjaweed gang wiped out by some mysterious phantom force.

They had to leave the area immediately and report what
had happened to their superiors—and hope they would not
be shot for delivering such bizarre bad news.

As soon as they could command their legs to move
again, they rushed back to their vehicle—a highly camouflaged Range Rover—intent on heading north at top speed.
That's when both men noticed another vehicle sitting atop
the next hill over. It was a plain white SUV, with a red cross
painted on the driver's side door. But it did not look like a
typical relief vehicle. It was festooned with antennas and
they thought they could see a weapon of some sort hiding
below its roof rack.

There was a lone man standing next to the vehicle; he
too was looking at the smoldering desert plain below, using

a gigantic pair of binoculars. The agents couldn't see his face or features, but he seemed strangely out of place. Too well dressed. Too well groomed. Something was odd about him. And he was definitely not an African.

When the man turned toward them, the agents felt a chill run down their spines. Suddenly both felt more afraid now than just moments before when they'd seen the rain of destruction come out of nowhere.

They quickly retreated to their vehicle, started the engine and prepared to speed away. That's when one looked over his shoulder at the man on the other hill—only to see the hillcrest was empty.

The mystery man had disappeared.

THE outpost of Kahlia Point consisted of a few huts, a dozen prefab buildings, a large satellite antenna and a helipad.

On the face of it, it looked no different from the dozens of other oil exploration research facilities found in this part of Africa.

Under normal conditions, the people stationed here would spend their days combing the desert in search of new wells to tap. Their buildings would be full of lab equipment, set up to determine the oil content of core samples taken from the ground beneath the burning sands. If substantial oil deposits were found, within a year, the pristine desert would become home to a small city of workers, derricks and pumps.

But while that invasion might still come to Kahlia Point, the "research facility" here was more about moving the population off the oil rich lands than actually digging for crude. This place was a covert supply station for the armed militias who'd been decimating the local tribes for the past few years. There was a substantial armory hidden here, as well as an ammo dump and refueling facilities. Though ostensibly operated by CNPC, the Chinese state-owned oil company, in actuality, Kahlia Point was run by SID.

Of the fifty Sudanese nationals who worked here, more than half were SID agents. They interfaced with the local militia gangs, supplied them with guns and money, and then let them loose in the desert to do their thing: get rid of the area's scattered population before the drilling began. By rights, these people should have been given a share if oil was found on their ancestral land. But what the government of the Sudan was doing here had nothing to do with being "right."

At any given time, more than half the SID agents were out in the field liaising with the militia gangs. This night, though, all were accounted for except two. They'd accompanied the Janjaweed gang on its latest attack, but nothing had been heard from the militia nor the two SID agents since sunset, when the assault on Aylala, fifty miles away, was supposed to commence. This was somewhat out of character for the SID agents, who usually kept in close contact with their base during any kind of operation.

Their colleagues' fears were allayed somewhat when they finally spotted the heavily camouflaged Range Rover carrying the two wayward agents heading down the dusty, straight-as-an-arrow road leading to Kahlia. The Range Rover was traveling at high speed, a bit odd as it was dark and its headlights were only partially illuminated. Once it was within five hundred yards of the outpost, the SID agents assigned to watch the gate along with two Sudanese Army soldiers gave the troops the OK to lift the barricade and allow the vehicle to pass through.

But the Range Rover never slowed down; by the time the soldiers reached the barrier, the speeding vehicle was so close, they had to jump away for fear of their lives.

The truck hit the barrier, splintering it to pieces, and kept right on going. Through the gate, it sideswiped another Range Rover parked close by, roared into the outpost, smashed into the well, ricocheted off another car, collided with a fuel truck and bounced off it, before finally smashing into the stone wall at the far end of the compound.

Soldiers and SID agents rushed to the wreck, where they made a grisly discovery. Both men inside were dead—but not from the crash. Rather, both had taken a bullet right between the eyes. Then they had been propped up in the front seat of the truck, its steering wheel tied in such a way that it would drive only straight. A boulder on the gas pedal completed the gruesome arrangement.

Most bizarre, though, were the signs placed around the necks of the two agents. Both were hastily written in the local dialect. Both read: *Dawali wekok* . . .

Loosely translated: "You're next."

Not a second later, there was a huge explosion right over the center of the compound. An airburst bomb had detonated in the worst place possible. It rained thousands of pieces of razor-sharp metal on all those below. A dozen people vanished in a bloody mist. At this, those Sudanese soldiers that survived vanished into the night. There were twenty of them, and they took off in all directions, out the front gate, the back gate, over the walls of the compound. Gone . . .

The SID agents had no such option. Where could they go? They didn't even know what was happening. More explosions were going off now—some in the air, some hitting important facilities around the base.

The water-pump shack went first. Then the power house, then the communications antenna, then the helipad. Then the barracks, the sewage pump, and the canteen.

The SID agents panicked. Some had sidearms, a few had AK-47s. But none of them were experts in firing such weapons. And who would they shoot at? The sky above them was clear and full of billions of stars. But they began blasting away nevertheless, all while seeking cover from this madness.

But then the ghostly barrage began systematically leveling any building the SID agents sought cover in. The agents were left scattering from one pile of rubble to the other, and each time there were fewer and fewer of them.

Finally, there was only one building left to hide in: the compound's ammunition bunker. Only a handful of SID agents were still alive, and they knew seeking shelter in the ammo magazine was suicide, but they had no choice. In a matter of seconds the research station had been reduced to a massive pile of burning junk. There was nowhere else to hide.

So the five men dashed into the ammo bunker—it was hit at almost the exact same time by the mysterious fire. Its six-inch-thick cement walls were obliterated, and an instant later, all the ammo inside blew up. The massive explosion rocked the desert for miles around, its monstrous mushroom cloud rising and disappearing into the night.

Once it was gone, all that remained was the sound of crackling flames and a column of belching smoke, drifting toward the stars.

Khartoum
Capital of Sudan

Mustafa Ziom was the leader of the Janjaweed militia.

He had under his command nearly two thousand desert fighters, most of whom were psychotic criminals and drug addicts with little or no formal military training.

But training wasn't needed in their line of work. All Ziom's militiamen had to know was how to shoot a gun and how to rape, pillage and kill. That was their order of battle. And they'd been highly successful at it for years. With no outside interference from any of the international powers, Ziom's men had run the desert sands red with innocent blood, all in the effort to clear the oil-rich wasteland of southern Sudan so petroleum marketeers and oil rigs could take over, making Ziom rich in the process.

Ziom himself was not a soldier—he hated the desert. Middle-aged, overweight and prone to rashes, he ran his army of psychos from an obscenely large penthouse in downtown Khartoum. Located atop the tallest building in the city, it was also the most expensive and luxurious, befitting Ziom as Khartoum's richest citizen. His building towered thirty-two stories over the shacks and slums on the south side of the ancient capital, overlooking the Ban River. On a clear day from his balcony window, Ziom could see the desert that had become the playground of his roving armed bands and had brought him so much wealth.

Ziom was hosting a cocktail party tonight. Two hundred guests were jammed into his place, drinking French wine, eating shrimp nuts from Jakarta and listening to trashy Euro-disco music. The guests were mostly low-level diplomats from low-level countries; the Syrians, of course, and the Pakis and the Iranians. Two North Koreans were stealing food. The Indonesian delegation was wondering when the call girls would arrive. About a dozen guests were Chinese.

Ziom was in the kitchen beating one of his Filipino maids with a spoon for not bringing out food quick enough when he heard a commotion in the main living room.

He took one more swipe at the help and then returned to the party, where he was startled to see a dozen soldiers in combat uniforms, their faces covered, standing near the buffet table.

They looked like they were from another planet—black combat suits, huge, oversized Fritz helmets, night-scope monocles, their belts weighed down with all kinds of equipment, with bandolier ammunition belts crisscrossing their chests and black ski masks hiding their features. They were standing around so casually, at first Ziom thought it was some kind of joke.

They saw him at approximately the same time he saw them. And suddenly they were not so casual. He knew at that point, this was no joke.

Suddenly Ziom was looking at a dozen gun barrels. At the same time he saw more of these soldiers on his balcony, appearing as if from nowhere. Where the hell are they coming from? he found himself thinking.

Ziom looked toward the front door of his penthouse, where two uniformed security men were always stationed—but they were nowhere to be seen. He looked into the crowd for his two plainclothes bodyguards. But they too had disappeared.

Finally he looked at the highest ranking of his Chinese guests—the man was looking back at him with an expression equal parts bafflement and horror. This just seemed too unbelievable: These otherworldly soldiers were crashing his party.

One soldier turned his gun toward the CD player and squeezed off three quick rounds. The stereo exploded in a spray of sparks and smoke; that was the end of the crappy disco music. Some guests were so startled by this, they dropped their cocktails, cheap German glassware smashing on the fake wooden floor. The soldiers began slowly encircling the guests, herding them in the largest part of the living room. Some of the Chinese were so frightened, they already had their hands over their heads, as if in surrender.

Still the mysterious soldiers had not said a word. Two went into the kitchen and let the indentured help go free. Others went through the crowd, pulling aside the women guests and frisking them for weapons. Then they too were allowed to leave.

This left only the male guests—and Ziom. The soldiers searched them all for weapons and cell phones. Anything found was broken in half and tossed off the thirty-second floor.

Then a small, ratish-looking man appeared out of the forest of soldiers. He was wearing the same kind of uniform as the others but did not have a helmet and was not armed, at least not with any weapon that could be seen.

He walked up to Ziom—an extremely rotund man—and stared him right in the eyes.

"I demand to know who you are . . ." Ziom began sputtering.

"My name is Lieutenant Moon," the diminutive man replied. "Sorry I didn't RSVP . . ."

With that, he delivered a massive punch to Ziom's temple. Ziom went down like a ton of bricks.

The guests stirred, but all the soldiers had to do was rustle their weapons and they fell back into their terrified, confused silence. Suddenly the small man was right in Ziom's face.

He was holding a package of photos. They depicted genocide victims of Darfur's violence. Dead bodies. Men, women, children. Entire families murdered. He was putting the pictures up to Ziom's eyes, forcing the gasping man to look at them.

"Do you recognize these people?" the man was hissing at him. "Do you know these kids? These babies? These women?"

Ziom was fighting for air, while weakly trying to push the man away. But he couldn't; he was too scared.

The soldiers continued to tighten the ring around the frightened party guests as more horrible photos were flashed in front of Ziom's eyes, each one coming with a slap to his face. Ziom was soon crying uncontrollably.

While this was happening, six of the soldiers broke off from the rest and went into Ziom's private quarters adjacent to the living room. They soon reappeared carrying boxes full of maps, data discs and weapons catalogs, all of which were written in Chinese with crude French translations in the margins. It was obvious from these translations that Ziom and his cohorts were working on even bigger plans to bring more weapons into the unstable region of north-central Africa and that those weapons purchases, paid for by China, shipped in by the North Koreans, were tied to securing the oil deposits indicated on the maps. It took only a few moments to put it all together.

Leaving Ziom to whimper on the floor, the man named Moon sought out the senior Chinese official at the party. He pushed the evidence into this man's face, especially the weapons catalogs. The Chinese man went pale. Moon nodded to the soldiers; they dragged the man out onto the balcony. To his horror they forced him over the railing and held him by his feet, thirty-two stories high, until he passed out from sheer fright.

Pulling him back from the brink, the soldiers then took the Chinese official's clothes off and threw them off the balcony, leaving him unconscious and naked on the porch.

The rest of the guests were on the verge of panic now, thinking they were about to receive the same treatment—or worse. So it was with some surprise that they responded to the soldiers, who started pushing them out the front door of the penthouse, essentially letting them go. Those who caught on quickly began running for the stairways, wanting to put as much distance between themselves and the crazy soldiers as they could.

Only Ziom remained. He was still flat on his back on the floor, his face red from being slapped, his eyes still watery from fear. He watched as the soldiers began wiring his penthouse with explosives.

Finally he blurted out a few words. He was trying to say something in English, but it was tinged with a heavy French accent.

"If you're going to blast this place and kill me anyway, why did you come here and announce it?"

"Because we're going to rob you first," the strange little man told him.

At that point, a wide-scale search of the entire penthouse began. It took another ten minutes, but the soldiers were able to uncover a strongbox containing a hundred thousand dollars in cash and a fistful of gold ingots.

Now the soldiers picked Ziom up off the floor and brought him to the balcony. When they kicked the unconscious Chinese official aside, Ziom was certain the soldiers were going to hurl him to his death.

But it wouldn't be that easy.

He suddenly noticed that a tiny helicopter was hovering nearby. It was not making any noise and looked like a giant, overgrown, angry bug. One man was flying it; another, holding a huge combat weapon, was strapped into the passenger seat.

Ziom hated flying, but he would have no choice in the matter. He was handcuffed, his feet were tied, and when the tiny chopper came very close to the balcony, the soldiers hoisted him up and strapped him to the aircraft's outside cargo rack. The strongbox full of cash was also loaded aboard. The copter dipped precariously from this added weight, but the pilot increased power to his hover and finally Ziom and the box were secured. Then the pilot cleared the building and started moving toward the south. In less than a minute, the helicopter disappeared over the horizon, heading for the desert.

Meanwhile down below, the entire building was being emptied out. Frightened guests and residents were astonished to see a huge black airplane sitting in the middle of the street right outside the building, its engines turning but making very little noise. The street made for an improbable landing strip—it wasn't very long and was fairly narrow, with other buildings and shops and shanties crowded along each side. It seemed impossible that the large plane could have landed here.

As more people ran out of the building, the mystery soldiers, their work done, exited the structure as well. Running up the plane's lowered ramp, they quickly disappeared inside.

Those people left on the street who dared to watch then saw the huge plane back up—a feat in itself—and turn 180 degrees. Its nose now pointing west, it started moving very quickly down the narrow thoroughfare. Just when it seemed it would smash into a row of buildings at the end of the street, four bright white rockets ignited under its wings and, incredibly, lifted the plane noiselessly into the air.

It climbed into the bright wash of stars overhead.

Then, in a blink, it was gone.

ZIOM'S penthouse blew up three minutes later.

The explosion was so loud, so violent, it shook all of downtown Khartoum. Debris scattered everywhere, the explosives inside being so powerful, the largest fragments were no bigger than a golf ball.

When the smoke cleared, the top six floors of the formerly luxurious building were gone. Reduced to dust, they blew away, scattering across the city like volcanic ash and leaving only jagged concrete and burning hot metal behind.

THE women of the village of Aylala were wailing again.

But this time they were not crying for their lives—they were whooping with anger and life.

They saw the helicopter coming from afar. Its buglike silhouette appeared out of the late-rising full moon, looking like one of the region's mythical gods, a flying deity that always returned the enemies of the desert people back to them for retribution.

The helicopter circled the village once; it was still lit by the fires smoldering from the aborted attack by the Janjaweed militia. The copter finally set down, but only long enough for the two men riding in it to jump out, untie the straps holding Ziom to the copter's strut and pull the murderous militia leader to the ground. Ziom had screamed just about the entire flight, but now the last thing he wanted was to get off the aircraft. He knew what lay ahead for him.

The two men also left the strongbox containing the cash taken from Ziom's penthouse on the ground nearby. The villagers had already gathered dozens of weapons from the dead fighters, so now, not only were they well-armed, but they would have currency too, with which to buy food, clothes and medicine and maybe even survive in this very harsh corner of the Earth.

The men climbed back into the helicopter and lifted off again; this just as the women of the village reached the landing spot, carrying broom handles, hammers and jagged rocks. The men in the tiny copter could hear Ziom's screams over the sound of their aircraft's engine as they rose into the sky. The higher they flew, though, the fainter the screams became, until they just faded away completely.

Only then did they know their work this long night was finally done.

CHAPTER TWO

There were military police everywhere.

In the corridors, watching the elevators, and especially outside Hearing Room 333.

This entire section of the House of Representatives had been cordoned off. No public tours, no administrative staff, no one but a select group of congressmen, Pentagon officers and intelligence officials were allowed past the ring of MPs. Even the building's usual protection service, the Capitol Police, were not allowed on the same floor as Hearing Room 333.

The room belonged to the Special Armaments Subcommittee. Charged with oversight of the country's new weapons systems, this little known but powerful group held the purse strings for highly advanced armaments that in most cases wouldn't be built for years. Everything they dealt with was classified. Which was why they did most of their work in secret.

But today was different. They were not only investigating a matter of grave national security, they were also looking into whether some highly classified equipment was missing, and the possibility that one of their own, a member of the committee itself, had been murdered by rogue U.S. forces using this same highly classified equipment. All this was one of the most closely guarded secrets in Washington at the moment, a place that practically floated on secrecy.

Thus all the security.

There was only one witness for today's hearing. His name was Doug Newman. He was an Army officer—a colonel, in fact. But at the moment, his status in the U.S. armed forces was very much in question. He'd spent the last two months under guard in the psychiatric wing of the infirmary at Nellis Air Force Base in Nevada. Previously he'd run a training camp deep in the Nevada desert, not far from the infamous Area 51. This place had been home to one of the most classified black ops units in U.S. military history, a group known as the 201st Special Operations Wing.

The unit's activities were so covert, even the higher-ups in the White House knew little about them. Their budget was a secret. Their equipment was highly classified, as were the names of the people inside the unit itself.

Just what the 201st was training for in the desert was also a closely guarded secret. It was known that they were made up of a hundred-man company of the 82nd Airborne, a platoon of Marine Armor, (including two specially adapted M1-A1 tanks), plus jet pilots from all three services, and that at least one of their airplanes was extremely heavily armed. But that was just the beginning of the story of the 201st. Even from the little anyone knew about them, they were "spooky," in more ways than one.

There were seven congressmen on the panel—an eighth chair was vacant. It belonged to the committee's ranking member, Representative Adamis Toole. As prior testimony had shown, he was no friend of the 201st; in fact he'd proposed cutting their funding and dissolving the unit before it had even completed its training phase. This was all very odd because Toole was now dead, killed in a mysterious plane crash in the Mediterranean two months before, along with one of the most wealthy and controversial oil princes in the Middle East. Officially, the plane—owned by the prince and heading for Monte Carlo with Toole as a guest on board—went down due to mechanical failure. However, whispers in the deepest reaches of the black ops world said that somehow, someway, the 201st had shot the plane down, killing the prince, the crew and their adversary, Congressman Toole.

And that was just one of the things the committee wanted to get to the bottom of during this hearing.

NEWMAN was brought into the hearing room under heavy guard.

He was wearing plain Army trousers and a shirt, but no indications of rank. He was a man in his sixties, shaved head, rock jawed. Comparisons to a 21st century John Wayne were not too far off the mark. He had a long history of service in the Army and especially in Special Forces. But the last twelve months of his life seemed to be a blank slate, officially anyway. Most of this coincided with the time he'd spent in the Nevada desert, getting the 201st off the ground.

The official focus of the hearing revolved around the extremely expensive equipment the 201st had somehow been able to acquire—deals with DARPA and other special weapons entities within the military and intelligence services had been previously revealed. The committee was especially interested in the 201st's half dozen aircraft. The first three airplanes, C-17 Globemaster cargo lifters, had been adapted for a kind of hit-and-run warfare. One had been equipped with non-lethal-ray crowd-control weapons to simulate real combat for the unit while it was in training. Another had been adapted to carry the Marine tanks; the third was outfitted for dropping the 82nd's paratroopers. The planes had been fitted with engines that made little noise and also had rocket-assist packages under their wings to get them off the ground after a very brief takeoff roll.

The odd thing was that the second set of planes—also three in number—were even more highly advanced. And much more expensive.

The hearing began. The committee chairman read a brief opening statement and then asked Newman directly: "What was your unit training for, Colonel, and why?"

Newman glanced at his court-appointed Army lawyer sitting to his left. The guy looked like he'd rather be getting a root canal than be here, serving as Newman's legal advisor. He pretended to be taking notes. When Newman nudged him, he nodded quickly, indicating that Newman should answer the question.

Newman collected his thoughts for a moment, then he began: "The 201st started off as one of several special operations groups assigned to train in Nevada inside a place known as Area 153. I was the unit CO. The reason we were formed was the CIA did a classified study of the worst-case scenarios the U.S. would face in the Persian Gulf region in the next ten years. According to the Agency, because the whole Gulf area was fragmenting so quickly, it was feared more radical Muslim groups than ever would rise up in the next decade. Specifically, the CIA told us the biggest threat would be from terrorist splinter groups run by a new type of religious fanatic called a 'warlord mullah.' These people were described as bloodthirsty, brutal, unreasonable holy men, very much in the spirit of al Qaeda, with plenty of money and access to weapons, including those of mass destruction. The nightmare scenario the CIA presented depicted a bunch of these bin Laden wannabes operating unchecked, with all kinds of WMD at their disposal. For them, 9/11 was just the beginning. The Agency told us they'd identified at least a dozen of these characters and were certain there would be more to come. It is my understanding that at first the Agency was at a loss on how to handle this new threat.

"Then the CIA discovered the majority of these mullahs apparently had something in common: They shunned the big cities and population centers of the Middle East and had gone back to their tribal roots. They built isolated compounds way out in the desert, under the pretense of starting new religious centers. They surrounded these religious forts with private armies. From the satellite photos, the Agency learned most of these compounds had what appeared to be super-hardened bomb shelters, bunkers that could withstand air attacks including cruise missile attacks. They found these shelters were hidden under mosques the mullahs had put up on their sites, thinking they'd be untouchable. So, the result of all this was we had an entirely new enemy: well-financed, well-connected radicals, sympathetic to al Qaeda, with access to security and WMD, and impervious to our best counter-weapons. And there was an additional problem: While some of these religious forts had been seen popping up in Iraq and Syria, the Agency told us they'd spotted others in places like Turkey, Jordan and Saudi Arabia, countries considered allies of the U.S.

"The CIA knew unless something was done about these mullahs, wherever they were, they would surely cause a lot of trouble over the next ten years. Though they might be just one step from living in a cave, they were said to be technologically astute and, soon enough, able to project power around the globe whenever they wanted. So, the 201st was formed to build a high-tech strike force to be ready to counter the warlord mullahs should they start any trouble. Or . . . at least that's what the original specs for the 201st said."

Newman stopped for a moment. A hush came over the room.

"Meaning what, Colonel?" one congressman asked.

Newman looked at his lawyer, who was sinking very quickly into his chair. Newman cleared his throat and said: "I guess it makes no sense to keep it secret now. The truth is, for want of a better term, the 201st was actually set up as an assassination team. A high-tech hit squad. Mobile. Quiet. A way to get these warlord mullahs before they could get us. That's really what we were about. Get in, knock off these people and get out, without being spotted."

A gasp went through those assembled. The two CIA representatives on hand for the hearing quietly slipped out a side door.

"But how were you going to do *that* exactly?" one startled congressman asked once things had settled down.

Newman took a sip of water and continued: "Because we were told these warlord mullahs had set themselves up in these bomb-hardened religious forts, we knew this type of preemptive mission couldn't be done by airpower alone. What was needed were people on the ground too, and heavy weapons to support them. The 201st put these things together, in an integrated system: paratroopers, tanks and one massive airborne gunship. Now, true, it would have been highly illegal, eliminating people who really hadn't done anything to the U.S. yet, and well-connected religious icons at that. Plus, to get caught doing this in a 'friendly' country would mean huge embarrassment for the U.S. government. But it was felt successful operations against the warlord mullahs would solve a lot of little problems before they became big problems. The CIA figured that it would most likely be one of these warlord mullahs who got ahold of a rogue nuclear weapon or bio weapon first, before any terrorist state could. Unlike places like Iran and Syria that might get nukes someday, the warlord mullahs weren't going to be affected by sanctions or diplomacy. The CIA said there was even a chance one or two of them had some WMD already. So, the thinking was they had to be whacked now, quickly and quietly, without the leaders of whatever country they were in even knowing it happened—at least officially, anyway."

The congressmen were shocked. They began whispering among themselves. Many of them were hearing about this aspect of the 201st for the first time.

Finally one asked: "But, Colonel Newman, how do we know if this warlord mullah thing is even true?"

Newman shrugged. "You'll have to ask the CIA that, sir."

"But you never actually carried out an operation against one, did you?"

Newman shook his head. "No, sir."

"And did you ever actually see one of these religious forts up close?"

"No, sir . . . just the Agency's satellite photos of them."

"But those could have been photos of anything—correct? Even possibly legitimate religious centers?"

Newman shrugged again. "I suppose."

"So there's a chance these religious forts don't actually exist?"

Newman began to say something but stopped. He suddenly wished his water glass was filled with gin. Or cyanide.

"That's possible, I guess," he finally replied.

The congressman pressed his attack: "But your unit did in fact see action, is that correct?" he asked. "About two months ago?"

Newman's head hung low. "Yes, it did, sir. But I don't think even this committee is authorized to discuss that."

"Well, is it true you sent your unit on an unauthorized mission against a terrorist group in Pakistan?"

Newman nodded slowly. "Yes, sir."

"And that this terrorist group had kidnapped your daughter, along with a few other Americans?"

"Yes—sir."

"And the result was?"

Newman bit his lip. "More than a thousand terrorists killed, sir—but . . ."

"But . . . what?"

"But all the hostages were killed too," Newman replied.

A silence came over the hearing room. Newman rubbed his eyes and shifted uncomfortably in his seat.

Finally the committee chairman said: "Let's move on."

Another congressman took up the questioning. "Colonel, I understand you had six planes at your disposal."

"True," Newman replied.

"Planes 1, 2 and 3, the training planes?" the congressman asked. "Where are they at present, Colonel? And what is their condition?"

"Those three aircraft are still in Nevada, sir," Newman said. "Or at least as far as I know. They were used round the clock for a long time, so I know that they were pretty beat up."

"And planes 4, 5 and 6?" the congressman asked. "The non-training planes."

Newman shrugged again. "They were not so beat up—or again, the last time I saw them they weren't."

The congressman looked confused, but plowed on.

"I want to concentrate on those last three aircraft at the moment," he said. "For instance, is it true that these three aircraft have the ability to . . . disappear?"

Newman rolled his eyes. He glanced at his lawyer again, but the man had sunk even lower in his chair. He wanted no part of the question—or shaping Newman's answer.

"I'm sorry, sir," Newman finally replied. "But that's classified."

The congressman's face turned crimson.

"But this is a classified hearing," the congressman insisted. "You can say anything you want in here. In fact, you are compelled to tell us. So, I'll repeat the question, as absurd as it sounds: Do these three aircraft have the ability to . . . to vanish?"

Newman looked at the lawyer again. The man came up for air long enough to sort of nod and shrug slightly.

"I don't think 'vanish' is the right word," Newman answered.

The congressman's face never lost its beet-colored tinge. "These aircraft—they cannot be seen. And not just on radar, but to the human eye. Is that accurate?"

Newman thought a moment, then said, "Under some circumstances, that is correct."

A loud murmur went through the room.

The congressman pounded the desk in front of him. "But how is that possible, Colonel?"

Newman shrugged yet again. "It's technology, sir. Classified technology."

"Is it magic?" the congressman shouted. "Something supernatural?"

"I don't believe so, sir . . ."

An aide whispered something in the congressman's ear. The politician nodded and shoved the aide back where he came from.

"Is this invisibility something gleaned from . . . and I can't believe I'm saying this . . . 'alien technology'? Something taken from a downed UFO—this Roswell nonsense, for instance."

Newman took a long sip of water. "I would not be in a position to know that, sir."

Another murmur went through the room. Those military officers in attendance were thanking their lucky stars that the hearing was closed to the press. Still, they were worried that if anything were leaked from the session, it would mean jobs, careers, pensions.

The chairman banged his gavel once and quieted the crowd. "Please, let's move on," he said in a raspy voice.

The congressman returned to his notes. "All right, Colonel Newman, let's leave the whole discussion about how these planes work for a moment. Do you know how much one of these operational planes, 4, 5 and 6, costs?"

Newman looked at his lawyer. The man scratched two words on the pad before him: *Tell truth.*

"I believe the cost is approximately two billion dollars each," Newman said.

Another gasp. The military's most expensive airborne weapons system—the B-2 stealth bomber—only cost a billion dollars each.

The congressman who asked the question looked like he was about to have a cardiac infarction. "*Two billion each?*" He fumed. "For a cargo plane?"

Newman moved the microphone closer to him. "Highly adapted cargo planes, yes, sir."

"Why may I ask do they cost so much? Leaving aside whatever makes them 'invisible.'"

Newman thought a moment, then said: "They are packed with weaponry and heavy lift capacity. Their flight controls are highly sophisticated . . ."

"Move on . . ." the chairman intoned again.

The congressman looked over his notes. "All right, Colonel," he began again. "Can you please tell this hearing where these three planes are now? These two-billion-dollar airplanes?"

Newman didn't even bother looking at the attorney this time. He took a nervous sip of water, cleared his throat and said: "They are currently missing, sir."

No murmuring this time. Now it was complete silence in the hearing room.

"Missing . . ." the congressman said. "As in unaccounted for?"

"That's right," Newman said.

"Did they crash?"

"No, sir . . . I don't think so."

"Well, does anybody know their location?"

Newman shrugged again. "I'm sure the people flying them know."

This elicited some laughter from those assembled, causing the committee chairman to bang his gavel and restore order.

The congressman was extremely frustrated now and it showed.

"Do we have any idea, any clue as to what part of the world these airplanes might presently be?"

Newman looked at the lawyer, who now appeared to be sweating profusely. He was shaking his head not so subtly.

"I'm really not sure, Congressman," Newman replied.

The congressman looked like he was about to explode.

"OK then, Colonel." Again, he fumed. "Can you tell me this: Is there a possibility these multi-billion-dollar airplanes are presently somewhere in . . . Africa?"

At this point, the lawyer sank so low in his seat he nearly disappeared. He was effectively leaving Newman on his own.

Newman thought another moment, then replied: "Well, Congressmen. I guess anything is possible."

The politicians had a hasty, huddled conference. Clearly agitated by Newman's strong, but evasive stand, they chose to hurl one last fur ball at him.

"What then would you think, Colonel," the chairman asked Newman, "if we told you that we are very close to finding these lost airplanes, and your lost unit, and when we do, we are dispatching a special ops team to bring them all back to face military justice of the severest kind."

Newman looked back at the chairman, just fifteen feet away, and had to repress the urge to spit in his face. He was being set up here and he knew it.

He began to reply, but then thought better of it. Instead, he leaned over to his anxious lawyer and whispered something to him. The lawyer looked even more uncomfortable than before, but Newman urged him to do as instructed.

The attorney wiped the perspiration from his brow, and then brought the microphone closer to him.

"Sirs," he began, "my client's only response to that is a line from his favorite book."

"And what is that?" the chairman asked.

The lawyer gulped and said: "'You can't stop what you can't see.'"

CHAPTER THREE

South Rift Drift
Southwest Sudan

The man named Mr. Yoyo had spent four days lost in the desert.

Stumbling, falling, crawling, he had no food, no water, no relief from the brutal sun. He'd been bitten by scorpions and sand ants. He'd been pecked at by vultures, trying to hurry along their next meal. He'd hallucinated that he was caught up in ocean waves; he'd dreamt that the sky was on fire. He'd seen mirages of emerald green oases, with trees and waterfalls. *Fata Morgana,* always just up ahead. Always out of reach.

But it was one of these visions that saved his life.

At the beginning of his fifth day lost, he'd stumbled toward one of the imagined oases, with its sparkling water and swaying palm fronds, and finding it was just simply more sand, more heat, more nothing, he finally collapsed and gave up. He couldn't go on, even though he knew he would never see his family or his tribe again.

It was only his good luck that his black, burned skin was such a contrast against the white-powder sand of the lower

Sahara. That's the only reason Lieutenant Moon saw Mr. Yoyo when he flew over him in his minicopter.

The 201st's intelligence officer was returning from a recon over South Rift Drift, a section of the Sahara where Darfur-type bandits were known to hide. Some of the oases out here were real, and when things got hot for the militia gangs, as they had now, they would sometimes lay low at one of the watering holes, allowing things to cool down.

Looking for these criminals was part of the deal. The 201st Special Operations Wing was on the lam—and the top-secret African Union military outpost at Wum Bakim, Cameroon, was their hideout. The AU officers had taken them in after the unit's unauthorized rescue mission in Pakistan and the horrific events that followed. In return, the 201st agreed to do what no one else on Earth had the guts or inclination to do: battle the genocide that was going on in Darfur. Just as long as they were able to do it secretly—more or less—then that was fine with the fugitives of Colonel Doug Newman's former unit. They were rogue warriors, on the run, guilty of every charge brought against them. But at least they were trying to do something good for the world.

While they were adept at long-range strikes against the Darfur criminals, like the one against the Janjaweed gang two nights before, it was important to the 201st to keep an eye on things closer to home too. The Rift Drift was barely thirty minutes' flying time from their sanctuary at Wum Bakim; as such it qualified as the local neighborhood. That's why Moon happened to be out here today.

He landed next to Mr. Yoyo's outstretched body and, with great care, fed him a few drops of water from his canteen. It took a while, but finally the tall black man opened his eyes and began breathing normally. He asked Moon in the local dialect of Nihilli if he was a saint in the Great Beyond.

Moon answered no, then, again with great care, lifted

the man into the passenger seat of the minicopter and took off, heading south.

It was amazing that Mr. Yoyo was able to recognize his village from a thousand feet up. But he got very excited when, ten minutes into their flight, Moon flew over the collection of straw huts located next to a real watering hole. His passenger began squealing again in Nihilli—and again, it didn't take Moon long to figure out what he was saying.

Moon put the copter into an orbit above the village and then set it down in the middle of the huts. The entire village came out to greet them—some were in shock, others were deliriously happy. They couldn't believe Mr. Yoyo was still alive and that they were seeing him again.

The village chief was quickly on the scene. He was able to speak a bit of English, enough for him to talk to Moon and Mr. Yoyo and piece together how Yoyo, the chief's grand nephew, found himself nearly dying in the desert.

IT all began two weeks before when a band of warriors descended on the village in the middle of the night. These people were not Africans—at least not the typical kind. They weren't black, they were brown. Arabs, from many miles away. They were heavily armed.

They shot anyone who tried to stop them, stole a lot of the village's supplies and then rounded up the five of the strongest men and forced them out into the desert with them. Mr. Yoyo was one of them.

He said a convoy of trucks was waiting for them in the dark. His captors tied him and the others to the last truck in the column and began whipping them so they would keep up as the raiders slowly drove deeper into the desert.

Their trip lasted all that night and into the grueling heat of the next day. Just before noon, the column reached its destination, a high-walled desert compound literally in the middle of nowhere. According to Mr. Yoyo, from horizon to horizon there was nothing around this place except sand. Here, the captives were put to work digging ditches, mixing cement and carrying water from one end of the compound to the other.

One by one the other captives died from exhaustion and beatings. On the ninth day, though, Mr. Yoyo woke in the middle of the night to find his guard asleep. He slipped out of the compound and walked into the desert. He was just minutes away from death when Moon found him.

THE story troubled Moon greatly. The kidnappers fit the description not so much of the Darfur bandits but of another enemy—the one that the 201st had been originally trained to fight: al Qaeda–like terrorists.

Such Islamic fanatics had been reported in Somalia and places like Djibouti, but this was certainly deep in the desert for them—and the wrong desert at that. Moon knew it was unwise to jump to conclusions, but he also realized he had to get as much information from Mr. Yoyo as he could.

He'd found the description of the trucks the kidnappers had used to be highly unusual. According to Yoyo, they were huge, with big tires and big engines, and they moved very slowly and deliberately. This seemed to be unlike any vehicle that would normally be employed to cross the desert—Range Rovers and such. And much too elaborate.

Moon pulled out one of his BlackBerrys, and after explaining to the villagers that it contained no bad demons or spirits, he searched for a page on military trucks. He showed the resulting images to Mr. Yoyo—but the weakened man couldn't identify any of them. He kept saying "bigger and thicker."

Moon called up images of civilian all-terrain trucks, but again Yoyo shook his head no. Nothing matched.

Out of desperation, Moon called up "unusual general purpose vehicles" and showed the images to Yoyo.

Incredibly he passed on all of them except for the last one. It was a picture of a Brinks armored truck. He excitedly indicated that's what the kidnappers' vehicles looked like.

Moon was stunned. A Brinks truck? Something used in the states for hauling money around? Why would anyone have one—or something that looked like one—out in the middle of the Sahara Desert?

But Mr. Yoyo reiterated that yes, this was the kind of truck the kidnappers had—had several of them in fact. But even bigger.

So, these possible al Qaeda types were out in the wrong desert, somewhere, driving around in huge Brinks trucks?

It didn't make sense.

But in Moon's business, few things did.

HE left the tribe his spare BlackBerry as a reward for their patience and help. Then he went aloft again and started circling a piece of desert about a half mile east of the village.

It took a while, but finally he spotted a series of tire tracks, punched into the dry sand. And just as Mr. Yoyo had said, they headed straight into the deepest part of this part of the desert.

Following the tracks while still flying the tiny helicopter took some doing, but Moon managed it for the next two hours, and finally found what he was looking for.

Mr. Yoyo had described the place he'd been brought to as a compound. It was a somewhat misleading description—something lost in the translation. What Moon came upon in the deepest part of the desert had high, thick walls complete with parapets, surrounding dozens of stone buildings and a battery of towers.

It was not a compound. It was a fort. Something from a French Foreign Legion movie.

And it was filled with weapons.

Moon put the copter in a shallow orbit about a quarter mile north of the fort, intent on taking pictures with his camera phone. His fuel was running low, and he had a long flight back. But he knew he had to gather as much information on this place as possible.

He flipped open his phone and put the camera on standby. Suddenly the sky around him turned bright red. At first he didn't know what was happening—but then his instincts kicked in. The red flare was coming from a rocket-propelled grenade someone had fired at him. He immediately turned the little copter over and went into a long, curving dive that put his eyeballs somewhere in the back of his skull. The RPG came so close to him, he felt the heat of its rocket motor as it streaked by. It missed, but only by a few feet.

Hands shaking, his flight suit suddenly bathed in sweat, Moon somehow righted the copter only to find his life-saving maneuver had put him directly over the fort. Now a storm of tracer rounds was coming up at him. Time seemed to stand still, something that frequently happened in combat. Moon could feel his heart beating right out of his chest, but he also started his camera phone clicking.

Dozens of people were shooting at him, but he was still able to snap some photographs and, in doing so, see some remarkable things. It was strange because, for a moment, he thought he was over not the Sahara Desert but the wilds of Nevada. Inside the fort were not only stone buildings, but a mosque and what were obviously bomb-proof bunkers, or at least the tops of them, surrounding it. There were also plenty of artillery pieces, 50-caliber machine guns and antiaircraft weapons.

And that was the weird thing: Save for the high walls, it was almost an exact snapshot of their old training ground inside Area 153—a mock-up of what a so-called warlord-mullah's religious fort would look like. That place that looked almost exactly like this one.

Moon actually shook his fist in triumph—even though tracer rounds were still whipping by him with a high-speed ferocity.

He turned the copter away and retreated to the north, letting out a yelp as he hit the throttles.

Goddamn, he thought. We finally found one!

CHAPTER FOUR

Wum Bakim
Cameroon

USAF Major Tommy Gunn collapsed on his bunk and prayed for sleep to come.

It hadn't been just a long day for him, or a long week. He hadn't stopped moving in nearly two months, day or night. He was exhausted, and he could feel it in every bone in his body.

Gunn was used to long hours. A career Air Force pilot with twelve years in, he was both a test pilot and a combat veteran. Prior to driving X-planes at Edwards Air Force Base, he'd spent two tours flying F-15s in Iraq, plus one tour as commander of a classified F-117 stealth squadron stationed on the Indian Ocean island of Diego Garcia. Hollywood handsome and built like a linebacker, Gunn had the instincts of a street fighter and the guts of a barnstormer. He was also brilliant—so much so, he was on the short list to begin training to fly NASA's newest spacecraft, the Orion, the vehicle that would take America back to the moon and then to Mars beyond.

Or at least he was before he was recruited into the 201st—and the 201st went on the run.

From top test pilot/astronaut in training to being wanted by the U.S. government on a multitude of charges, despite destroying one of the most dangerous terrorist groups in the world? It was not an understatement to say Gunn was leading an interesting life these days. Maybe too interesting.

And never had the hours been this long.

Sleep deprivation was now an occupational hazard for him. As field commander for the 201st, planning and flying the missions against the Darfur gangs while trying to stay invisible and keep the multibillion-dollar planes in good shape all fell onto his shoulders. There was no time to eat most days, never mind sleep. Worse, his stash of amphetamine pills was getting perilously low.

But now, this night, the unit was finally on stand-down. They'd flown their biggest mission yet against the Darfur bandits two nights before, whacking the head Janjaweed, Ziom, and greasing a few hundred of his mooks. Before this they'd carried out similar attacks against smaller, more isolated militia groups, just to see if the 201st's ghostly method of operation worked against such squirrelly opponents. The answer was yes—and the Janjaweed had paid the price.

But planning and carrying out the big operation had taken time, and then the next forty-eight hours was spent doing post-mission maintenance on the airplanes, not an easy thing with tool kits that contained little more than hammers and screwdrivers. Getting the planes hidden back under their special camouflage nets was also a long, time-intensive job.

But finally, all the work was done and the unit was given the day off, their first since coming to Wum Bakim. Which was why Gunn was mercifully asleep as soon as his head hit the straw pillow, the sounds of the deep African forest outside playing like a lullaby in his ears.

But the respite lasted no more than two minutes. Because

before he even started to dream, someone was shaking him awake.

He opened his eyes to see the familiar face of Lieutenant Moon looking down at him.

"I'm sorry, sir," Moon was telling him. "But something has come up. Something very important."

JUST one hut over, Navy Lieutenant Amanda Faith O'Rourke lay wide awake, her eyes open, her body sweating, gloomily contemplating her spare surroundings. This hut. This base. This place—none of it could ever be mistaken for her home in L.A. She'd thought that place was minimalist? Wum Bakim had it beat by a mile.

She was as hot and exhausted as the rest of the unit. Trying to hide in plain sight did that to you, especially when the temperatures hit one hundred degrees before midmorning. She'd kept track: seventeen hours sleep in the past eight days, thirty-two in the past twenty-one. Not good for someone whose job was piloting a large airplane. Not good for anybody, in fact.

She closed her eyes and slowly rubbed her hands all over her lithe, naked body. It was an old Tzu massage trick her first modeling agent had taught her. A good way to relax and let sleep come. But it wasn't working tonight.

She'd grown up in a Navy family. Her grandfather had flown Banshees during the Korean War. Her father had flown F-4s over Vietnam. Her older brother had flown F-14s during the first Gulf War and, more recently, F/A-18s over Iraq—until he was shot down and went MIA. She'd inherited their skills along with her mother's good looks to become a three-headed monster: a premier Navy fighter pilot, a NASA shuttle trainee and, most unusual, a well-known photo model.

It was a good gig. The Navy loved her celebrity status; her layouts were good PR for both Naval Aviation and

NASA. Her modeling agency loved the fact that she was this gorgeous, intelligent, independent woman who aspired to travel to the stars. And for a while, she'd been having the time of her life. Until a few months ago, when the 201st came calling.

Why did they want her for such a weird, highly classified, even illegal mission? She didn't know. Her family was all about service to the country. Maybe the military assumed hanging tough was in her genes. But never did she think it would end up like this, flying a humper like the C-17, herself a veteran of hand-to-hand combat with the terrorists in Pakistan, with more horrible sights locked in her brain than she could ever hope to get out, and now wanted by the U.S. government? More than six years of work, schooling, study, training for NASA, and here she was, in the middle of the jungle, in a forgotten corner of the forgotten country of Cameroon, fighting the nastiest bastards on Earth, but wanting nothing more than to step back onto U.S. soil just one more time.

She took a deep breath and kept massaging her body, now glistening with sweet perspiration. Finally, sheer fatigue overcame her. With each passing breath, she slowly sank into thankful slumber, as always wondering if she'd ever see her home again.

The next thing she knew, she was being shaken awake by Lieutenant Bing, pilot of the 201st's paratroop plane.

"They want us in the ops hut," he told her awkwardly, trying not to look at her naked body. "Something big has come up . . ."

GUNN and Moon were hunched over a makeshift photo table when Amanda and Bing walked in. The unit's Marine CO, Captain Steve Cardillo and the paratroop commander, Captain Bruce Vogel, were also on hand.

It was one hour past sundown and the jungle around them was alive with the screams, hoots and hollers of the vast army of nocturnal animals that surrounded the base every night. It was hot inside the simple tin hut; the men were wearing shorts and sneakers. But Amanda was wearing just a stretched-out T-shirt and flip-flops. Her long blond hair, a perfect mess, her beautiful features having no need for makeup, she was so gorgeous, it was distracting, even at a time like this. Especially for Gunn.

They were going over the photos Moon had taken in his recon sweep of South Rift Drift. He'd returned just a half hour before, after a harrowing, slow-speed, fuel-starved trip back to Wum Bakim. He told them how he'd found the half-dead Mr. Yoyo and how that led him to discover the very unusual place in the desert. The photos of the fort were crude, small and shaky. But still, they showed something they'd all heard a lot about but had never seen before, until now.

It was the broken record in their heads: The 201st had been put together to eliminate the so-called warlord-mullahs, the religious madmen said to be building heavily fortified forts in the deserts of the Middle East. The unit's mission was to secretly assassinate these troublemakers before they could obtain WMD with which to attack the West.

But because the unit was shut down before their training was complete, the 201st never actually went up against one of the warlord mullahs and, as time went by, especially since coming to Wum Bakim, they had come to wonder if any of these mullahs actually existed or whether they were just the fancy of some especially imaginative CIA analyst.

But now, looking at Moon's photos, what they saw was an almost exact copy of the mock religious fort against which they had honed their skills back in their Nevada training ground, a place that had been built based on CIA satellite photos: many low buildings, lots of weapons, one building looking like a mosque, complete with minaret, with evidence of at least one underground bunker nearby. Suddenly the whole idea of the warlord mullah had taken on some credibility.

But what was strange about all this was that it was here in Africa. The CIA had warned that the warlord mullah idea would spread throughout the Middle East, and specifically around the Persian Gulf—that was the theory. So, even if it were real, would it have jumped all the way to the Dark Continent already?

"Real or not," Moon told them, "we have to do something about this place. If a Janjaweed-type militia has any kind of connection with one of these warlord mullahs, then that could be big trouble. With the money and access to all kinds of weapons these religious thugs are supposed to have, to let them loose in this region would be catastrophic. And even if that's not the case, whoever is in that fort shot a bunch of people in Mr. Yoyo's village and then killed four of his tribesmen. And they shot at my helicopter. Even though they are way out there in the middle of nowhere, they're obviously up to no good."

At that point, a very tall, sunny black man walked in. He was Colonel Mdosi, CO of Wum Bakim. Originally from Senegal, he'd been educated at Oxford and the Sorbonne, was a veteran of the French Special Forces and a major force in chasing down the various bandit gangs causing so much misery in the Darfur area, a couple hundred miles to the east, as well as other rebel groups throughout Africa.

He was also a close friend of Colonel Doug Newman, the man who'd put the 201st together. When things got hairy for the team after their small unauthorized war in Pakistan, Newman reached out to Mdosi. He knew the colonel was operating out of the secret African Union base at the northeastern tip of Cameroon. Though there was a long runway here, Wum Bakim was more of a listening post than anything else, a place to eavesdrop on the many different groups who would exploit Africa or bring terror to its peoples. Newman knew Mdosi was being financed by both the British and French intelligence services to pay for his operations and his tiny twenty-man army in return for a steady stream of intelligence. Mdosi had been doing his thing quietly for several years, practically undetected, even by U.S. Intelligence. Thus, his hidden base was the perfect hiding spot for the rogue 201st.

They briefed Mdosi now as he studied the recon photos. He readily agreed with their assessment: Bad characters had obviously taken up residence in what appeared to be an old French Foreign Legion garrison. But Mdosi was further troubled by something else he saw. He pointed out one particular building located in an isolated corner of the fort.

"I don't like the looks of this structure," he said. "It appears more solidly built than the rest of the buildings, like it's a weapons dump or something. Religious fort or not, maybe these guys plan on selling arms to one of the rebel groups in this area—or a lot of them. At the very least, we can't let that happen."

Gunn looked around the table. They were here at the kindness of the African Union and the deal was they would help them whenever they could. This was one of those times—plus it would answer a lot of lingering questions for the 201st.

It didn't take much discussion. They were all in agreement.

The fort would have to be attacked.

"Sure, why not?" Bing concluded. "I mean, what else do we have to do tomorrow?"

THE 201st's airplanes were invisible.

Or at least they could be, under the right conditions.

And it didn't have anything to do with alien technology

or UFOs. It was actually a simple method—but one that cost more than a billion dollars per plane.

The unit's aircraft were typical C-17 Globemasters packed with some very un-typical technologies. At 175 feet long, with a wingspan of almost the same length, a standard C-17 resembled an airliner on steroids. Along with the gigantic C-5 Galaxy, Globemasters were the workhorses of the Air Force in its role of moving Army troops around the world and keeping them supplied. C-17s could fly anywhere on Earth in just a matter of hours, due to their high speed and aerial refueling capability. They could land on rough, unprepared surfaces and take off the same way. They could operate in any type of environment, from the Tropics to the Arctic, in any kind of weather, day or night. As a way of projecting power, they were an awesome aerial platform.

What made the 201st's C-17s different was their skin. Each plane was painted in dull, non-reflective black. Imbedded in this paint was a matrix of tiny twinkling sensors, tens of millions of them. These sensors could detect stars, star formations, clouds, atmospherics or any mix thereof that appeared above the aircraft and re-create them exactly onto its bottom. As such, the aircraft, which were also equipped with silent engines, could pass overhead at night and not be seen by anyone on the ground because what they thought they were looking up at was nothing but the stars. In other words, under the right conditions and with all their additional stealth gear working, the airplanes could indeed become invisible.

But there was more. The lead C-17, known as the Fireship, was the largest airborne gunship ever built. The USAF had an airplane called an AC-130 Spectre, a propeller-driven converted cargo plane that carried four large weapons that stuck out the left side of its fuselage. To attack a target, the Spectre's pilot put the plane into a left-hand bank and opened up, usually with devastating results. A child of the Vietnam War, the Spectre was primarily used against troop concentrations and hardened targets.

The 201st's Fireship was that same idea—multiplied by four. It carried sixteen massive weapons along with four times the amount of ammunition and four times the amount of technology to make it all work.

The inside of its enormous cargo bay looked like a Rube Goldberg nightmare, with ammo belts and power lines running in every direction imaginable. But there was some method to the madness. Looking in from the rear of the plane, the first weapons one saw were a pair of M102 105mm howitzers, a field gun that had been deployed to support U.S. Army infantry units for years. Next was a trio of 20mm M61 Vulcan cannons, not unlike those used on fighter jets such as the F-15 and F-16. They could each fire three thousand rounds a minute. Following the Vulcans were four Mk-44 Bushmaster 30mm cannons—long, scary-looking weapons that fired airburst rounds. These were the weapons that had leveled the SID base at Kahlia Point.

Next to the Bushmasters were four 7.62mm GAU-2 mini-guns. They were similar to the Vulcans, with two differences: They could fire four thousand rounds a minute, and they were usually loaded with incendiary rounds. Next came a pair of 40mm Bofors cannons, extremely high-powered antiaircraft guns adapted for airborne use. A shot from these guns could penetrate fifty millimeters of armor plate at almost a half mile away.

The last weapon in this murderer's row was the fiercest one of all: a Phoenix CIWS gun. This was a monstrous Gatling gun used to protect capital naval ships like aircraft carriers and cruisers. It was radar-directed, with six barrels, and fired a 20mm shell. It could also fire four thousand rounds per minute, over a very large area. It was able to throw out so much lead, so quickly, nothing in its path could escape. Along with the Vulcans and the miniguns, this is what had swept away most of the Janjaweed militia.

All this firepower was directed through gun stations cut into the lower left side of the aircraft and controlled by the pilot via an LCD screen. Installed just above the flight computer, this screen displayed icons for each weapon. Once the pilot was ready to unload on something, he would sight the target automatically and then select his weapon of choice by touching the weapon's icon. The fire control computer did the rest.

There was so much firepower contained in the Fireship that during the 201st's battle in Pakistan, while they were attacking a mountain stronghold belonging to the much feared PKD terror group, Gunn mistakenly opened up with all sixteen of the airplane's weapons at once—and wound up blowing off the top of the thirteen-thousand-foot high peak.

The unit's other two planes were similarly equipped with stealth devices and the magical Star Skin. The number two plane, also know as the Jump Plane, was outfitted to carry the 82nd's paratroopers. There were more than ninety of them at present with the 201st. The number three plane— also known as Heavy Metal or, more simply, the Tank Plane—was outfitted to carry two M1-A1 tanks, plus their Marine Corps crews.

Together, the three planes were their own self-contained air-land strike force. They wielded more firepower than the military forces of several small countries combined, Cameroon included.

GUNN was checking his small air fleet now.

Five hours had passed since their meeting ended; it was now three in the morning and even hotter than before. Once they'd decided to hit the fort, they knew it was best to do it quick. Unlike going against the Darfur gangs, which took a lot of surveillance work just to find them and their intended target, the fort was stationary, as were the people in it. When an opportunity like this presented itself, it was mandatory to jump on it right away.

Planning, logistics, getting everyone suited up and the big planes refueled took three hours. Then it took just about every able body in the 201st another hour to push, pull and cajole the three big planes out from under their specialized camouflage netting—this after spending as much time the day before pushing them back into their hiding places. Ironically, the camo netting was nearly as expensive as the planes themselves. It was actually a mosaic of electromagnetic images taken of the surrounding terrain and printed on top of each other like photographs. The fabric itself was computer-generated and overlaid thousands of these images to create a realistic impression of what would be on this piece of ground at Wum Bakin if they weren't. The netting also deflected light and heat instead of absorbing it, preventing it from being penetrated by infrared satellite cameras. It might have been the best camouflage ever invented—it was certainly the most expensive.

The 201st had used the super camo netting to hide their base in the Nevada desert, and somehow Newman had gotten some the magic netting to Colonel Mdosi even before the 201st knew they would soon be calling this place home. It worked even better here than it did in Nevada.

Mdosi's men had set up three large tents using the super camo netting as the covering material. The netting blended in so well with the colors and textures of the surrounding jungle, the illusion held until you were within just a foot or two of the "hidden" structures.

But Mdosi only had three small trucks on the tiny base, and even revved up all the way, they couldn't move a massive C-17 on their own. That's why so much muscle power was needed to get the planes out from under the tents so their engines could be started and they could be made ready for flight.

This was finally done by 0315 hours. The sun came up in this part of the world around 0530 hours. Gunn wanted to commence the attack on the fort before daybreak and be done with it by sunrise. This meant they had to really chop-chop if they wanted to keep to their hastily arranged schedule.

By 0345 the aircrews for the paratroop plane and the Tank Plane had fired up their engines. Gunn, Amanda and Bing checked their Star Skin matrixes, one of the last things the team did before taking off on a mission. They signaled Amanda's copilot first and then Bing's. The undersides of both planes suddenly lit up with hundreds of tiny white and bluish lights, perfectly mimicking the night sky above. Each plane inched forward a little, and in both cases the illusion remained intact, with most of the "stars" underneath seeming to move only slightly, while a few new ones appeared under the planes' noses and a few old ones disappeared off their tails.

Gunn gave Bing a thumbs-up. The skin was working as advertised.

"Let's do it just like we practiced in Nevada," he said to the young pilot as they watched the last of the paratroopers load into the back of his plane.

Bing gave him a quick salute. "I can already see Vegas off in the distance," he said. With that, he climbed into the Jump Plane, kicked up its engines and rolled onto the main runway.

Gunn then returned to Amanda's plane. He found the beauty queen pilot checking over her front landing gear.

This was something Gunn always tried to arrange—to see her alone before they went on a mission. Whether she knew he was doing this or not, he didn't know. She would never let on if she did, just like she would never, ever give him any indication that she knew he was hopelessly in love with her.

"No heroics needed today, Lieutenant," he told her as she finished checking her nosewheel. "We did this so many times in Nevada, it should be a cakewalk."

She smiled at him—she could see right through him, of course.

"If I remember right, Major, we only did the Nevada drill correctly one time," she said, balling up her hair and putting her crash helmet on.

This was true; the unit had only successfully "attacked" their Nevada training site once before their funding had been cut. But Gunn laughed anyway—he couldn't help it. She always managed to zing him.

"You got me there," he said. "But seriously, this will be by the book, OK?"

She became serious too. The landing beacon on the front gear was lighting her face in a way that made her look positively radiant.

"I know," she said.

At that moment, if they were in a movie, he would have kissed her. But he didn't. Instead, he just gave her a quick salute and she was gone, disappearing into her huge airplane and closing the access door behind her.

Gunn felt his chest tighten; it always happened like this. They were in a dangerous business, she and him. All of them. They were highly trained and had all seen combat before. But there was always a chance something could go wrong, and this might be the last time he ever saw her, or she him.

So, he just took a deep breath of the hot African night air, got his emotional shit together—and then climbed into his own aircraft.

The three huge planes took off two minutes later. One

right after the other, their rocket assists pushing them up quickly into the star-filled skies.

Mdosi and his men watched them ascend into the heavens and circle the base once.

Then as always, the three airplanes reactivated their Star Skins—and disappeared, just like that.

CHAPTER FIVE

South Rift Drift

As always, Gunn's Fireship went in first.

He maneuvered the huge airplane up and over the desert valley east of the old French fort, then did a sharp bank to the left. The target was now right off his nose. It was 0430 hours. The sky was clear and still full of stars.

Perfect conditions.

He reduced speed, and double-checked his Star Skin integrity. It was working 100 percent. He flipped down his reverse infrared goggles and switched them on. Unlike standard night-vision goggles, RIFs identified cold spots in the target area and filled in temperature differences around them. This method allowed the user to see nearly three times as much in low-light conditions as with regular night-vision apparatus. It also gave everything a cool blue otherworldly glow.

What Gunn saw now corresponded perfectly to Moon's recon photos, but with much more detail. The fort was about a quarter-mile square, surrounded by a ten-foot wall. There were dozens of old stone buildings within, with narrow interior streets crisscrossing around them. There was a scattering of vegetation, fig and palm trees mostly, and Gunn could see artillery pieces, rocket launchers, and anti-aircraft guns hidden among them. It *was* amazing, though. This place looked almost exactly like their combat training simulator back in the Nevada desert.

And just like at that place, one building here stuck out. In the middle of this fort was a mosque.

THE 201st numbered 145 people total, counting pilots and ground personnel; 120 were on this raid. No matter what they took on, they were usually outmanned. But . . . they could appear invisible, they had massive firepower and they had surprise on their side. Added together, it was supposed to even the odds, or even throw them slightly in their favor. At least that's how it was supposed to work. Now would come a real test.

Gunn flew over the fort at just one thousand feet. There were no indications that he'd been spotted. He could see no one below pointing any weapons at him; in fact he couldn't see anyone down there at all. But nothing was certain in combat—and, invisible or not, Gunn knew he couldn't fly around like this forever. He opened up a secure line to the other two planes and relayed what he saw to Amanda and Bing.

"The Moonman was right; it's like they used the same blueprints for this place as they did for our old playground back in Nevada," he told them. "Except there's a wall surrounding it—and those look like real weapons down there . . ."

Gunn checked the time again. It was 0435 hours. They had at least a half hour of nighttime starry skies left. Again, it was perfect timing.

He checked with his gun crew in back. Everyone was ready, as were the sixteen awesome weapons they were carrying.

Gunn put the plane into a shallow orbit above the fort, then called back to his crew again.

"Initiating" was all he said.

Then he tipped the AC-17 on its left wing and pushed nine icons on his fire control panel—his two artillery pieces, two Bushmasters, two Vulcans, the two miniguns and the frightening CIWS gun.

"Weapons engaged," he said into the mic. Then he pushed the computer's fire button . . . and suddenly night was turned into day.

The bright flash from all those weapons going off at once blinded Gunn and his crew. It was an unintended result of the Star Skin. Its millions of sensors picked up light not just from stars but everything around the aircraft. When the guns went off, their muzzle flashes bounced off the fuselage and then were reflected back as increased heat and light, making for a spectacular light show for anyone unfortunate enough to see it on the ground.

The nine separate streams of fire went across the fort like a huge fiery scythe. Buildings simply disappeared, vaporized by the concentrated fire. Barracks, gun towers, fuel tanks, ammo supplies—they all started going up as if caught in a tidal wave of flame. Turning even harder left, Gunn took out a power station, an administration building and the fort's water tower. In the same barrage, he destroyed the fort's front gate, blowing a hole in the wall two hundred feet wide.

Around and around he went—three times, four times, five, his weapons firing nonstop. Some of the secondary explosions were gigantic. Gunn could feel their shock waves from a thousand feet up. The flames they'd created spiraled up into the night, brilliant colors of orange, red and even blue. The smoke was tremendous. Debris was being thrown so high into the air, Gunn could hear it hitting the bottom of his aircraft.

The attack lasted just ninety seconds. That's all that was

needed. No one fired back at him. He saw no movement at all among the firestorm he'd created. He keyed his helmet mic and called back to the other two planes.

"OK—the table is set," he said. "Be careful . . ."

AMANDA acknowledged Gunn's message and turned her big plane south. She'd been doing figure eights about a mile north of the fort, waiting for the gunship to do its thing. Now it was her turn.

She called back to the cargo bay. The two Marine tanks and their crews were ready to go. Also riding along were three of Mdosi's men who would serve as translators if need be, and Lieutenant Moon and his minicopter. While the rest of the unit was engaged in the attack, Moon would get airborne as soon as she set down and serve as the 201st's aerial eyes and ears while the battle progressed.

The terrain in front of the fort—indeed for miles in every direction—was as flat and hard as a typical big airport runway. The C-17 was a robust machine and was built for landing on unprepared airstrips, so touching down wasn't Amanda's concern. It was what would be waiting for them when they got there. Her job was to get the Marine tanks into a position as close as possible to the target without getting her aircraft and everyone in it blown to pieces. It was akin to landing in the middle of a battle—or at least that's how they'd trained for it.

But as she came upon the target, she realized this would not be like the training. Back in Nevada, people used painful microwave weapons to shoot back at them. But Gunn's airplane had done such a good job devastating the fort, Amanda couldn't imagine anyone aboveground still being alive inside, never mind shooting a real weapon at her. After ninety seconds on the wrong end of the Fireship's fusillade, the fort looked like an atomic bomb had hit it.

Still she had to be careful. At 750 feet altitude, she reduced her speed to a crawl, just 110 knots. The fire and smoke coming from the fort were like a huge sandstorm with flames sprouting out of its middle. She flipped her RIFs to full power and brought the big plane down to 500 feet. She was about a half mile from the front of the fort now—she could see that Gunn had blasted a hole so large in the wall she could almost drive her plane right through it.

At 250 feet altitude, she lowered her landing gear and yelled back to the Marines to be ready; they started their tanks' engines and got into their battle positions. At 100 feet, Amanda turned on her plane's nose lamp as an extra precaution should she not see any random boulders on the flat desert. Anytime the nose lamp came on, a TV camera also positioned in the nose was activated, allowing her to land purely by watching the TV screen on her control panel if she needed to. This sort of thing was helpful in bad weather, but she wouldn't need it now.

At 50 feet and just moments away from landing, she eased the throttles just a bit more, and prepared to activate her landing rockets—they would fire as soon as she touched down, quickly slowing her landing roll. Her finger was on their activation button, when suddenly something caught her eye in the landing-assist TV screen. It was a truck of some kind, a Range Rover maybe, with a huge red cross painted on its door. It drove right in front of her—dangerously close. Covered with blowing sand, it disappeared before she realized it was even there.

The plane touched down a second later. Amanda hit the retro rockets and braced herself for their reactive impact. Once they ignited, it was like slamming on the brakes in a car going 100 mph.

The rockets kicked in, and indeed, it was like the plane had hit an invisible brick wall. This, along with standing on the real brakes and reversing engines, combined to stop the

C-17 in less than 200 feet. Amanda immediately pushed the big plane to the left, going into a smooth 180-turn. At the same moment, she lowered the plane's big rear cargo door. The two tanks inside, their engines warm, their crews in place, exploded from the cargo bay even before she completed the pirouette.

The Marines hit the desert floor hard and fast. Their barrels were already facing in the right direction—in front of them was the blasted out hole in the fort's wall. They started shooting immediately, even as their drivers pushed on their throttles and started moving toward the burning fortress.

Looking over her shoulder, Amanda could see that the tanks had deployed perfectly. She let out a breath of relief. Then she saw Moon's copter roll down the ramp. He got its rotors spinning quickly and in seconds he was gone too.

That's when Amanda thought back to the white Range Rover with the Red Cross on its door, driving away from the fort at high speed and vanishing into the desert.

"Why would the Red Cross be out here?" she wondered.

LIEUTENANT Bing also saw the white Range Rover roaring across the desert floor, but he was much too busy at the time to pay much attention to it.

He'd brought his plane right over the fort's west wall just about the same time Amanda was landing. He was flying very low and very slow, nearly at stall speed, this so all his paratroopers could get out and land as close to their tiny drop zone as possible. The big C-17 was shaking angrily in response, its engines fighting to keep everything airborne, Bing fighting the controls to stay straight and level. It was the usual ten seconds of sheer terror.

But still, everything was going according to plan. The paratroopers were jumping en masse out the open cargo door, departing in ragged alignment, deploying their T-13 "short jump" parachutes, and floating down to the flat plain just west of the fort—just where they wanted to be. Bing could see the troopers hitting the ground, bouncing back up right away, their weapons ready, and racing toward their assembly points. Best of all, Bing couldn't see any counterfire, which was no real surprise. Judging by the damage already inflicted by the AC-17 and now the Marine tanks, he couldn't imagine anyone inside the fort having the fortitude to oppose this sudden invasion from the sky.

But then again, the paratroopers weren't there to fight the people on the ramparts, if there were any. Their fight would be underground.

All this happened inside those ten crucial seconds—including Bing seeing the white Range Rover. With all the excitement and confusion typical of any combat action, he didn't think much about it again.

CAPTAIN Vogel, CO of the 82nd Airborne paratroopers, was one of the first to hit the ground. He gathered in his chute and snapped the safety off his M4. His men were floating down all around him. One thousand feet up, he could just barely sense Bing finally accelerate the big C-17 and literally disappear into the night.

Vogel couldn't hear any return fire coming from the fort. The entire place was engulfed in flames, so this wasn't a shock. The 82nd's task was to go underground, where an unknown number of enemy fighters were probably hiding. But to get no return fire at all seemed a testament to the AC-17 and the training all of the 201st had gone through a million years ago in Nevada. Time well spent, Vogel thought.

As soon as he had a squad of twelve men around him, Vogel started running toward the fort. More paratroopers were close behind, everyone moving swiftly through the darkness courtesy of their RIFs. Vogel led them in a line along the western wall, trying their best to see through the smoke that was billowing everywhere. They reached the blasted away hole in the fort's entrance just as the Marine tanks did—again, perfect timing on the part of the 201st.

The two tanks screeched to a halt in front of Vogel. Captain Cardillo, the tank unit's CO, relayed a series of hand signals to the 82nd CO; Vogel replied in kind. Neither had taken any fire from the fort, and they were ready to proceed.

Now came the hard part. Gunn's AC-17 had certainly softened up the target for them. But again, their training told them that in the case of these warlord mullahs, if they were attacked overwhelmingly, the chances were good that their hard-core soldiers along with their leaders would lock themselves away in any bunkers hidden beneath their mosque. The idea was that any kind of soldier, Western or Muslim, would refrain from wholesale attack on a holy place—and in many cases that was probably true.

But not when it came to the 201st. Just the opposite, in fact. They were in the business of blowing mosques apart.

That didn't mean it would be easy, though.

The paratroopers took cover behind the two tanks and together the strike force entered the fort. It was like walking into hell. Fire and smoke were everywhere, but also great quantities of white ash were falling on them like some bizarre otherworldly snow. It was like trying to navigate a city that had been nuked, and the falling ash made it all look weirdly winterish. The 201st soldiers were soon covered with it.

They saw no enemy fighters as they inched forward, not even any bodies. But again, after what Gunn had done to this place, this was no big surprise. Following a map hastily made from Moon's recon photos, the strike force spread out through the burning fort, hitting some key points and checking the few buildings that were left standing. But still they found no one, dead or alive.

Somehow through the thick smoke, they located the road that served as the fort's main thoroughfare. It was littered with burning trucks, artillery pieces, large guns and rocket launchers—enough equipment to supply a small army had been caught out in the open by Gunn's bolt from the blue. It took all the power the tanks had to push through some of it; the trailing paratroopers found themselves running gauntlets of flame just to keep up with the Marine M1-A1s. Meanwhile, the solders continued checking every structure still standing. But again, no one, living or dead, was found.

IT took longer than expected, but the strike force finally located the spot where, according to Moon's recon photos, the mosque should be. What they found instead was just another pile of smoking rubble with a wall of flame rising from it.

This was expected. If the CIA had been right all along, the concrete bunkers built beneath these holy buildings were so strong, even a direct hit by a cruise missile wouldn't put a dent in them. But everything—and every person—had a weak spot. The 201st's paratroopers were expert in looking for them.

Vogel gave another series of hand signals and his troopers immediately encircled the devastated building. Under the protection of the Marine armor, their goal was to locate any means of access to what lay beneath the smoking rubble.

It didn't take long. A few minutes into the search two troopers found a large steel-reinforced door beneath the debris. It was flush against a horizontal concrete pad, just about where the rear entrance to the mosque would have been.

Vogel and Cardillo examined the door and agreed it was

what they'd been looking for. The paratroopers' sapper squad was brought up; they applied a plastic charge to the door and suggested everyone take cover. They activated the charge and the resulting explosion blew the door off its hinges. But looking in, the sappers discovered yet another steel door about ten feet beyond the first. And this one was as thick as a bank vault.

The sappers quickly determined that no plastic charge would dislodge this behemoth. Vogel conferred with Cardillo, and in seconds the Marine CO had moved his tank up to the area in question. It took a few moments of awkward maneuvering, but finally the Marines were able to put the muzzle of their huge 122mm cannon directly on the second entryway. Those soldiers in the vicinity quickly took cover and then Cardillo fired a shell point-blank into the door. There was a huge storm of sizzling sparks and a long sheet of flame as the barrier was reduced to hot metal and dust. When the smoke cleared, the sappers found that the Marine tank had done its job well. Trouble was, there was another door beyond it, just as thick, just as heavy.

Another round of tank maneuvering ensued. This door was thirty feet down, so deep that it required Cardillo's tank to put its right-side track up on a pile of rubble and then turn its turret so that it was sticking almost straight down. The acrobatics looked strange, but when the tank fired yet another shell, the third time proved to be the charm. Finally the 201st had broken through to the mosque's one and only bunker.

Weapons up, gas masks on, a select twenty-member squad went down into the smoking hole, Vogel in the lead.

Beyond the third blasted door was a narrow vertical passageway containing a set of rickety metal stairs. They seemed to drop right into the middle of the Earth itself. Vogel flipped down his RIFs to see that the stairs went down about fifty feet to a concrete landing, where he saw . . . yet another door, this one made of thick wood.

Moving carefully, he reached the concrete landing and then just stopped and listened. He could hear nothing coming from the other side of the wooden door. He set a plastic explosive against the door's sill and started unwinding its fuse. But before he could activate the *plastique*, he was surprised to hear the door squeak open on its own.

Very weird.

Vogel held his men in place. Then, again moving very carefully and slowly, he toed the door open further, stuck his M4 in ahead of him and fired off a burst. No one fired back. He tried it again, but still no response. There was no noise at all coming from inside the bunker. Nothing was moving; everything was just dark and quiet.

Finally, Vogel set his RIFs on high power, pushed the door open and looked in.

He was immediately nauseous. He vomited heavily, staggering back against the metal staircase. Were his RIFs playing tricks on him? Had he suddenly gone insane?

He took a deep breath and looked inside the bunker again. That's when he realized that what he'd seen was real—and absolutely horrible.

"Goddamn . . ." he gasped. "What the hell happened here?"

GUNN was in his twenty-second orbit of the burning fort when his headphones started crackling.

It was Vogel. He sounded uncharacteristically troubled.

"Sir—we have a situation down here," the paratrooper CO began. Gunn looked at the burning target below.

"What kind of situation?" he asked.

Vogel hesitated before answering. Then he said: "A 'Flash-Delta' situation."

Gunn felt his body freeze up. Flash-Delta was an unofficial all-encompassing special ops term for something words couldn't describe, as in "freaky-deaky." Despite the comical name, it was not a phrase that black ops operators used lightly.

"'Flash Delta'?" Gunn asked him. "Are you sure?"

Again there was a delay in Vogel's reply. Then he said: "I think you better see for yourself, sir."

GUNN put his plane down on the hard sand and rolled up as close as he could to the remains of the fort. Amanda's plane was several hundred yards off to his left, as was Bing's. A few hundred feet above, Moon was circling in the minicopter, serving as their lookout while the rest of the 201st was on the ground.

Gunn climbed out of the AC-17 and took a long look inside the fort. He was astonished at the extent of the devastation. It appeared much worse from ground level than from the air. Flames and ash falling. Smashed and burned equipment. Smoke everywhere. But, strangely, no bodies . . .

He hurried down the rubble-strewn street, following a paratrooper's directions to the blown-to-bits mosque. So far, just about everything was as Gunn expected it to be. The fort was flattened, there was a bunker under the mosque, and as far as he knew, this was where most of the people in the fort had fled when the attack began. Nothing really freaky-deaky—yet.

He finally found what was left of the mosque and spotted the blasted out doorways. He passed the Marine tank standing guard nearby and went down the rickety metal stairs. He was struck by how eerily quiet everything was.

He stopped at the door, took a deep breath and then stepped inside the bunker—and for the first time in his life, he felt he'd really seen hell.

Bodies. Lots of them. Everywhere . . .

In one corner of the large concrete room, there were at least a hundred corpses, stacked like a pile of cordwood. All of them were dressed in combat gear; all had been shot or stabbed. Yet many still had guns and knives in their hands. As improbable as it seemed, it appeared they'd all died while fighting one another, and then someone stacked their bodies almost as high as the ceiling. This was why there'd been no opposition for 201st's attack on the fort. All its defenders were down here, dead.

But that was not the most disturbing part of what he saw. There were more bodies here—civilians, another hundred or so. They were lined up in rows in the center of the room, men mostly, but also many women and children. These people were not run-of-the-mill gang fighters or militia types either. Some were well dressed in new camos and new boots. Judging from the size of some of the adults, they were well fed too.

These people were not Africans—they were definitely Middle Eastern; the color of their skin gave that away. Nor had they been killed in the fighting or by the effort the 201st had made to get into the bunker.

Rather, they'd been butchered or, more accurately, cleanly sliced into pieces, even the children, and their body parts rearranged in bizarre, pornographic positions.

Gunn had been in combat situations before. He'd been inside the terrorist stronghold at Bora Kurd at the height of the killing frenzy and madness there. But like Vogel and the other combat veterans on the scene, he'd never seen anything like this.

"Who are these people?" he finally asked Vogel, watching as the 82nd's medics went over the corpses, trying to make some sense of the carnage. "I thought anyone connected with a warlord mullah would be wearing rags and sandals—and definitely not have women and kids with them."

Vogel just shook his head. "Your guess is as good as mine," he replied. "These people weren't rag-tag. They had money. Well dressed, well fed. Some still had valuables in their pockets. And it looks like they'd been living out here for a while. Funny place to take a vacation."

Gunn looked at the remains of five or maybe six women lying in a row nearby—it was hard to tell. Those with clothes still on were wearing upscale Middle Eastern garments, something seen on people in Persian Gulf super malls. Close by were the remains of some teenagers, girls and boys, horribly dismembered and posed as if in horrific sexual acts. They were wearing chic safari-type clothes, as were even the youngest children. It was some of these young victims that had been placed in the most hideous positions.

It was just too much to take. Combat veterans though they were, this was indeed Flash-Delta.

Vogel and Gunn retreated back up the stairs to the rubble-strewn street, leaving the unlucky medics alone in the real-life Bosch painting. Vogel nervously lit a cigarette.

"That won't be easy to forget," he said, blowing out a cloud of smoke. "Like I don't already have enough stuff keeping me up at night."

Gunn could only shake his head in agreement. "This is a not a Janjaweed thing," he said. "Not an internecine fight or a feud. Sledgehammers didn't do that."

"But what is the point of it?" Vogel asked him after another few puffs. "To leave them there . . . like that?"

"Someone wanted to leave a message," Gunn said. "To make it clear that they're some kind of sick force to be reckoned with."

"But someone like who?" Vogel asked. "I mean, those people were killed not too long before we got here."

A voice behind them said: "Maybe it was whoever was driving that Red Cross truck."

They turned to see that Amanda had come up behind them.

"Is it as bad as I hear?" she asked them, putting a kerchief over her nose and mouth.

"You can't see it," Gunn replied. "Just take our word for it, it is."

She looked at him with a surprised expression. "I can't see it?" she asked. "Why?"

Gunn changed the subject. "What Red Cross truck are you talking about?" he asked her.

Amanda told them what she'd seen. Just a flash of white going by her nosewheel camera, a truck with a red cross painted on its door. The driver was moving extremely fast, no doubt spooked by the fort being obliterated and obviously surprised that a huge plane was nearly landing on top of him.

This was the first Gunn and Vogel had heard about any vehicle.

"Lieutenant Bing saw it too," she told them. "We just talked about it a few minutes ago."

She started to brush past them, heading for the bunker stairs. But Gunn stopped her again. "I mean it, Lieutenant, it isn't a good idea that you go down there."

She just looked back at him strangely. "Excuse me, Major—is that an order? Or did you suddenly become my father?"

That hurt Gunn so much, he nearly crumpled to the ground. They stood there for a few moments—a sort of standoff. Then she put the kerchief back over her mouth and gently nudged him aside. He finally let her go.

Vogel nervously lit another cigarette as they both watched her descend the stairs. "She's got to learn, I guess," he said. Then after blowing out a long stream of smoke, he asked: "This truck thing is strange. Maybe it was a Red Cross person who had seen what happened here and was going for help? Or someone just trying to get out of our way?"

Gunn pulled out his sat-phone and started punching in a number.

"Maybe we can find out," he said.

LIEUTENANT Moon answered Gunn's call on the second beep.

He was still circling the fort, looking out in every direction, making sure no one was in the neighborhood watching the 201st do its thing.

He too had seen the mysterious Range Rover leaving the scene and heading west just as the attack was beginning.

Now that hostilities had ceased, Gunn wanted Moon to try to find the white and red vehicle again. On getting the order, Moon immediately turned the minicopter west and gunned its tiny engine up to maximum speed.

It was only a few minutes later when he thought he'd spotted his prey. Some twenty miles from the burning fort, over a small mountain range, Moon came upon a road winding its way through the desert. On this road he saw not one but about two dozen white Range Rovers. They were heading north, all of them marked with the sign of the Red Cross and a few of them even flying large Red Cross flags.

You've got to be kidding me, Moon thought.

His plan had been to somehow disable the Range Rover if he caught up with it. He had his M4 with him. A surgical one or two shots across the truck's bow would have done it, or maybe in its tires if it refused to stop. But this—there was no way he could fire on a convoy of relief trucks.

He tracked the column for a few minutes, but the desert was so vast, it was impossible to tell where it had come from or where it was going—or whether the vehicle he'd been chasing had joined it, or was somewhere else entirely.

Besides, it was getting near dawn—and that meant the unit's "invisible" planes would lose a lot of their cloaking ability soon.

Finally, Moon just gave up and turned the copter back toward the burning fort. The relief convoy kept on going north, disappearing over the next set of hills and finally out of sight completely.

Moon pushed his throttle ahead, but then something caught his attention off to the right. It was a column of smoke, rising up from behind a sand dune. He steered the minicopter in that direction and, upon passing over the dune, saw a burning vehicle below, hanging off the edge of a narrow pathway that just barely cut between the sand dunes.

It was a Range Rover, he could tell, even though it was totally engulfed in flames. And though the last of its paint was just burning away, he thought the vehicle could have been painted white, but there was no way of telling for sure. He could see no bodies, however. No one was around the burning vehicle at all.

Was this the truck seen leaving the fort at high speed at the beginning of the attack? Or had that vehicle joined the convoy he'd spotted and this was something else?

He went lower and started circling. He saw footprints and then a large circular outline made by blowing sand. He'd seen patterns like this before: They were left when a helicopter landed in the desert. They were unmistakable.

So what happened here? Had a helicopter attacked this vehicle? Or had the helicopter rescued the person after the vehicle crashed? Or had the driver intentionally crashed the vehicle and let the waiting helicopter pick him up? Or was it none of the above? It was impossible for Moon to tell.

He took a few pictures on his camera phone and once again headed back toward the fort, more perplexed than ever.

This time he took a more direct route over a deep desert valley, formed by narrow columns of sharp, craggy rocks. He was halfway over this valley when he glanced below—and saw yet another Range Rover. This one was indeed white and had a Red Cross on its door and had apparently crashed into the valley from the road up above. But the vehicle looked old, as if it had been at the bottom of the gorge for years. Still, it was so weird that he'd actually spotted the thing.

His fuel was running low; he had to get back to the unit. So he circled this valley just once, took a few pictures and then headed east again.

The desert is a strange place, he thought.

GUNN was still standing next to the stairs leading down to the bunker when Cardillo appeared out of the smoke and falling ash. Vogel had returned to the bloody bunker to help his medics try to sort it all out.

Gunn was pretending to jot down notes, but what he was really doing was waiting for Amanda to emerge from the horror show below. He was hoping she'd fall into his arms and apologize and tell him she should have taken his advice. But as each minute passed and she didn't come up, he knew the likelihood of anything like that happening was remote.

Cardillo approached him after positioning one of the two tanks at the end of the fort's main street. He and his men had driven around the entire fort and had confirmed that there was no opposition anywhere.

"What do you think is going on here, Major?" the Marine CO asked him, nodding toward the hole leading down into the bunker. "It seems anyone who was here wound up down there, dead."

Gunn could only shake his head. "Something happened

here between yesterday and this morning. Something worse than whatever we could have done."

Cardillo wiped his ash-strewn brow with his hands.

Then he said: "I know this will sound funny—but do you want to see something really strange, Major?"

"Stranger than what's down there?" Gunn asked.

Cardillo shrugged. "Maybe," he said.

THEY made their way to the western edge of the devastated fort; two of the few buildings left standing were located there. Made of heavy blocks of stone, one looked to be a small prison; the second Gunn immediately recognized as the building that had given Mdosi the creeps back in the pre-strike briefing.

Oddly though, this building was not an ammo dump as Mdosi had feared. Instead, it was a garage. Inside were three trucks.

But they were not ordinary trucks.

They mostly resembled the typical generic lorry that could be found all over Europe, the Middle East and Africa, a vehicle about half the size of a U.S.-style tractor-trailer. But these three trucks were hardly typical. First, they had steel plating welded on just about anywhere it would fit: the doors, the hood, the fenders. Their wheels were apparently made of reinforced steel, and their tires of the hardest rubber imaginable, the same as used on military vehicles like the Stryker. The cab windows were thick and obviously made of bulletproof glass. The steering wheel, accelerator, brakes and shift all seemed more elaborate than they should be. For want of a better word, the trucks were armored. Or better yet: bombproof. And they were also built to carry things. Their cargo bays were at least able to hold forty cubic feet of something.

"Could these be the 'Brinks trucks' that Moon's friend told him about?" Cardillo asked.

Gunn shook his head. "They must be. But what are they really? They're too big, too expensive, too everything to be out here in the middle of nowhere."

Cardillo agreed. "They also look like they could take a direct hit from just about anything and have it bounce off. Even if you'd targeted this building, I'm not sure it would have made a dent in these things. Plus it looks like there might have been more than just these three here."

He pointed to a series of tire tracks that could barely be seen on the rubble-strewn ground. There were five slots in the garage, three trucks and two sets of tire tracks.

"Two left here, sometime recently," Cardillo concluded.

"But what the hell are these things for?" Gunn wondered aloud. "They almost look like something used in a mine— but much more elaborate."

"The question is, what are we going to do about them?" Cardillo asked. "They're too big to bring back with us."

Gunn just shook his head. "Let's see what a grenade or two will do."

He and Cardillo tossed hand grenades into the backs of the overly armored trucks. They were hoping to ignite the gas tanks on the giants, but after three tries, it proved fruitless. The grenades did little or no damage to the vehicles. Their gas tanks were armored, as were the filling pipes, which were also triple-locked. The result was like throwing hand grenades at a twenty-foot-thick wall.

Gunn checked his watch. It was now 0445. They'd been on the ground fifteen minutes, not very long at all. But the sun was coming; the eastern horizon was just beginning to soften with bare light. Like vampires, the 201st didn't operate best during the daylight. They had to fly back to Wum Bakim while it was still dark. It was time to go.

Two clicks on Gunn's sat-phone sent an order to all of the 201st's officers that they had to get moving. But just then, Gunn saw movement in the rubble near the prison building. Gunn and Cardillo had their weapons up in a flash.

They approached the battered jailhouse and discovered three African women huddled next to a large piece of wreckage. Barely clothed and very frightened, they were trying to hide. It was also clear that all three were blind.

Gunn helped them out of the rubble while Cardillo called for the medics and a translator. Gunn gave them his canteen and the three women drank from it greedily. One of Mdosi's men arrived quickly and started to translate.

Gunn asked him to ask the three what they were doing out here. The women kept saying: "Dwilly . . . Dwilly." Prison. They were prisoners here.

"'Comfort women,'" Mdosi's man added. "Women on hand to rape at will."

"Why are they blind?" Gunn asked.

"They say these people burned their eyes out so they couldn't look back at them while they were raping them," the translator replied.

"Class act," Cardillo said angrily.

Gunn asked the three women where the people who rebuilt this place originated.

They all shook their heads violently. It was clear they didn't want to talk about that, at least not now. But through a torrent of tears, the oldest of the three did manage to tell them that she and the others had "seen" one man here—the Devil himself—even though they were without their eyes. And they were afraid for their lives because of it.

Gunn's sat-phone rang. It was Vogel, asking what they should do with the people in the bunker. Gunn told him to take lots of pictures—and then burn the place. They had to be off the ground in five minutes.

He turned back to the three women. "Let's bring them with us," he told Cardillo; the Marine officer signaled for the medics to take care of the women. "Once they are fed and not in shock, maybe they can fill in a few more missing pieces."

Their attention turned back to the garage and the three weird trucks. Cardillo looked over at Gunn and shrugged.

The rest of the unit was out of the fort by now, including the tanks. The airplanes' engines were starting up again. They had to get going.

"We'll just leave them," Gunn told Cardillo, stopping to take a few photos of the vehicles with his camera phone. "I'll try something else."

Cardillo signaled the last of his men and, together with Gunn and a few stragglers, finally left the bombed-out, decimated fort.

IT was now 0450 hours. All three planes were back in the air.

As the others circled nearby, Gunn put his huge gunship in a tight circle one more time above the burning fort. He lined up the garage containing the armored trucks and let fly with his Bushmasters. They impacted all over the garage, blowing away its concrete walls and roof. But when the smoke and flames cleared, the three unusual trucks remained, smoking, dented, but still more or less intact.

Gunn went around again, this time adding his two artillery pieces to the barrage. The fire and smoke were blinding as always. But once again, when they cleared away, he could see the trucks were only slightly more battered than before.

He went around a third time, calling up his Vulcan cannons and the awesome Phoenix CIWS gun and adding them to the Bushmasters and the M102s. This barrage lit up the waning night for miles around and absolutely flattened both the garage and the small prison building next to it.

But again, when the smoke cleared, the three trucks were still more or less in one piece, still upright, their tires still supporting them, smoking heavily, but much more than the three piles of metallic dust that they should have been.

Gunn couldn't believe it.

The one-sided attack, the carnage in the bunker, the bizarre trucks.

He checked the time. Just 0455 hours—and already it was one of the strangest days of his life.

CHAPTER SIX

Wum Bakim

The Fireship landed with its usual thump, its brakes screaming and throwing up a storm of sand and dust in its wake.

Gunn applied a minimal amount of the wing-mounted retro-rockets, further slowing the huge gunship. He quickly rolled the AC-17 to the end of the runway as Amanda was coming in right on his tail. Turning left, he saw her touch down, applying just a bit of her retro blasts as well.

He braked the big airplane to a stop and just sat there for a moment collecting his thoughts. The mission had been a success. They'd destroyed the religious fort just as they'd been trained to do—and indeed there was no doubt that's what the place had once been.

But what they saw after the attack was anything but clear. Who were those people in the bunker? Who had so brutally killed them? And "killed" wasn't even the right word. They'd been ritualistically slaughtered, with no evidence of any resistance, at least not against whoever orchestrated the hideous massacre. But the way the bodies were positioned after death, or possibly while being killed . . .

those images would never leave Gunn's mind. The three blind women claimed they'd seen the Devil himself—and Gunn was starting to believe them.

He took off his crash helmet and wiped his furrowed brow. That's when he noticed that something else was odd. The base runway lights were still illuminated. Usually Colonel Mdosi's men shut them off as soon as the 201st's planes touched down. In this case, the Jump Plane was a few minutes behind him and Amanda—and Gunn had radioed the base that this was the case. So the lights should have been extinguished as soon as he and Amanda arrived, to be turned back on only when Bing's plane was within thirty seconds of touching down. It was a small thing, but a critical one. The air base had to stay secret from everybody—the locals, the 201st's newly acquired enemies, spy satellites, both friendly and not. Everybody . . .

Keeping the lights on could expose them in ways that might prove disastrous.

Gunn secured his flight deck and climbed out of the gunship, heading for the Ops building. The jungle was quiet—that was also weird. Even though it was just 0525 hours, this part of Africa had so much nocturnal animal activity it was sometimes quieter at high noon than in the dead of night.

He walked by Amanda's airplane and gave her a thumbs-up.

"Someone forget to hit the off switch?" she called down to him, also noticing the still-glowing runway lights.

"I'll find out," Gunn called back up to her.

Ten seconds later, Gunn walked through the Ops building door and into Colonel Mdosi's office. The normally smiling officer was sitting behind his desk, looking very stiff, his nearly seven-foot frame all tension and right angles. And he was sweating—this Gunn had never seen before.

He looked Gunn right in the eye and said: "I'm sorry, Major. They came from nowhere."

He nodded to the other side of the room. Gunn turned and saw a dozen weapons pointing back at him.

"Unstrap your sidearm," a muffled voice ordered him. "Then put your hands over your head."

AMANDA lingered inside her cockpit, eyes still on the burning runway lights. She secretly wished she'd heeded Gunn's advice and not gone into the bunker. Those images would be burned into her brain forever, as would the mystery of how anyone could do anything so grotesque and inhuman. What she'd seen back there made what gangs like the Janjaweed did seem like a picnic.

But her stomach was getting tight now and it wasn't entirely from the horror viewed at the old fort. Something was not right here at Wum Bakim. She could feel it.

Her copilot was a young Air Force pilot named Stanley. She leaned over and tapped him on the knee.

"Contact Lieutenant Bing," she said quietly, looking into Stanley's eyes. "Tell him there might be some debris on the runway, that he should be careful."

Then she climbed off the flight deck, gave a quick salute to Moon and the Marines in back, and opened the access door to step outside.

She was met by the barrel of an automatic rifle pointing right between her eyes.

"Don't move," a voice ordered her. "Unstrap your weapon—let it fall to the ground."

Amanda did so, slowly, her eyes adjusting to the glare of the runway lights and the total darkness beyond. About a dozen armed men were pointing guns at her. Another dozen were in position at the back of her aircraft.

They were all wearing black camos, goggles and ski masks covering their faces. Their weapons were flashing bright red laser pointers everywhere.

This can't be good, she thought.

* * *

AMANDA was marched into Mdosi's office, where Gunn and the colonel were sitting under heavy guard.

Gunn exchanged dejected glances with her as she was put in a chair right next to him. As soon as she was seated, one of their captors announced: "Our orders are to hold you all here until higher authority arrives."

"So you're arresting us?" Amanda asked him.

"Call it what you want," the man replied.

"Who sent you?" Gunn asked.

The man chuckled. "You know better than to ask that, major."

Gunn took stock of their captors. They were all wearing the same style of black uniform, their faces covered with ski masks. They were all carrying the same type of weapon: rather elderly M16s. So they were probably Americans. But they weren't typical Army special ops. Gunn studied their footwear. It looked highly waterproof. Were these guys SEALs maybe?

"Give me a hint," he pressed the man. "A name. A unit."

The man waved away Gunn's questions. "We get orders. We follow orders. End of story. Besides, what difference does it make? You've been caught. Now just sit tight and wait for the warden to come."

Those words hit Gunn like a sledgehammer. *Now* he knew what this was all about—and he'd feared this day since the moment they'd left Nevada for their rescue mission to the wilds of Pakistan. From the moment their wheels left the ground he'd known—they'd *all* known—that because they were stepping on the wrong side of the law, eventually Uncle Sam would come looking for them.

Now that reality had apparently arrived.

In those dark moments when the 201st's senior people had discussed this scenario, it was assumed that once they were caught, they would be looking at a minimum of twenty

years in prison for a variety of crimes. Unauthorized use of
U.S. military equipment. Being AWOL. Maybe even deser-
tion. The death penalty was always a possibility—only
there were more than a hundred of them, and they couldn't
imagine the military shooting that many of their own. But
for people like Gunn, for whom flying was everything, the
thought of sitting in a cell for the next two decades made
going before a firing squad seem like an attractive alternative.

He felt the worst for Amanda, because he knew the
military would not go easy on her, for fear of a backlash
from the Tailhook crowd. So she too would be severely
punished, as would Newman and the other officers of the
renegade band. They'd all agreed that when this day came,
in return for full cooperation, they'd ask that their enlisted
personnel get off easy. After all, they were just following
orders, like good soldiers do. It might work and it might
not—but the 201st's brass knew that after what they'd all
gone through, trying to save the noncoms would be essen-
tial. The same would go for Colonel Mdosi and his men.

"How long do we wait here like this?" Gunn asked the
masked men. "We just returned for a mission. Our people
are tired."

"So are we," the spokesman replied quickly. "It wasn't
easy finding you guys. So you'll stay like this for however
long it takes."

"But what if we decide to just walk out of here?" Amanda
asked him.

"We have orders to shoot you," the man replied emphatically. "Simple as that."

Gunn slumped even deeper into his seat. He'd always tried to steer clear of pessimism, but all hope seemed
lost now.

Until he saw the face at the window.

It was Lieutenant Bing. His features were blackened with

camouflage paint and he had his RIF night-vision goggles on, but it was unmistakably the guy everyone called "Bada." He was looking in the small, cracked window right behind Mdosi's desk, surveying the room, while managing not to be seen by anyone except Gunn.

But this was not good. The masked men were under the impression that they'd captured the entire unit—and so was Gunn until this moment. But Bing had not landed at the secret base because, Gunn would learn later, Amanda had tipped him off. Bing knew something was wrong, and now he was here, looking in the window, assessing the situation. It showed real courage and good thinking, but Gunn knew it was also a recipe for disaster, as Bing and the paratroopers his plane carried probably had no idea these weren't exactly hostile troops holding them captive.

Blue on Blue . . .

It was the term for people on the same side shooting at each other. Friendly fire. A fuckup in communications. It's what got Pat Tillman and many other good soldiers killed over the years. It was a symptom of the confusion of combat—and at the moment Gunn could understand how Bing and the 82nd guys might be confused. They didn't know what he, Amanda and Mdosi knew.

He felt a shiver go through him.

If the 82nd came in shooting . . .

As it turned out, Bing and the paratroopers had the secret base surrounded.

Warned off by Amanda, Bing had expertly set the Jump Plane down on a rough road about a klick from the base. Then he and Vogel's paratroopers had doubled-timed it up to Wum Bakim to find it had been taken over by an armed force, origin unknown. Armed men were standing around the two landed planes and guarding the front of the Ops building. Others had corralled the 201st's enlisted personnel as well as Mdosi's men, Lieutenant Moon and all the

Marines, under the camouflage tents and had them under heavy guard as well. In all, Bing counted about fifty armed intruders spread out around the small air base.

Because of their superior infiltration techniques and knowledge of the surrounding terrain, the 82nd had encircled the place within minutes of arriving. But now they were faced with the question: What to do next?

It called for some advanced recon. That's why Bing had volunteered to bypass the mysterious soldiers and steal up to the rear of the Ops building. But surveying the situation inside only added to the confusion. He saw more armed men with their weapons trained on Gunn, Amanda and Mdosi, but he'd seen no indication who the masked intruders were or what they wanted.

Bing made his way back to where Vogel had positioned himself. The 82nd's CO and a squad of his men were stationed just off the south end of the runway, laying low in the thick jungle. Bing told Vogel what he'd seen.

"And no idea who they are?" Vogel asked.

Bing could only shrug. "None," he replied. "They're dressed in generic combat suits. They're carrying M16s. They've got their faces covered with ski masks. Could be anyone."

Vogel shook his head. "We've been making a fuss around here lately. I guess no matter how quiet we tried to be, it was just a matter of time before someone came looking for us. They might be mercs, hired by someone to spank us. Or maybe a rebel gang, here to rob us—and then slit our throats."

"Well, either way, we've got to hit them first," Bing replied.

"Roger that," Vogel replied. He made a series of hand gestures to his men nearby—and they in turn passed them on to the paratroopers surrounding the base.

The plan went around silently. The paratroopers' half

dozen sniper-rated soldiers would move into position and pick off as many of the intruders as possible. Then the rest of the paratroopers would move in. Half the force would take out the soldiers holding the 201st personnel under the camo netting; the others would assault the Ops building and those standing near the planes. The paratroopers outnumbered the assailants two to one. The problem was that pulling off the rescue without getting any 201st people killed was a virtual impossibility.

"But we gotta do what we gotta do," Vogel said, jamming a fresh clip into his M4. "They'd do the same for us."

He and Bing synchronized their watches. "Three minutes for everyone to get in position," Vogel said. "Then we go in shooting."

GUNN was sweating now.

The face at the window had disappeared, but he knew things were happening in the jungle around the base—he could sense it, that's how in tune he was with the 201st. The paratroopers obviously had these guys surrounded, and at any minute they were going to try a rescue with guns blazing.

Moments before all this, he'd thought the worst thing that could happen was they'd all go back to the U.S. to face prison. Right now, he would have given anything for that outcome. What they were looking at was a bloodbath between Americans deep in darkest Africa, all of them dying anonymously. A Blue on Blue battle here would be so highly classified, the details would never see the light of day. And there was nothing any of them could do about it. To tip the intruders that the paratroopers were outside would just lead to another kind of gun battle. Yet there was no way to warn the paratroopers to hold off.

Gunn had never felt so low than at that moment.

What a weird place to end, he thought.

* * *

VOGEL had taken two dozen men and positioned them just opposite the camo tents. They could see at least twenty of the intruders holding guns on the airplane crews, Moon, Mdosi's men, the three blind women and the Marines.

Luckily, the intruders had the hostages sitting, and they themselves were standing. Perfect for the snipers' head shots.

Vogel then doubled back and joined a third squad of paratroopers laying low in the grass right next to the pair of parked C-17s. The largest group of armed men watching the airplanes was just twenty yards away.

Vogel checked his watch. Two minutes to go . . .

Meanwhile Bing had taken another squad of paratroopers and cut around the front of the runway, where a half dozen of the intruders were standing a few feet from the entrance to the Ops building. They would handle these guys once the snipers started shooting and then join in the attack to liberate the building itself.

He checked his watch.

One minute to go . . .

ANOTHER face appeared at the cracked window.

Gunn saw it, and this time so did Amanda. It was one of Vogel's paratroopers. He was holding a sniper rifle. He was signaling them that they should get ready to hit the floor.

Amanda knew what was happening now; after all she had been the one who warned Bing that all was not right at the base. So, in a way, she would feel responsible for any bloodshed that followed.

What if we just told them? she thought. Told them they were surrounded by the 82nd Airborne? No—she was sure this would cause gunfire as well. Even if they did believe her.

But she didn't know what else to do.

VOGEL checked his watch again.

Twenty seconds . . .

He signaled his snipers. They were ready.

Fifteen seconds . . .

He checked his men along the runway. They replied with a silent thumbs-up.

He looked back at the paratroopers stationed near the camo tents. Another thumbs-up.

He checked with Bing. He too was ready.

Ten seconds.

Vogel checked his own weapon. It was locked and loaded.

He stopped for a moment and said a silent prayer that the very minimum of 201st personnel would get hurt in what was to come.

Then he raised his hand—and started to give the signal to open fire . . .

But suddenly . . . Vogel saw a glint of light above the base. It distracted him just long enough to hold off giving the firing order.

His men saw it too. It was a helicopter—but not a typical one. It was right over them, hovering silently.

"What the fuck is this?" Vogel thought aloud.

The aircraft started descending, and it took a few seconds for Vogel and the others to realize this was an EC-135 Eurocopter, probably the most expensive nonmilitary copter in existence. Considered the Ferrari of rotary craft, this one was painted in weird black camouflage paint with a small forest of antennas stretched along its underside.

It landed on the edge of the runway, no more than twenty

feet in front of Vogel and his men. The hatchway opened and a man in an all-black combat suit stepped out.

Vogel's men were on him in an instant, roughly tackling him and forcing him to the ground. Other paratroopers had their weapons on the copter's crew in a flash. But some of the armed men standing near the airplanes had seen the helicopter's arrival and a half dozen ran over to investigate. They didn't seem surprised to see the black EC-135, but when they saw the paratroopers holding the crew on the tarmac, their weapons went up immediately. The same was true with the armed men at the Ops building and those guarding the two C-17s. They suddenly realized that paratroopers were all around them.

A standoff . . .

The paratroopers had their weapons trained on the intruders and the intruders were aiming back. No shooting yet, but one wrong move, and they'd all be dead.

That's when Vogel turned over the tackled man—and realized he knew the guy. He was Mark Downes, U.S. Special Forces Command, the same organization the 201st used to work for. The last time Vogel had seen him, Downes was a captain. Now he was wearing the eagle insignia of a full colonel.

At that moment, someone shot off a flare. And then someone else killed all the lights in the buildings and then along the runway. And then a fire broke out somewhere.

And suddenly the night air echoed with the cry: "Don't shoot! We're Americans!"

The paratroopers, not knowing what else to do, jumped the startled intruders guarding the camo tents and began pummeling them. Mdosi's men and the Marines joined the fray, helping the paratroopers overwhelm the intruders guarding the aircrews.

Meanwhile an even larger fight broke out around the expensive helicopter, quickly spilling over to the front of the Ops building. Vogel was at the bottom of one pile of opposing soldiers brutally punching and kicking one another. So many people were yelling "Blue on Blue!" his ears were hurting. And flares kept going off, as the fists continued to fly and the copter's huge rotors were still spinning at high speed, blowing everything around, including some human beings.

It was complete madness for a full minute, until someone let loose with a long burst of tracer fire just over the heads of the main fight out on the runway. The sound of the machine gun was enough to freeze everybody. "Confirmed Blue on Blue!" someone started yelling. "Stand down!"

The piles next to the copter broke up gradually, and soon enough, both Vogel and the person he'd tackled were on their feet.

Vogel just couldn't believe it was Downes. The guy was like a saint inside Special Ops Command. One of the few military people permanently assigned to Area 153, Downes was not only a bigwig in Delta Force, he was also a member of several other deep black op units. Vogel was very disheartened to see Downes's lip was bleeding and his eye already sporting a shiner. Assaulting a superior officer had just been added to his long list of offenses.

Downes brushed himself off and then started yelling orders—to everyone.

"Stow all weapons! Next person who discharges his weapon sees a firing squad!"

With that, complete silence came over the air base. Even the copter's pilots started shutting down their engines.

"Who is the senior commander here?" Downes demanded to know.

It was at that moment that Gunn and Amanda walked out of the Ops building, having left Colonel Mdosi's office in the confusion once the lights had gone out. They joined the gaggle of disheveled people next to the swank EC-135.

Gunn was also shocked to see Downes; he'd only heard

of the legendary officer, had never met him. But in that instant, Gunn knew Downes was the perfect person the government would send to find the 201st and bring them back to justice. Especially now that he'd been bumped up to colonel.

So he walked up to him and saluted somberly.

"Major Gunn," he said. "At your service, sir."

FIVE minutes passed, and while not calming down completely, things at Wum Bakim did come under some semblance of control.

All weapons on both sides had their ammo clips taken out and the safeties locked on. Downes's men took up positions around the helicopter; the 82nd stood along the edge of the jungle. Both sides eyed each other suspiciously, nursing their many busted lips and bruises.

Returning to the Ops building, Downes, Amanda, Moon and Gunn sat down at a long table; Vogel, Bing, Mdosi and Cardillo stood nearby, keeping an eye on their troops out the window.

Downes had a wet cloth up against his eye. He seemed too young to be a colonel—but if anyone was on the fast track, it was him. He was a small man, with a sophisticated air about him that made him seem like he was in his early thirties. Yet again, rumors were that he'd served in the notorious pre–Area 153 training ground called "War Heaven"— and that was in the late 1980s. Maybe one of the secrets of that old testing range was the secret of youth.

Laying the wet cloth aside, Downes seemed to regain enough of his composure to address those in the room.

But before he could speak, Gunn spoke instead: "If you are here to ask us to surrender, Colonel," he began, "then I have to tell you, I think you came a long way for nothing."

Downes looked surprised, but not insulted.

"An interesting opening statement, Major Gunn," he said. "Which means I must tell you that there are so many people who are calling for your heads, I hear they had to be talked out of just sending a few cruise missiles over and putting an end to this thing here and now."

"People are mad at us?" Gunn replied angrily. "Why? Because we eliminated a thousand al Qaeda–linked terrorists? Or that we stopped something that was going on in Pakistan that our entire armed forces could not stop? Or that we prevented a nuke from being smuggled into the United States?"

"I think it's more that you did all that by stealing three of the most highly classified weapons systems known to man," Downes countered.

"But what difference does that make?" Amanda growled, speaking for the first time. Gunn looked over at her—and he couldn't believe the words that came to his head. But, no exaggeration, she *did* look beautiful when she was mad. "Would these friends of yours rather have another big hole somewhere in Manhattan?"

Downes shook his head. "They are no friends of mine, Lieutenant. Though I'm sure a few of them are friends of Congressman Toole—or should I say, the late Congressman Toole?"

"He was just as bad as the terrorists we snuffed out," she said. "We heard him, plotting with that billionaire prince. They were intent on wreaking havoc in the Persian Gulf, in the U.S., and anywhere they could. The world is better off without both of them."

Downes gave her a sort of half salute. "Preaching to the choir," he said. "But still, you can't disagree that you've broken many, many laws. Military laws. National security laws."

Gunn and Amanda fell silent. Hanging on the fringes of the conversation was Lieutenant Moon. He said: "So that's why you're here? To bring us back to justice?"

Downes chose his next words carefully.

"Not exactly," he said. "Actually, I'm here to offer you a deal."

A ripple went through the room. Gunn was suddenly sitting straighter in his seat.

"Such as?" he asked.

"There's a new terrorist group that's popping up all over Africa," Downes began. "They are well financed and well trained—and Al Qaeda–connected of course. They are starting brushfire wars everywhere as a diversion for something else. Simply put: Help me find them and there will be much consideration in studying any charges that might be brought against you in the future."

Gunn was stunned. They all were.

But Gunn asked quickly: "Does that stand for everyone involved? Colonel Newman as well?"

Downes nodded. "Everyone's case will be considered."

A long silence in the room. Never had any of them thought that there might be a way of out of this mess.

Finally Moon spoke up again: "You say these terrorists are starting little wars as a diversion for 'something else'? What would that be?"

"Procuring a rare form of yellowcake uranium," Downes answered. "To be specific, so-called 'Yellowcake 212,' which, by certain chemical processes, can be enriched quickly and in small quantities and turned into fissionable material in a short amount of time. It's only been found here in Africa, so far, and we believe these terrorists are buying it, stealing it, grabbing as much as they can for eventual processing into nuclear weapons."

Another murmur went through the room.

"But it gets worse," Downes said. "We believe all this might also involve a person named Adolph Kaiser."

The normally unflappable Mdosi shifted uneasily in his seat.

"You've heard of this guy?" Gunn asked him.

"You haven't?" Mdosi asked.

All of the 201st's officers shook their heads no—except Moon. He suddenly looked as uncomfortable as Mdosi.

Mdosi said to Moon: "Do you want to tell them or should I?"

Moon became very nervous.

"Be my guest," he replied.

Mdosi took a deep breath, as if thinking about where to begin.

"No one is sure who Adolph Kaiser is," he said to start off. "Or even if he exists at all. Some rumors say he's a U.S. intelligence agent or SOF, or ex-KGB posing as a U.S. agent. Others say he's East German, or even Middle Eastern. What's clear is, if he is real, he's extremely wealthy. He owns vast quantities of Middle East oil and vast gold reserves—the only two currencies that speak loudly these days. Supposedly, he sneezes and the world's economy changes. But he's also a terrorist. Or better put, he's an *uber*-terrorist. Someone who, quite simply, wants to control the world—financially, politically and militarily.

Vogel audibly scoffed at this.

"You've been watching too many movies," he told Mdosi. "No one like that can be real."

Mdosi looked at him very coldly. "And yet here we are, talking about him."

Gunn cut through the tension. "OK—just tell us the story."

"Which one do you want to hear?" Mdosi asked. "That he was the person who arranged for bombs to be put into the World Trade Center the day before the towers were hit? Or that he fired the missile at the Pentagon that everyone thought was an airplane on 9/11? Or that he shot down that airliner over Queens, and TWA 800 over your Long Island? Or that he's been able to burrow his way deep into the U.S. intelligence services and does his dirtiest work from there?"

"Which one makes the most sense?" Bing asked.

"None of them," Mdosi replied. "That's the madness of it."

To the surprise of all, Mdosi produced a bottle of Glenfiddich scotch from his desk drawer. He poured out a glass for each person, then leaned back and began again.

"You ask me, 'who is Kaiser?'" he said. "Let me start at the beginning. Like I said, at first nobody believed he was real—and many still don't. Nobody I know has ever seen him or known anybody who's seen him. No one I know has ever had any direct dealings with him. But to hear some people in the intelligence world tell it, anybody could be working for him at any given moment. That's just it: You never know. You're in the world of special ops, you get orders from on high, you go out and do it, and you don't ask who was pushing the buttons or why. Turns out in the past, SOF people were doing Kaiser's bidding without realizing it. He was manipulating those orders from on high, and with all the layers of secrecy, no one knew it until it was over and done with. That's his mojo, his power. What's the line from that movie? 'The greatest trick the Devil ever pulled was convincing the world he didn't exist'? Kaiser would do something, or get people to do it for him—something small. But days, weeks, even years down the line, it paid off, at least for him. And then, just like that, he'd be gone again."

Another murmur went around the room. "But how can that be? This guy must have an entire army working for him," Amanda said.

Mdosi shook his head no. "Just the opposite. He works alone. Why? Because if you don't have any people, then you don't have anyone who will betray you—again from that movie. But when I was working for French Intelligence, we saw fingerprints on many things that just had to be his. Arms sales. Oil futures manipulation. Military incidents started specifically to create international crises, just so he would gain some huge economic advantage, and put the screws to the rest of us. He's brilliant. But he's also brutal. Bloodthirsty. Soulless. And just about invisible."

"So, you believe in him?" Gunn asked Mdosi.

The colonel laughed darkly. "I don't want to—but he still scares me. He doesn't just kill you. He kills you twice—three times. More . . ."

Vogel scoffed again. "But like you just said, this is too much like that movie."

"*Casablanca*?" someone asked.

"No, the other one," Vogel said. "It can't be real. *No one* person could be like this."

Gunn turned to Moon. "What about you, Lieutenant? Do you believe all this?"

Moon lifted himself up a little. He said: "The story most told is this one. When he started out, he was running guns somewhere in the Middle East or the subcontinent, depending on what version you want to believe. Some people he was working with stole money from him, just to test his resolve. Kaiser waited, bided his time, let things cool down. But then, when the time was of his choosing, he went after these people. He tracked them down and he didn't just kill them, he killed their wives, their kids, their parents and their parents' parents. He burned down the towns where they lived and blew up the places they had frequented. He poisoned their water and their food. He laid waste to these people single-handedly—and then he just vanished, for years. He'd become a ghost. Something to haunt adults and kids alike."

"Then there's the more recent stuff," Mdosi added. "Scary on a global scale."

"What do you mean?" Amanda asked.

"Do you remember when the price of gasoline went sky-high everywhere two summers ago?" Mdosi asked. "Just before the stock market meltdown?"

"Don't tell me that was his doing," she said.

Mdosi nodded gravely. "One of the reasons the oil speculators went crazy was that one day back then the Israeli Air Force conducted a mock attack maneuver out over the Med. One hundred airplanes, flying this way and that. People thought sure they were rehearsing to attack Iran's nuclear facilities. Truth was, no one knows who gave the order for the IAF to conduct that mock attack. It didn't come from their top military people or their cabinet or the Mossad. The IAF got secret orders they thought were legitimate and off they flew. When it happened, oil futures went through the roof and they say Kaiser made himself about forty billion dollars in one day. Now, can you imagine someone having the power to wend his way through the Israeli security system and actually deliver orders to those guys and convince them they are real?"

Mdosi drained his drink. "They say he's done many other things like that—sent false messages to the Iranian Navy to buzz U.S. warships, or approach tankers, or paint U.S. aircraft with SAM missile radars. He's set off bombs simultaneously in the Kashmir, to get India and Pakistan fighting; some people blame the Mumbai Massacre on him. He's blown up oil pipelines and made it look like Iraqi insurgents did it. He's even left his fingerprints on some NASA mainframe computers, hacking into things like shuttle launch schedules and secret military payloads. All these things have a domino effect and usually they result in a financial windfall for him, while the rest of the world's banking systems go down the drain. The problem is, one day, the Iranians *will* attack a U.S. warship and the U.S. will fire back. Or the Iranians *will* sink a tanker and block the Strait of Hormuz, or the Israelis *will* bomb Tehran—and then it will be utter chaos, for the entire world. Which is just what Kaiser ultimately wants."

Moon wiped the sweat from his brow. He was usually a cool customer, but even he looked worried now. "You've heard that there's a twenty-five-million-dollar bounty on bin Laden?" he said. "Well, it's fifty million dollars for Kaiser. It should be a billion or two. If you lead any Western intelligence service to him, dead or alive, the money is all yours. Not that you'll live long enough to spend any of it."

Another silence descended on the room.

Finally Gunn said. "OK, let's say he's real. What does he have to do with us? Or us with him?"

Everyone turned to Downes, who'd been silent through most of the discussion.

"Because this Yellowcake Gang has stolen from him," Downes said. "He'd secured a large quantity of this rare element and they took it from him, and now he wants it back. Maybe they don't know it yet. But they will, once he catches up with them."

"Which is what you want us to do?" Amanda said.

Downes nodded solemnly. "With the technology you have in your aircraft, especially the ability to fly undetected at night, you are the perfect choice to find the Yellowcake Gang before Kaiser does. And do so as quickly as possible."

Gunn thought a moment, then said. "Africa is a big place, despite what Sarah Palin thinks. If these Yellowcake guys are as savvy as you say, it might take us a while to cover the ground we need to find them."

"That's fine," Downes said, dryly. "Just as long as you do it in a week's time. After that the deal is off."

"A week?" Amanda gasped. "That's all we get?"

"That's all I can give," Downes said. "There's a big clock at work here. Many different things are in motion at once, things I cannot tell you about. So, whatever you do, you have to do it in a week."

Gunn and the others were aghast—and Downes could see it.

"However, I do have one big clue for you," he said. "Something that might make it easier." He took a photograph from his pocket. It showed a large, slightly weird-looking truck.

"The Yellowcake Gang is driving around in vehicles like this," he said. "Their cargo holds look typical, but they are solid lead. They can carry yellowcake without letting anything leak out. They can also take strafing and maybe direct large bomb hits. If they were armed, they'd be unstoppable, but they only stand out if you're looking for them. Find them, and you'll probably find the Yellowcake Gang."

He passed the photograph to Gunn, who looked at it, shook his head slyly, and then passed it over to Amanda. She looked back at him, flashing her million-dollar smile.

Gunn then reached into his pocket, took out his cell phone and called up a picture he'd taken during their last mission. It showed the three strange trucks they'd found inside the religious fort.

He passed the cell phone over to Downes and said: "Colonel, I think on this one, we might be way ahead of you."

PART TWO

7 DAYS
TO FREEDOM

CHAPTER SEVEN

Wum Bakim

Downes and his expensive helicopter were gone before the sun finally peeked over the rubber trees to the east.

Gone too were the soldiers who'd briefly held Wum Bakim. After Downes's departure, they simply walked down the narrow road leading out of the secret air base, climbed aboard several trucks they'd hidden nearby and drove off into the jungle. And that was it. The strange occupation was over.

Who were the mystery soldiers? No one knew. They were definitely not Delta Force—everyone at Wum Bakim would have been dead at the first sign of opposition. Marine Recon? Not a lot of jarhead SOFs around Africa. SEALs maybe, based on the waterproofed boots theory? That seemed the most likely answer. But even after the donnybrook that followed Downes's arrival, none of the intruders ever removed his ski mask, so it was really hard to tell who they were.

Just how Downes had found the 201st was also a mystery. He'd ignored all questions on the subject when asked about it. Though the 201st's godfather, Colonel Doug Newman, knew Downes fairly well, or as close as anyone could know the secret ops superstar, no one in the 201st believed Newman would have disclosed to their enemies in Washington where they were hiding. Unless, of course, Newman knew that Downes was going to make them an offer they couldn't refuse. But even then, it seemed unlikely that the ultra-loyal Newman would have told anyone about Wum Bakim and who was lying low there.

So Downes must have found them on his own.

Before he left, Downes had provided the 201st with an especially powerful sat-phone and a number. They were to call it under only two circumstances: if they found the Yellowcake Gang or if it looked like their mission was a failure. At no other time should they use the phone; that's how tight the security was on this.

Downes also agreed to a list of things that Gunn said the 201st needed in order to conduct their weeklong search. Topping this list was more aviation fuel. As the mission might be taking the unit to many distant parts of Africa, they would require lots of gas—and a means of getting it into their trio of ghostly planes.

What this meant was an aerial refueler. Downes promised that one would be dispatched to Wum Bakim within twenty-four hours.

NOW the 201st had to get to work. Their very freedom depended on it.

No sooner had Downes disappeared than the unit's officers were back in the Ops building, anxiously looking at maps of Africa spread out on the floor in front of them.

Besides their ability to go invisible, the unit's trio of C-17s were also loaded with highly advanced targeting gear, including futuristic ground-imaging radar systems. Based on the same technology used in the latest fleet of J-STARS battlefield command planes, the 201st's GIR could look at wide swaths of territory in real time and search for specific targets, moving or stationary. As some of the unit's ground techs were wizards at adapting the planes' GIR sets, what they hoped to do was load in everything they knew about the Yellowcake Gang's heavy duty transport trucks and then tell the GIR to locate them, at the expense of everything else.

Along these lines, they planned to give the GIR some clues to look for. First of all, they fed in the pictures Gunn had taken of the trucks during the attack on the religious fort, synching them up to the GIR's photo recognition system. Furthermore, they knew the armored trucks were put together with vast quantities of lead, and lead held heat in a way different from other elements, something else the GIR could key in on. The trucks also would be radioactive, or more so than other similar-looking vehicles, another characteristic that would help in the search. They would also be moving rather slow, due to their heavy weight. Once all these things were factored into the GIR's search commands and combined with the unit's RIF night-vision capability, the radar sets should be able to find anything resembling the weird heavy trucks, if they knew where to look.

But that was the important thing: Where to look?

With the help of codes found inside Lieutenant Moon's high-security laptop, the 201st were able to access a top-secret CIA database that pinpointed locations throughout Africa where Yellowcake 212 processing facilities might be found. These locations included a dozen sites in Tanzania, Niger, the Congo, Malawi and Mozambique, as well as several dozen more secondary locations scattered throughout central and southern Africa. It made sense that the Yellowcake Gang and their two remaining trucks might be lurking somewhere close to one of these locations, ready to buy or steal the precious bomb-making material. That's why as soon as night fell, the 201st intended to take off, go invisible and start flying low over these places, their GIR and RIFs turned up to the max. If they found something that looked promising, then they'd take steps to either confirm their suspicions or dispel them, including putting boots on the ground to get an up-close look if necessary. And if they hit the jackpot and actually found the damn trucks? All they had to do was push the button on Downes's sat-phone and give him the good news. It was their understanding that he would take it from there.

The plan was daring and high-tech, just like the rogue unit itself. Still, it was soon apparent that there was a problem. They had a lot of ground to cover, and even under the best of circumstances, search missions like this took time and luck—but mostly time. And time was something they didn't have a lot of. After calculating the distances between the primary targets, they concluded that finding two ordinary-looking, if very heavy, trucks in the vastness of Africa could take weeks.

Or maybe even months.

But still, they had to try.

MOON eventually joined them.

He arrived in the tiny operations room, sunglasses firmly in place as always. It was now 0830 hours.

"I've been trying to debrief the three blind women," he told them, pouring himself some coffee. "I got bits and pieces from them, but they can't talk very much. They're still in shock."

He studied the maps the others had scattered across the floor. Because he was the unit's intelligence officer, it was important that they explain to him what they had in mind for the upcoming mission. They told him their plan to use the planes' GIR and RIFs to search for the yellowcake trucks at the locations indicated by the CIA database. Moon listened intently, took a few notes and agreed it was their only hope. Then it was his turn to give them as much background as possible on the people they'd be looking for.

"To begin with, just for the record, I think there's no doubt that it was the Yellowcake Gang who was operating out of that fort we squashed," he said. "The evidence certainly points that way, especially the three lead-lined trucks we found there."

There was no disagreement from those present.

Moon continued: "And from what I could determine by the photographs taken in the bunker, from the clothes those people were wearing and so on, I'm sure the Gang is made up of Arabs—Yemenis mostly. They've got nothing to do with this Darfur business; they are a different breed of evil, I guess you'd say. And while they were probably among the first practitioners of this warlord mullah philosophy, it didn't do them much good in the end. There were about two hundred of them at the fort originally, plus their officers and imams, who travel with their wives and mistresses and kids. Those are the dead civilians we came upon in the bunker."

A dark silence descended on the room as those who'd witnessed the horror inside the bunker relived it all over again.

Moon quickly broke the spell.

"As we know, the three blind women were the Gang's prisoners," he went on. "And what they went through is almost beyond words. They were raped repeatedly. Tortured. Beaten. Awful stuff—and all just for fun. Their eyesight was taken away by acid poured directly onto their pupils—that's how these Yellowcake characters like to play. The three of them are so traumatized, they can't even tell me where they're from. At least not yet.

"But from the little I got out of them, I learned this: They were kept in the prison most of the time they weren't being abused. That's where they were when whatever happened in the bunker happened, and that's where they were when we descended on the fort. But prior to all this, whenever they were let out of their cells, they managed to hear some interesting things, including the gang members discussing Yellowcake 212 and how they were all so hot about looking for it, in return for guns and money.

"That's why the gang was out in the middle of the desert in the first place. They used to store the stuff at the fort until they got enough to move it to the next stop, which would usually be some al Qaeda middleman's location. It was he who would pay them off. But the women also said the gang had another hiding place, even more remote than the fort, and about half of the gang stayed there most of the time, processing the stuff or just holding on to more of it."

Moon took a sip of coffee and went on: "Now, the women indicated that about two weeks ago the gang was all hopped up, very excited. Somehow they'd made a big score in Yellowcake 212 and had found a place where they knew they could get even more. I think that's where their convoy of trucks was coming from when the gang invaded my friend Mr. Yoyo's village and took him and his fellow villagers prisoner.

"The women believe that the night before our attack, two of the trucks left fully loaded with 212. Once they were gone, the gang had a huge celebration, as this was the beginning of another big payday for them. The three women were taken from the jail and were being passed around to the fighters as usual. But then they said that around midnight someone uninvited suddenly showed up—'the Devil himself' is how they keep describing him, even though they couldn't see him. And suddenly everything got quiet. At some point, they were put back into their jail cell and they didn't hear another sound, until we came along."

"And you think this guy they described as the Devil is this character Kaiser?" Gunn asked.

"It makes the most sense," Moon replied. "He's trying to

find the Yellowcake Gang too, because somewhere along the way, they ripped him off. If he was just one step behind them, when he came upon the fort and found out his Yellowcake 212 had already left, he obviously wanted to leave a message behind for the other members of the gang, the ones at the second hideout. The message was that he was someone that didn't screw around when it came to exacting revenge—and that his brutality had no limits. It sounds like his MO."

Mdosi was nodding in grim agreement. "He knows how people's minds work," he said in his deep French accent. "He knows that whenever those bodies in the bunker were found—whether it was the next day or in a year—word would go around about what was done and the horrible way it was done. And for those people in the know, speculation who did it and why would all fall back to Kaiser and his myth—which is probably his greatest creation. It would only make his legend that much stronger and last that much longer. And it would also make the next person who thought about crossing him think twice."

"By that theory then," Gunn said. "Either someone connected with Kaiser or Kaiser himself was in that Red Cross truck you guys saw."

"Could be another piece of this puzzle," Moon replied with a shrug. "I saw for myself how good that person was at turning invisible. There one moment, gone the next."

"But how could one man so viciously murder all those people?" Amanda asked with a shudder. "I mean, some were obviously innocents, the women and children—but there were more than a hundred fighters in that bunker too. And many of them looked like they died fighting each other."

"That is part of his power," Mdosi said gravely. "They say he can control men's minds, and while I don't believe that—though anything seems possible with him—I do believe that he can convince people that he can control them. And when you think about it, that's all it really takes."

Gunn drained his coffee. "Yeah, well, again, he sounds like a lot of fun," he said, turning back to the maps. "But let's hold off on the ghost stories for now and figure out how we can do an end run around this guy."

He paused a moment, then said: "Before he does the same thing to us."

CHAPTER EIGHT

South Central Niger

Karl Steng and Bors Laght ran the huge Seguidoa uranium mine located in south-central Niger.

The place encompassed ten square miles, a once tranquil valley now strip-mined down to the bone, with rivers of contaminated slurry running through it. When the warmth of the day went away, the chemicals in the slurry would create an evil-looking yellowish mist that would hang above these rivulets, giving the entire valley a strange almost incandescent look.

More than five thousand people worked at the mine, though they weren't really employees. Many of them lived on land nearby that was owned by the mining company. The company charged such exorbitant prices for the shacks they occupied, most of the people who spent long hours digging in this enormous pit weren't getting paid anything. In fact, many actually owed the company money. That was just the way it was in Africa. The strong preyed upon the weak, the richer got richer and the world went round and round.

Steng and Laght were ruthless to their workers—that's

how their European bosses wanted it. They'd been paying off the UN Committee for Worker Safety for years, necessary as there were usually a half dozen fatalities at the mine every week. Or sometimes, because of the heavy machinery used there, there could be that many deaths in a single day. All for what amounted to a relatively small amount of usable uranium and an even smaller amount of yellowcake.

It was an hour after sunset. The workers had just dragged themselves back to their shantytown and Steng and Lacht were counting the day's receipts from their half dozen canteens, which charged the workers for their meals eaten while working. Their office was situated on a high plain that overlooked the big hole in the ground. Beyond their office was a large hard desert area, and beyond that was the jungle.

They were the only people on the site at the moment, or at least that's what they thought.

It was by pure coincidence that Steng stepped outside the office at that moment to light a cigarette. Steng looked down into the huge hole they'd dug in the middle of the once-pristine landscape and saw the faintest hint of movement. He thought at first it was an animal roving the huge pit, looking for scraps dropped by the workers during the day.

For this reason, he reached inside the office door and retrieved his Mannlicher Luxus high-powered hunting rifle. He was not above shooting the local wildlife—also strictly forbidden—especially if it was an animal with a valuable coat he could sell.

The Mannlicher had a long-range sight that featured something called a Star Scope, a very rudimentary form of night vision. It was enough, though, to enhance Steng's eyesight to the point that when he aimed the rifle toward where he'd seen the movement, instead of seeing a wild animal, he saw three shadowy humans instead.

They were moving in and out of the line of battered trucks used to haul away the results of the day's mining. They certainly weren't workers—they were dressed all in black and were wearing military-style helmets. Steng's first thought was that they were the police, snooping around the site.

He called for Lacht to come out right away. Then he increased the power in his Star Scope and tried to key in on one of the three intruders. If they were police, they weren't locals. The local constables usually dressed as badly as the workers at the mine. These three guys, on the other hand, were wearing very modern uniforms.

Steng called for Lacht again, this while he loaded a shell into the rifle's chamber. He had every right to shoot anyone trespassing on the grounds—especially at night. So why not?

He took aim at one of the figures as all three were looking up under one of the trucks' radiator grills. Steng was morbidly curious: Why were these people interested in these old, good-for-nothing trucks?

He called for Lacht a third time just as he was about to fire on the intruders. When Lacht didn't respond, Steng took his eye off the night scope for a moment and looked behind him. He saw Lacht finally—but he also saw two enormous individuals standing on either side of him, one of whom was holding a massive weapon to his partner's head.

These two people were dressed in military uniforms and carrying military weapons. They were dressed all in black, with large helmets and goggles and other gear that looked like props from a sci-fi movie. In other words, they were dressed like the three people Steng had spotted down in the pit.

He was stunned. Lacht looked like he was going to pass out from fright. What were these guys doing here?

Before Steng could ask, one of them spoke first.

"You speak English?"

"Yes," Steng replied.

"Then you'll understand this: Lower your weapon or your boyfriend here will get a haircut."

Steng dropped the rifle. One of the mystery soldiers kicked it over the side of the pit wall; it clattered 250 feet to the ground below. This attracted the attention of the three men skulking around the trucks. They waved—and then started running away from the trucks and toward the far end of the huge, open pit.

"OK," one of the two soldiers said. "Second question: Ever hear of Yellowcake 212?"

The two mine bosses just looked at each other.

"What's going on here?" Lacht demanded to know. "Who are you people?'

"We're tourists," one of the solders replied, raising his weapon again. "Now answer the question."

"Yes—of course, we've heard about it. Everyone in the business has."

"Do you mine it here?"

Both men started to reply—but then both stopped. Yellowcake was not something they wanted to discuss with anybody, and especially not Yellowcake 212.

Steng suddenly grew a set. "Look here, we don't know who you are—or why you're asking these questions. But this is proprietary information you're inquiring about and we don't have to tell you anything."

Both soldiers sort of shrugged. "OK—your choice," one said. "However, it's probably best you tell us what we want to know."

"And why is that?"

The soldiers didn't respond. Instead one simply pulled out a laser designator pen, held it over his head and blinked it three times.

Suddenly it was as if the night sky had opened up and

the fires of hell were falling out of it. Sixteen long, bright, blinding streaks of red and orange light lit up the open pit mine as well as the jungle for miles around. They all impacted at once on the first line of huge trucks parked at the bottom of the pit. Then, just as quickly, the light and the fire were gone.

"What the fuck?" the mine bosses cried out in unison.

They couldn't believe what they'd just seen. The line of trucks had been reduced to a line of burning junk.

Steng started stuttering. "How? When? What the . . ."

Lacht began to say something, but his partner stopped him. "We can't . . ."

Suddenly there was another bright flash—and the mine's nearby power shack was reduced to cinders.

Steng was speechless. Once again, Lacht began to say something. But he didn't speak quickly enough. Another bolt from the blue and the cable rig, which lifted the mined materials from the bottom of the pit to the top, was suddenly blown to pieces.

"You boys get the point yet?" one of the two soldiers asked.

The mine bosses were almost too stunned to talk. "How—how can you possibly do that?" Lacht gasped. "There's nothing flying around up there!"

The soldiers just shrugged again. One said: "We're not only tourists—we're magicians too. Now please— Yellowcake 212?"

Steng was finally able to speak. "We have not produced any here," he said. "Not yet anyway. But . . ."

"But what?"

"But we were about to start. We have orders, new customers. We just built the processing plant."

He pointed to a large Quonset building on the other side of the pit. It was constructed of shiny aluminum and looked brand-new.

There was another laser signal to the heavens—and then

came two more monumental flashes out of the night sky. And suddenly this building too had been reduced to ashes.

The two mine bosses were now close to a state of shock.

By this time the three soldiers who'd been poking around the mine's trucks had joined them up on the hill. They were dressed and armed just like the first two.

As the two mine bosses were watching their processing building dissolve away into nothing but smoke, one of the soldiers started inflating a bright orange balloon via a canister of helium. This took just a few seconds and soon the balloon was twenty feet across and trailing five yellow cords. This man then sent the balloon aloft, as each soldier attached one of the cords to his belt.

Despite this odd behavior, the soldiers remained nonchalant.

"You are now out of the yellowcake business," one said. "Or we'll be back . . ."

Suddenly the cords became taut and shot upward, taking the five soldiers with them.

Just like that, they disappeared into the night sky.

SAMUEL Obeea had worked in the uranium mine at Shinkolobwe since he was a child, a total of forty-two years. Located in the Katanga province in the Democratic Republic of the Congo, the mine was part of a three-hundred-mile-long belt of uranium rich ore that stretched deep below the ground from here to the border of Gabon.

Obeea was a shaver, meaning it was his job to go into the lowest, deepest part of the mine shaft and, with little more than a pick and shovel, attack any new outcrop thought to contain the precious bomb-making material. He'd been doing this for so long, his lungs were full of grit and his fingers were worn down to the knuckles. So much dust and powder had gotten in his eyes over the years, his pupils had a whitish color to them. He was bent over and stooped, his back muscles locked in a permanent crooked position.

Uranium from this mine had been used to make the American A-bomb dropped on Hiroshima. But history aside, Shinkolobwe had a checkered past. It had been shut down many times over the years by the International Atomic Energy Commission and the UN due to appalling work conditions and because it had been declared an environmental disaster zone. But no matter how many times the mine was closed, it always opened again shortly afterward, simply because the Congolese government couldn't afford to have it not working. Bribes were paid, the police and the army told to look the other way. This was the reason all mining at Shinkolobwe was done after sundown.

The mine owners didn't pay the people who worked there. Most were prisoners or other lawbreakers. Others were captured army deserters. Still others, like Obeea, were indentured to local tribal chiefs. The mine owners dispensed food once a day, and the workers lived in crowded shacks built on the slag heaps surrounding the pit. If they had family in the area, the mine canteen would dole out a cup of rice and coarse grain to them every other week. That was it as far as incentives went. Essentially, the workers at Shinkolobwe were slaves. Like Obeea, most were just trying keep themselves and their families from starving to death.

Obeea had seen many horrible things at the mine over the years—friends and coworkers crushed by equipment, killed in falls, dropping dead from simple exhaustion or malnutrition. It seemed to get worse every year, as he got older and the mine's owners got greedier.

The reason for this greed was that the mine was a large

producer of not only yellowcake uranium, but lately, an offshoot of that precious element called Yellowcake 212. Even the most confidential news at the mine eventually filtered down to the two thousand lowly workers who broke their backs here every night. The word was that the mine's owners had several very wealthy clients looking for Yellowcake 212—and they were ready to pay millions for it. Which meant everyone here would have to work even harder, or die trying.

This night was brutally hot and Obeea was feeling sick, tired and old. His family lived just a mile away, yet he hadn't seen them in more than two years because, even though he was able to get food for them, families weren't allowed near the site, day or night, as they were considered a distraction. There was a small chance that a worker trying to leave the site would be shot by the company guards. But that made little difference. If a worker escaped, he could never come back, ever. And that meant no job, no food, and eventually starvation. That's why, bad as it was, few people ever wanted to leave.

THE workers at Shinkolobwe got their fifteen-minute meal break halfway through their twelve-hour shift. While most workers ate their meager rations inside the mine itself, Obeea would usually climb the gantry leading out of the pit and scramble up the tallest slag hill overlooking the large hole in the ground. Here, he would spend those few precious minutes looking up at the stars and thinking about his wife, who was so close, yet a million miles away.

So it was this night. Break time came, and he climbed out of the hole and perched himself atop the enormous mound of slag. Lying back, he let the stars take him away.

But tonight, something was different.

Obeea was counting the stars to the east when he saw

something very strange. The sky was moving, rippling, as if the stars were an ocean wave. He'd never seen anything like it.

He was quickly on his feet, his eyes straining to comprehend what was happening above him. He heard no sounds, but the stars *were* moving, of this he was sure. But something was also moving through them—and it was getting closer.

Obeea didn't know what to do. Should he tell his bosses? Should he run back to the mine and hide? Or should he just fall to his knees and pray?

Before he could decide, something else happened: He saw tiny stars suddenly appear beneath the ripple. Little white stars, falling from the sky. And just as soon as he thought this, he realized these weren't stars at all. They were angels floating down from heaven.

And just as suddenly, these angels were landing all around him under great swaths of cloth. But now they didn't look so much like angels. Up close, they looked huge and were dressed all in black and were carrying enormous weapons. That's when he first realized that they were soldiers, the biggest he'd ever seen.

And in seconds, Obeea was surrounded by them.

He held his hands over his head as if to surrender. He didn't know what else to do. Two soldiers approached him while the others began sneaking down into the pit. The two soldiers seemed as surprised to see him as he was to see them. One of them patted him on the shoulder and indicated he didn't have to keep his hands over his head. This helped calm Obeea down a little.

"Speak English?" the soldier asked him.

Obeea did, but just a little he'd picked up over the years from others in the mine.

The soldier pulled out a photograph and showed it to Obeea. He asked Obeea if he had ever seen anything like what was depicted in the photo.

Obeea looked at the photo. It showed a large truck, with a large cab and gigantic wheels. It was much different from the mining trucks that were a fixture at the mine.

He shook his head no. "Something like that, I would remember," he told them.

"How about yellowcake?" the other soldier asked him. "Ever heard of it?"

Obeea nodded vigorously. "They make it here. Lots of it."

"Where?" the soldier asked

Obeea pointed out the three processing buildings that had just been constructed on the site. "In there—that's their special place."

The soldier patted his shoulder again and then told Obeea: "Thank you. Go on home now. Take the rest of the night off."

That's when Obeea started crying.

The soldiers insisted that everything was all right, that he could go.

"But I can't go home," he told them. "I can't take the night off. I have no money. I must stay here, or my family will be without food. That's how it works here."

The two soldiers looked down into the mine and seemed to understand what Obeea was trying to tell them.

That's when one reached in his pocket and came out with a gold ingot. It glistened in the bright starlight. Obeea's eyes went wide. This was enough gold to make him the richest man in his village, richer even than the chief.

The soldier put the ingot in Obeea's hand and closed his fingers around it, so he would hold it tight.

"This is a gift from the United States of America, my friend," the soldier said to him. "Don't ever forget that, OK?"

Obeea couldn't believe this was happening. "I will always remember," he said, still crying, but now with tears of disbelief and joy. "And a million times thank you."

"OK—so now, go home," the soldier said.

Obeea decided to take their advice. He looked to the sky again, but the stars were no longer rippling. He considered this a good sign. He started making his way through the jungle back toward his home, the gold ingot still tightly wrapped in his hand. About a minute into his journey, he heard three loud explosions coming from behind him in the mine. He didn't turn around to look at them, though. Somehow, he knew what they were. The processing buildings, the ones just constructed to handle Yellowcake 212, were being blown to smithereens.

He reached the mine's outer fence and easily slipped under it. Once he was safely beyond the mine pit's perimeter, he plunged back into the jungle and began singing and laughing with joy.

"I only hope I can remember where I live!" he cried.

AMANDA had been aloft for seven hours—way too long as it turned out. Her fuel reserves were very low and her crew was very tired.

They'd flown over five uranium mines in that time: two in Mozambique, two in Tanzania and a fifth on the northern edge of Gabon.

The combination of the ground imaging radar and their reverse infrared night-vision capability was astounding. Her techs had merged the two into one visual display, and viewing it was like looking down on the big blue Earth at high noon. They could key in on suspect vehicles and make them show up on screen in variations of red or orange depending on their heat signatures. Plus, anything showing yellow indicated some degree of radioactivity.

Everything worked great—and when combined with the C-17's ability to fly quiet and invisible at night, they really did make the near-perfect aerial spy platform.

But there were problems. First of all, most vehicles around

uranium sites were radioactive. That was just common sense. Second, they were learning that most uranium mine owners in Africa were basically slave drivers. And based on this mentality, any vehicles on-site were worked to the max too, meaning they were all burning red-hot as far as their heat signatures were concerned. As for hits on the GIR's photo recognition system, they'd had some close calls, but none matched up exactly with the pictures Gunn took of the Yellowcake Gang's trucks back at the religious fort.

Nevertheless, Amanda flew over these sites, sometimes as low as five hundred feet, trying to catch a glimpse of something—anything—that might be useful in future searches. But what they saw instead looked like scenes from an old Tarzan movie: thousands of native workers, toiling nonstop in the night, under appalling conditions, surrounded by a nightmare landscape of environmental disaster and armed guards.

And nothing to indicate that the Yellowcake Gang or their weird trucks were anywhere nearby.

AT 0300 hours, after flying over another site in Tanzania and again finding nothing, Amanda took the big plane up to forty thousand feet and waited.

She was at a predetermined coordinate, a spot just over the coastline of southeast Nigeria. It was here that she was supposed to meet the unit's on-loan refueler, the aerial gas truck promised to them by Downes.

Having put the C-17 into a mile wide orbit, she watched the time tick by. She had no idea what kind of a plane to expect. There was no radio contact during these missions, of course, and even using a sat-phone was out of the question. But if something didn't happen soon, she would have to turn back to Wum Bakim, with her tanks running dangerously low to empty.

How long do you wait for someone that you're not sure

is even coming? That was the big question. She went round and round, telling herself that in five minutes or five more orbits, she'd just bag it and turn for home, hoping they could make it on fumes.

But with each go-round, she could see the Atlantic Ocean out in front of her. There was a half moon tonight and the light it cast seemed to stretch on forever. She imagined she could see a hint of land, out on the horizon. It looked warm, full of lights, inviting. In her mind it was the edge of the United States, just waiting for her, a short flight away. It was a nice fantasy—but it also reminded her of how much she wanted to go home.

These thoughts were interrupted when she saw a large, dark shape rising out of the clouds off to her left. At first she was sure it was an old airliner. It looked big, ugly and unwieldy.

But when she saw the plane's navigation lights start blinking, she knew this was the aircraft she was supposed to meet. Downes's flying gas trucks had arrived.

But what kind of plane was it? It wasn't a KC-10 Extender, the USAF's premier aerial refueler. Nor was it a KC-135 Stratotanker. This was an old, Russian-built something or other; even at night and eight miles high, that much was unmistakable.

Amanda looked over at her copilot, Lieutenant Stanley, who just rolled his eyes. "Why do I feel we've just been transported back to the 1950s?" he asked.

She turned toward the old plane and it turned toward her. A hose and boom was being reeled out from its aft section, two dim lights blinking at the end of the hose. Amanda tried to line up the nose of her plane with the rear of this one—but because the refueler was bouncing all over the sky, it took a few minutes of white-knuckle maneuvering to get the angles right. Finally, once she was as close to straight as she'd ever get, she started moving in toward the drogue.

The C-17's aerial refueling system was built to match up

with U.S., NATO and allied planes. What she saw coming toward her at the end of the hose was none of these. Rather it was a universal adaptor. But gas was already leaking out of it, leaving a thick trail of white vapor streaming behind it. Still, she moved in closer. With Lieutenant Stanley calling out the distance and speed numbers for her, Amanda gently pushed the big airplane right up to the waiting nozzle. It seemed to take forever, but somehow she was finally able to snag the adaptor.

Fuel started flowing into her tanks—for about three seconds. Then a wave of turbulence hit. It gripped both airplanes and started bouncing them all over the sky, breaking the connection.

Amanda fought the controls to stay steady and somehow rose up to hook onto the nozzle again. This coupling lasted a little longer—about ten seconds before the aerial refueler started dancing wildly, breaking the connection a second time.

Undeterred, she went in for a third hookup, snagged the hose and this time drank greedily. This connection lasted about a minute, before once again, poor flying by the refueler pilots caused it to be broken.

But she'd had enough. They'd taken on the bare minimum of fuel to fly back to Wum Bakim safely. That's all she needed.

Still, she was furious at the people flying the big, ugly refueling plane.

She couldn't radio them or call on a phone. So she had Stanley send out a message by flashing their navigation lights in Morse code.

Her message was: "Do you know what you are doing?"

The reply came back as: "No—we are just following orders."

* * *

Wum Bakim

Gunn checked his watch.

It was now 0500 hours.

He hadn't slept all day; in fact he hadn't slept since before the attack on the religious fort. For the last twenty-four hours he'd been doing a nonstop juggling act, mostly trying to determine the most efficient way to fly to and from their primary search targets. Once he'd come up with the three different flight plans, he'd had to brief the unit on them, get the planes pulled out and on the runway and then get them and himself off the ground, each plane with its own search list.

From there, their strategy was simple. If a plane crew thought they'd located one of the yellowcake trucks, they were to do everything possible to verify it, because 100 percent confirmation meant a call to Downes on the super sat-phone—and a free ticket home for them all.

Gunn and his crew had been just that cautious at the Seguidoa mine earlier that night. They'd detected high readings of radioactivity on the mine's trucks and a near hit on the GIR's photo recognition system. While Gunn remained aloft, driving the AC-17, a squad of paratroopers he had on board jumped into the mine to investigate—but nothing was found. And even though it gave them good operational practice in using their drogue balloon personnel retrieval system, as well as flattening several yellowcake processing plants, it had been the beginning of a frustrating night as their other primary sites had come up empty as well.

Gunn had landed back here at Wum Bakim around 0430 hours. Bing's Jump Plane came in right after him; they reported no luck as well.

Now Gunn was standing at the end of the runway, anxiously awaiting the third plane. Amanda was still out there, somewhere. Her search list had brought her the farthest away from the base, so when Mdosi got an anonymous call that Downes's aerial refueler would be available to them this night, times and coordinates were passed on to her just before she took off. Everyone knew, though, that she had to meet this gas truck in order to have enough fuel to get home.

And now she was overdue.

Gunn checked his watch again: 0510 hours. Amanda should have landed twenty minutes ago. He drained his twentieth cup of coffee of the day, but his caffeine genes had gone to sleep long ago. (Though he hated to admit it, he'd given Downes a list of other things he needed for this unorthodox mission. He was actually waiting for these other things as much as he'd been waiting for their extra jet fuel.)

Finally he saw three faint lights moving across the sky: two red and a blinking green. Gunn signaled Mdosi's men up in the base's tiny control tower to turn on the runway landing lights. Amanda's big C-17 came roaring over the treetops a few seconds later, setting down with a screech and a touch of retrorockets. Gunn felt a huge weight lift off his shoulders. At least she was still in one piece.

But suddenly he heard jet engines overhead, loud ones. He looked skyward and saw another set of navigation lights circling high above Wum Bakim. It was as if the pilot was wondering if this was really the place to set down. Gunn had his handheld laser designator out in a flash. He began blinking it in groups of three, and eventually he saw the plane blink its navigation lights three times in response. Contact had been made. The big noisy plane started to descend.

He lost sight of the aircraft for a few minutes as it began a wide turn and lined up with the runway, but he could hear it getting closer . . . closer . . . closer.

And those engines. That noise. Something didn't seem right about it.

Finally the roar got so loud, Gunn had to block his ears. In the next moment a gigantic aircraft appeared over the trees, went right over his head and set down with a violent bump.

Its engines were positively screaming—no engine silencers on this creature. The runway lights went out immediately after the plane touched down as per their security rules at Wum Bakim. As a result, it was hard for Gunn to see exactly what kind of plane it was. So he pulled down his RIFs and adjusted them for low-light conditions.

That's when he saw it.

It was neither a KC-10 nor a KC-135. In fact it wasn't a U.S. military aircraft at all. It was, instead, a Russian-built IL-76. Smoking and sounding awful, it looked like a bucket of bolts with wings attached.

"What the fuck is this?" Gunn murmured angrily.

As Amanda's plane taxied by him, he saw her up in the cockpit just shrugging and shaking her head.

Gunn waited as the fuel plane taxied its way back down the runway and came to a noisy, smoky, uneven stop in front of him. He saw the pilots working feverishly to shut the plane down, but paying him no attention at all. Finally the side access door opened and a man in a 1960s-style flight suit stepped out. He saw Gunn and saluted.

"Are you in the right place?" Gunn asked the man.

The man looked stumped.

"Are you Russian?" Gunn pressed him.

The man shook his head no. "Ukraine," he said. "We are here to help with you."

At that point another man emerged. He walked right up to Gunn and shook his hand vigorously.

"Captain Vistok, at your service," he said.

"Also Ukrainian?" Gunn asked.

The man nodded. "We are loan for you from Ukraine Air Force. You need gas for few days? We have gas."

Gunn was livid. He'd been expecting nothing but the best from Downes—and this plane looked like it had been old back in the 1950s. It had a high tail, four huge engines and a top-side wing that looked like it was about to fall off. It vaguely resembled the old C-141 Starlifter, a USAF cargo plane built and just about retired in the last century.

"Are you sure Colonel Downes sent you?" he asked the captain.

The refueler pilot just laughed. "I don't know who send me," he said. "We get orders, so we are here. Three main tanks full inside my airplane; a few smaller ones to spare as well. We refuel you on ground or in air. Our flight receptacles are universal, can match anything being flown by anybody."

Gunn still didn't know what to say. That's when the pilot reached into his pocket and came out with a bag of tiny white pills. He handed them to Gunn. "I am also told you had need for these?" he said.

Gunn looked at the pills. They were his beloved "bennies"—as in amphetamines, his crutch since his days back in Nevada. A few could keep him up for an entire day without sleep. A few more and he could stay awake for a week.

His spirits immediately changed. Anything seemed possible now.

He looked back at the two men and then said: "Can I get you guys some coffee?"

THE second night of searching proved even more miserable than the first.

The plane crews, all except Gunn, spent the daylight hours sleeping, or trying to in the brutal heat. With no good hits on their primary sites, Gunn went over the uranium location maps again and came up with a dozen more possible targets from the secondary list, six in western Nigeria and six along the Gabon-Congo border.

At 1500 hours, all crews were roused and the laborious process of dragging the three big planes out from under their camouflage tents was begun. The Russian-built refueler had been stationed at the opposite end of the runway and covered with a blanket of shrubs and tree limbs woven into a series of large fishing nets. It was low-tech but sufficient to hide the gawky plane from prying eyes.

Each of the C-17s had been topped off the previous morning, so the three aircraft were ready to go from a fuel point of view. Now each crew had to be briefed on their targets. As they had the night before, they split up the paratroopers, each plane getting about thirty of the 82nd Airborne soldiers. The Jump Plane also took one of the tanks.

The overall plan was also as the night before: If you see something that leads you to believe it's one of the yellowcake trucks, try to confirm it somehow, either with the paratroopers or, if the target is heavily guarded, by landing and using the tanks to get up close and personal. The 201st's planes were adapted to set down on rough surfaces and could take off in less than two hundred feet thanks to their rocket assists, so they had a wide option of landing sites. Get all the proof you can, Gunn told them—and if it's solid, then the winner gets to make the call to Downes.

But things got off to a bad start this night. No sooner were the three planes ready to go than a massive rainstorm swept across Wum Bakim. Occasional storms were typical in this part of Africa, but this weather system was like a category 5 hurricane.

It delayed their takeoff by two hours. Then once the bad weather cleared out, the Jump Plane lost 50 percent of its power during its takeoff roll. It was only the quick thinking of Lieutenant Bing in applying his retro rockets that kept the big plane on the ground and not careening into the air with not enough power to achieve flight. It was quickly determined that watered-down gas had caused the Jump Plane's shutdown—gas that had come from one of the aerial refueler's three main storage tanks. This meant that additives had to be put into the Marine plane and the gunship and their engines run up for thirty minutes to allow the fuel dryer to do its work. As a precaution, the Jump Plane's tanks were completely drained; it would not fly this night. Its suspect fuel, along with that remaining in the refueler's number one storage tank, was put into barrels to be disposed of later on. And while the gas inside the refueler's other two main tanks was checked and found to be OK, the incident just added to the less than confident attitude everyone had toward the Ukrainian aircraft and its crew.

And it only got worse from there. The gunship and Amanda's plane took off after they'd divided up the targets: She headed to the Nigerian search areas, while the AC-17 went down toward the Congo and Gabon. But if anything, the weather grew worse. As soon as Gunn got airborne, he saw nothing but nasty storms heading east, right into their noses.

He battled them for about thirty minutes, but when there was no end in sight, he turned around and hoped Amanda had the good sense to do the same. While the ground-imaging radar could see the terrain below in most types of weather, the atmospherics skewed it to the point where it didn't have the accuracy needed to look for much of anything, never mind two trucks in a million.

Gunn landed and again found himself out on the runway, this time in the pouring rain, waiting for Amanda. She finally returned as well, and the relief was almost enough to knock him off his feet. The smartest thing he could have done at that point was to get some sleep.

But no—while the rest of the unit turned in again, he simply took two more amphetamine pills, made a pot of coffee and stayed up the rest of the night, once again study-ing the maps scattered on the floor of the Ops building, looking for additional targets to fly over the following night.

THE third night it seemed like their luck had changed.

After checking her Nigerian targets from the night be-fore and finding nothing, Amanda flew over a uranium pit near a place called Lawi, Malawi. The weather was clear this night, with plenty of stars to mask her big plane.

The Lawi pit was close to a river that ran along a dis-puted border with Tanzania. The fairly large city of Tumba was also close by. There was a highway of sorts leading both to Tumba and the pit and it was on this highway, at 0230 hours, that Amanda's GIF/RIF display screen spotted two huge trucks, both carrying a lot of heat and excess ra-dioactivity, moving very slowly and close together.

These two vehicles looked so much like what they were searching for, Amanda brought the huge plane down to a belly-scraping altitude of just 250 feet and went over them so slowly she thought her four big, quiet engines were going to stall. The display screen didn't lie, however. The two trucks were glowing, moving slow and even rating high on the image recognition scale. In short, they looked like the Yellowcake Gang's Brinks trucks.

So Amanda decided to make sure.

She pulled the big plane around and landed it on the highway about a quarter mile behind the slow-moving trucks. She released the Marine tank and watched as it drove around in front of the airplane with a dozen of the paratroopers hanging off it. Then she started moving down the highway too, taxiing the big plane behind the tank, act-ing as if the road were one long taxiway.

They were able to catch up with the two trucks fairly quickly. When they were just a few hundred feet behind them, the paratroopers jumped off the tank and ran up to the trailing vehicle.

But just as they were about open the back door of this truck, there was a tremendous explosion. The blast was so powerful it lifted six of the paratroopers up into the air, throwing them back thirty to forty feet. It also hurled the cab of the second truck into the rear of the first truck, causing an even larger second explosion.

When Amanda saw the explosion, for one brief moment she thought the truck was carrying Yellowcake 212 and that it had somehow detonated and that by their actions, they had unwittingly set off a nuclear explosion.

But as it turned out, once the 201st soldiers went through the wreckage of both trucks, they discovered what they'd stumbled upon was a rolling methamphetamine lab, a mobile operation that had been making the illegal highly addictive drug for shipment to South Africa, where its use was soaring.

Just what lit off the explosions was never made clear. No one in the 201st fired a weapon. And there was a reason the trucks were driving slow: One of the chemicals used to make the drug was extremely volatile, unstable, and apparently radioactive.

In any case the twin blasts had rocked the countryside, which meant the 201st's exit had to be a quick one.

Luckily the paratroopers' armor plating had saved them from any serious injuries, though all suffered burns to their hands and faces. These wounded troopers were helped back onto the plane, and then the tank was loaded on board. Amanda used the C-17's unique ability to actually go in reverse—unheard of in most aircraft, big or small—and turned the plane around into the wind. With everyone safely aboard, she got the huge plane off the ground in less than two hundred feet, with a grand assist from her wing-mounted rockets.

In all, the team had been on the ground less than ten minutes. And while in some small way they'd helped stem the flow of crank into South Africa, in their search for the yellowcake trucks, the night had been a complete bust.

ON the same night, Gunn ran into a situation of his own.

He'd overflown a site on the border of Zimbabwe and Mozambique. It looked much like the others: a large pit in the middle of the jungle, a scar on what would otherwise have been an idyllic lush African setting. And like many places they'd passed over, this mine was doing its dirty work at night, under the glare of harsh arc lights.

It was 0300 hours, and they were getting the typical hits on their combined GIR/RIF display screen: some radioactivity on the mine's several dozen trucks. Lots of heat signatures from the same vehicles. They had learned it was best to search not just within the confines of the mine itself, but also a mile or two outside its perimeter, where the Yellowcake Gang's trucks might be lurking.

They were in the middle of doing this when they heard an unexpected sound coming from their defense suite. It was their air defense radar. Unknown aircraft were heading in their direction.

This was interesting, to say the least. They hadn't run into any other "unknown" aircraft since the search mission began. African skies were not as crowded as other places around the globe, at least not around central Africa. There were local carriers—bush planes and the like and the occasional used airliner coursing its way through the skies. But nothing like what was found in the skies over Europe, parts of Asia or the U.S.

But now as the radar indications grew, their advanced aircraft identification processor told them that these were military aircraft heading their way. More specifically Grippens, Swedish-built fighters that were on par with the U.S. Navy's F/A-18s. Not airplanes to fool around with.

Gunn knew of only one country in Africa that could afford to fly the Grippen: South Africa. But at the moment, the AC-17 was at least a few hundred miles *north* of South Africa.

"Why are these guys way up here in the middle of the night?" Gunn wondered aloud.

He asked his copilot, an African-American named Mike Robinson, to check their defensive systems, especially their Star Skin integrity. Robinson reported that because it was a clear night, with many stars, their cloaking technology was working at 100 percent. The AC-17 also had many other stealth characteristics—including the same radar-absorbing paint carried by the B-2 stealth bomber. Plus they had a passive electronic jamming capability, which would make an opposing aircraft think its communications and search radar equipment was on the fritz before suspecting that it was in fact being jammed on purpose.

So the only problem with this being-invisible stuff was the threat of a midair collision. While it was true that one couldn't stop what one couldn't see, that didn't mean crashing into that same thing wasn't a distinct possibility.

They'd completed two overflights of the mine, and while they were getting some interesting indications on the periphery, they were not enough to risk sticking around to get into a fender bender with one of the approaching Grippen fighter jets.

Gunn passed the word to the crew that they were exiting the area. The Grippens were still twenty miles away to the south. Gunn calculated that if he did a long power turn to the northwest, then he'd clear the area before the fighters arrived anywhere near their airspace.

But then the air defensive suite started buzzing again. More unknown aircraft were incoming, but from another direction.

"Who the hell could this be?" Gunn asked.

Robinson was on it immediately. He ran the new unknowns through the aircraft identification processor and the answer came back that the aircraft were probably MiG-21s.

"You're kidding," Gunn replied. "Someone still flies those things?" Robinson pushed a few more buttons, then replied. "The Ugandans still do."

Gunn looked over at his copilot. "South African Grippens? Ugandan MiGs? What's going on here?"

Robinson called up Google on his flight computer and made some inquiries. "According to this, there's been bad blood between these two countries for years. Who knew?"

Actually Gunn was aware that there were always little known conflicts popping up between neighboring and sometimes not so neighboring countries on the African continent. Occasionally these conflicts flared into international incidents, but most times the general public never even heard about them. But South Africa and Uganda? Who knew, indeed.

Gunn already had the big gunship halfway into its escape turn when the MiGs were spotted. Now he'd unintentionally lined himself up with the trio of ancient fighters flying down from Uganda.

This was trouble. The MiGs might be old, but they could still move at nearly twice the speed of sound. Same with the Grippens. It was a quick lesson in triangulation. The Grippens were accelerating north, the MiGs were pouring it on coming south. Gunn was currently at 6,000 feet; the oncoming fighters were converging at 6,200 feet. The big invisible gunship was caught right in the middle.

This meant the only one way to go was up—and quickly. Gunn pulled back on the controls and the AC-17 suddenly stood on its tail. Jamming the throttle to max, he gave the takeoff rockets a goose as well, pushing them even higher, faster. His crew and the paratroopers held on tight as they ascended in a quick and violent fashion. Anything not tied down in the plane wound up bouncing off the rear cargo door.

It lasted all of fifteen seconds, but by the time Gunn leveled them off at 45,000 feet, they were able to look down and see the two groups of fighter planes begin to engage in a meaningless, anonymous dogfight over the deepest, darkest jungle.

"Strange place," Gunn said, and not for the first time, as he turned and headed for home.

THE fourth night Mother Nature struck again.

This time it wasn't just hurricane-force winds, it was fifteen straight hours of solid, torrential rains.

None of the airplanes ever got off the ground, that's how bad the conditions were. At one point, the rain was so heavy, a nearby river overflowed its banks and flooded the runway itself. Side-by-side the 201st ground personnel and Mdosi's troops used shovels, buckets and even brooms to prevent the water from spilling onto the airstrip. But it was a losing battle from the start.

It was a testament to the unit's aircrews that they remained on board their aircraft throughout the entire day and night, just in the slim hope that a break in the weather and the flooding would allow them to take off and at least do an abbreviated night of searching.

But it was not to be. At 0200 hours, Gunn made the call and told all aircrews to return to their billets—there would be no operations until the weather broke.

It turned out to be a very frustrating twenty-four hours, as they all felt one more day of the seven allotted them had been totally wasted, and they were certain Downes didn't recognize rainouts.

But as bad as the fourth day was, the fifth day was probably the worst of all.

The weather broke finally, at least enough for all three planes to get airborne. They flew over places with names like Womboosa, Mozambique; Tongu, Namibia; and Imouraren, Niger. Sometimes they met up with the refueler and sometimes it got lost. They'd quickly learned not to count on it and simply took on extra fuel before takeoff, just in case. Gunn, for one, was never able to hook up with the winged Ukrainian antique; it was never where it was supposed to be when it came to refueling him.

The real problem, though, was that on this very long fifth night, none of the three planes came upon anything even close to resembling one of the Yellowcake Gang's trucks. Not a whiff. Nothing. It seemed like they were getting worse at searching for the mystery trucks, not better.

Each plane landed, its crew exhausted and roundly demoralized. What faced them the next day was hours of more aircraft maintenance, more mission planning and more brutal heat—mixed with the realization that they had only two nights left before their time was up and their deal with Downes went kaput.

And the weather forecast for that evening was calling for more torrential rains.

THE morning of the sixth day found the usual suspects gathered in the dreary Ops building again. Gunn was there, along with Amanda, Bing, Cardillo, Vogel and Mdosi.

Their spirits were at rock bottom. Mdosi had poured them all some of his prized scotch, yet no one was drinking it. That's how bad it was.

Outside, it was raining.

"What the hell are we doing here?" Bing said, going over the spare aerial photos of some of the targets they'd visited in the past few nights. "I mean, we saved a few souls. We stuck it to some of the money-hungry characters who own these mines. We even blew up a drug lab. But what about our own skins? Who's going to save us?"

Mdosi nodded grimly. "Between the Darfur missions and all this, you've done more for this continent in two months than anyone else has in the past twenty years."

No one could argue with him, but this did not lift their dark mood. They all agreed on one thing: They wanted to go home, to return to America, preferably without wearing handcuffs. But between the weather and their bad luck while aloft, the chances of doing that were fading quickly.

Bing finally said: "Maybe we should just call Downes and tell him we can't do it."

The groan in the room was universal.

"Or—we could always run again," Cardillo suggested.

Another groan. The thought of taking off and hiding somewhere else was extremely unappealing, even if another hideout could be found.

Gunn put his head in his hands and tried to massage his weary temples. The news had gone from bad to worse this morning when they learned that in addition to the six paratroopers hurt in the meth lab explosion, nearly two dozen of their ground personnel and just about all of Mdosi's men had come down with jungle fever, most likely because they picked up a water parasite of some kind while trying to prevent the runway from flooding during the last big rainstorm. The unit's medics were treating the afflicted, but they were all expected to be bedridden for at least another few days..

The planes were showing signs of strain too. The C-17s were hardy and well constructed. But no high-tech military aircraft was built for so much intense flying in such a short period of time under such primitive conditions. True, the mechanics kept a close watch on everything, but when going balls to the wall like the unit had been doing, it was always the unknowable thing that fucked up. Could they take two more nights of dangerous flying, trying to hook up with the unreliable refueling plane, and questioning the quality of the fuel when they did? All the landings, all the takeoffs, the unpredictable weather—it would take just one little malfunction and one of the big planes might turn out to be nothing more than a hole at the end of the runway—taking at least a dozen souls with it, or maybe many more.

"Maybe Bada is right," Vogel said, voice filled with resignation. "Maybe we just call him. Tell him we failed. Get it over with."

Gunn felt his heart sink to his feet. He was all messed up anyway. No food, no sleep, bad coffee, his stomach twisted in knots from taking too many pep pills. Finding two trucks hiding somewhere on a continent? Downes had asked the impossible. Now Gunn wondered if that had been the plan all along. Had they been set up to fail? We gave them their chance and they fucked it up. Hold that train to Leavenworth.

He took out the sat-phone and stared at it, his fingers hovering over the activate button. Pushing it wasn't just the easy thing to do—it was probably the smart move too. Could he really live with himself knowing he could have called a halt to this madness and saved some lives, but didn't?

He sat there for a full minute, just staring at the shiny yellow phone, not wanting to look at any of them, especially Amanda. Never before had he felt the burden of leadership so heavily—but in the end, he was left with this: The 201st was a collection of hardworking, dedicated, loyal people. But sometimes it was just impossible to do the impossible.

So he made his decision. His thumb sought out the sat-phone's activate button.

He started to press down on it . . .

That's when Moon walked in.

* * *

THEY'D seen little of him in the past few days because he'd been doing double duty too: writing intelligence briefs to help the planes' crews on their nightly missions, while still trying his best to get information from the trio of traumatized comfort women. He was here to announce that he'd finally achieved a breakthrough of sorts.

"I'm ashamed to admit it, but I gave those poor women alcohol," Moon revealed to the grim-faced group. "It loosened them up and they could finally talk in more than three syllables at a time."

"Did you learn anything earth-shattering?" Amanda asked him.

Moon pulled out his notebook and started reading over his notes. "Earth-shattering? Well, maybe. They belong to a tribe called the Wumbu, who are distant relatives of Mr. Yoyo's tribe. They were ashamed to admit that to me before, because they felt they'd disgraced their families. Their village is about fifty miles west of the fort, right where the desert ends and the jungle begins. Some bad characters named the Ubai run this village—and it turns out they are allies of the Yellowcake Gang. The Ubai are Africans and they're about a couple dozen in number. They moved into the Wumbu village a few months ago and have been doing a real number on the people ever since. I guess you can say they're cut from the same cloth as the Janjaweeds, without the good manners.

"The blind women told me their fellow Wumbus know a lot about the Yellowcake Gang, because they are buddies with these Ubai characters. In fact that's how the three women wound up at the fort in the first place. The Ubai gave them to the Yellowcake guys as a present, because the Yellowcake guys gave them weapons and ammunition."

Bing slammed his first down on the table. "If I hear any

more of this crap, I might swim home," he said. "I'm just sick of how people treat each other over here."

"But, listen to this," Moon went on. "Like I said before, the women heard about the Yellowcake Gang's second hideout. Well, now they tell me it's in a place called the *Dashi-dagumba*, which means the deepest part of the jungle, or, more accurately the Lost Valley. This is where the gang hides when the heat gets too high. And it's even more isolated than their fort in the desert."

"How can that be?' Amanda asked. "I thought that fort was as nowhere as you could get."

Moon shrugged. "Well, the *Dashi-dagumba* is even more so, simply because it's so hard to get to. The women talked about having to go down a haunted river and facing all kinds of weird things along the way. And that's just the beginning of it."

Vogel just rolled his eyes. "Again—someone's been watching too many movies."

But Moon was unfazed. "We've been flying all over Africa looking for these Yellowcake guys. And maybe we'd find them eventually, once they came out of hiding. But we've already burned through five nights with no results. I say it might be time to change tactics—or at least think about it. If what these women told me is true, then what the Wumbus have to say could be very valuable information for us."

Another murmur went through the group. If nothing else, the 201st was high-tech. Lost valleys? Haunted rivers?

Not exactly their style.

Moon pressed his case. "The gang is probably not a bunch of dumb ragheads, not all of them anyway. At the very least, some of them must know how to handle this Yellowcake 212. Plus, they must be pretty bold to rip off this guy Kaiser. Somehow they must have found out what happened at the fort, either before or after we got there. If they did, and if this magical hiding place of theirs exists, then logic says that's probably where those two trucks are. And probably where Kaiser's stolen 212 is too. But only the Wumbus can tell us how to get there."

The group was exhausted, numb and dejected. At this point, they just wanted to go to sleep for the next year or so, even if it meant inside a jail cell.

It was Gunn who finally came to life. He set the satphone aside for a moment and asked wearily: "But if these bad characters are still running this village, how can we get in there and get the information from the Wumbus? Bombing the crap out of the village is out, I assume?"

Moon nodded. "From the way the blind women described the place, it would be impossible to do an air strike on it without killing a lot of innocent people. Going in shooting would produce the same result. These Ubai guys have heavy weapons, RPGs. We could whip them, no sweat. But there would be a lot of civilian deaths too. However, I have another idea on how we can do it. *If* we want to do it."

The 201st's officers glanced around the ops table. Hightech? Low-tech? Did it even matter anymore?

Finally Mdosi spoke up. "I have a lot of confidence in American ingenuity," he said. "And yes, I'm sure if you looked hard enough, long enough, your radars and tracking gear would find these yellowcake people and the material they're trafficking in.

"But I should remind you, we are in Africa. And as you are finding out, things are a little bit different here. Things that might seem odd outside our shores are commonplace here."

He paused for a moment and then added: "If it was me and if I had a chance to talk to some spirit-induced villagers who might tell me a shortcut to this problem? At this point, I would take it."

He turned to Moon and asked. "You say you have a plan?"

The intelligence officer smiled, albeit briefly. "I do," he said. "I call it my 'Baboon Plan.'"

CHAPTER NINE

Chad

The village of Wumbu sat in a large open clearing on the edge of the Samu Rift, the dividing line of desert and jungle in northwest Chad.

This spot had been inhabited by the Wumbus for untold generations—and they had lived here in peace until two months ago when the Ubai arrived.

These intruders came from the north, where all bad things came from. To the simple people of the Wumbu, it seemed that a difference in their religions was what caused the Ubai to take over their village, abuse their women, steal their food and force all the village's people to be their personal and sexual slaves.

The Ubai always carried guns, and if one of the villagers did the least little thing wrong, the Ubai took delight in shooting that person to death, no matter how much the villagers begged them not to. It seemed like a game to them. They were just thugs—fighters who had fled the wildest of the Darfur region and settled here, to live off the hard work and blood of the Wumbus. This was the way of the world in many parts of Africa. The strong preying on the weak. It happened in Darfur. And for the last two months, it had been happening to the Wumbus. As a result, the Wumbus were slowly starving to death.

So it was strange then that when two villagers found the burning truck full of food, they reported it immediately to the Ubai instead of keeping the food for themselves. The gunmen, woken by the two villagers as they were slipping into an early morning qat stupor, roughly ordered the men to take them to the burning truck.

The villagers led them to the road close to the nearby lake, a winding path that ran off from the desert and went through the jungle all the way to the border of Cameroon and beyond. And sure enough, there was a 2.5-ton truck there, its engine smoldering, its cabin abandoned. The gunmen ordered the villagers to stand aside while they carefully checked the back of the vehicle.

It was filled not just with food, but good food—canned meats, sauces, sweets. And lots of liquor.

The Ubai had hit the jackpot.

IT took an hour, and a long line of Wumbu men and boys, to carry the contents of the truck back to the village.

The booty was brought to the largest hut in the village— the place where the two dozen Ubai could usually be found. The starving villagers gathered outside the hut, sitting in the burning sun, listening to the Ubai gorge themselves on canned ham, canned peaches and British whiskey. They were wondering if the gunmen would throw them a scrap, a piece of discarded food.

But that didn't happen.

Morning turned to noontime and the Ubai continued to overeat and drink. The villagers were smart enough not to stand outside the main hut for too long; it would be too easy for the drunken gunmen to start using them for target practice, something that had happened in the past. So the villagers retreated to their huts, still starving, still frightened, with nothing to look forward to but more hunger and fear as the afternoon approached.

But there was a surprise waiting for the Wumbus.

By mid-afternoon, all the Ubai were dead.

The food and liquor they'd consumed had been poisoned with antifreeze and watered-down aviation fuel.

Just like that, the Wumbus were free.

THE so-called Truth Hut was full.

The elders of the Wumbu tribe were on hand, in full regalia, sitting in what passed for the village's holy place. Sitting with them were Gunn, Amanda and Moon. They'd squeezed into the minicopter for the half-hour flight to the village, this after the unit's Jump Plane had delivered one of Mdosi's trucks as the bait that proved to be the Ubai's undoing.

The tribe greeted the Americans like deities; that is, after it was explained to them what had happened. The Wumbu elders were impressed at how the Americans had rid them of the Ubai, for they knew something about baboons too. Essentially, many baboon troops were made up of bullies and non-bullies. Should a baboon troop find an unexpected cache of food—like in a garbage dump, for instance—only the bullies of the group will share in the feast, as a means of prolonging the pecking order. But should the food be tainted or poisoned, only the bullies will die. And in one clean sweep, the baboon troop is transformed. Mdosi knew how these things worked, and so did Moon. That's how the 201st had got rid of the Ubai.

So now life was back to normal for the Wumbus, thanks to the Americans. It was time to return the favor.

Accompanying the 201st contingent was a man named Adi Umu. A longtime friend of Colonel Mdosi, Umu was an ex-mercenary who'd fought with Mdosi all over Africa and in secret ops in the Persian Gulf. Both had been employees of Blackwater and other security firms.

After twenty years of being hired out for combat, Umu had decided to hang up the weaponry and start a guide business. Tours, hunts, archaeological digs, he was considered an expert on this part of Africa. And the deeper you wanted to go into the jungle, the better.

Now he was here to act as a middleman for the 201st. They needed information, and the Wumbus knew things that they wanted to know. Priority number one: What was the secret of the Lost Valley?

But as grateful as they were, the Wumbus were reluctant to discuss the *Dashi-dagumba*. They believed anytime they talked about the Lost Valley, it brought bad luck upon their people.

This was why Umu was on hand. He was a short but muscular man, with a gregarious personality and a sunny demeanor. And he knew the ways of the locals. He suggested the Wumbu elders enact a smoke ceremony to help them decide whether to divulge the story or not. The elders discussed this, and eventually agreed.

They called for their ceremonial smoking pipe. What arrived was an enormous bamboo bong with a bowl the size of a Fritz helmet. The bowl was filled with an herb that looked a lot like marijuana. A torch was brought in and the bowl was lit. Each elder took several huge puffs, exhaling the smoke slowly and letting it drift around the interior of the hut. In seconds, everyone on hand was enveloped by the sweet-smelling haze.

After reciting a few passages from their holy books, the elders deemed themselves finally in touch with the good spirits. Smiling and red-eyed, they were ready to tell their story:

About a month before, at the behest of the Yellowcake Gang, the Ubai had forced six Wumbu men to accompany the gang to that place deep in the deepest part of the jungle, the uncharted territory known as the *Dashi-dagumba*. Similar to what happened with Mr. Yoyo's tribe, these half dozen Wumbus worked as slaves for the Yellowcake Gang, hacking out a road through the jungle that led to the gang's "second" hideout. According to the elders, four of these men succumbed not to exhaustion, but at the hands of night demons who "turned them inside out." The other two captives escaped, but only one made it back home. Even before the Ubai could kill him, this man died of something akin to delirium-induced fits. But he talked madly before he passed away, and the tale he told, of going to this haunted place and making his way back, was enough to curl the toes. Monsters, ghosts, demons, hellish heat, drowning rains, strange noises coming from everywhere—it was so frightening, even the Ubai forbade the villagers to talk about it.

Then, four days ago, the Yellowcake Gang returned and hastily took another six Wumbus as slaves to basically do the same thing, again hack out the road leading to their hideout. None of these men ever returned.

So where was this place where the Yellowcake Gang was hiding? How could one get to the *Dashi-dagumba*? The Wumbu elders puffed on their smoke pipe again, had a brief conference among themselves and then agreed to reveal all.

To get to the Yellowcake Gang's hideout, one had to go down the haunted Ingus River, as opposed to going in the other direction. Just saying the Ingus name aloud caused several of the elders to gasp and shrink back. Anyone traveling down this river would have to navigate its many twists and turns, be wary of the Stone Age–type tribes that were rumored to still inhabit its banks, be prepared to fight off a variety of strange creatures that lived in, around and above it, then find the exact spot where the Yellowcake Gang usually stopped and made the Wumbu slaves hack their way into their extremely isolated hideout. In the words of the Wumbu elders, what happened after that was "unknowable."

Gunn, Moon and Amanda sat there, taking it all in, trying to not to breathe too deeply, but mostly failing in that. Gunn finally turned to Umu and asked: "Why can't we just fly over this place? Find it from the air?"

Umu put the question to the Wumbu elders, who responded that the *Dashi-dagumba* was so hidden in the darkest reaches of the jungle, and possessed such a canopy of vines and overhanging trees, that even the deadeye snake eagles couldn't find it.

"Translation?" Umu told him. "Your radar would be hit and miss at best."

THE tribe elders needed a bathroom break, so Gunn and Amanda left the hut and sought the shade of a nearby rubber tree.

"Those guys should be scriptwriters," Gunn said, offering her his canteen. "They tell a hell of a story."

"That's the problem," she replied, taking a sip. "That ain't exactly tobacky they're smoking in there."

"I know," he said, sipping some water himself. "But assuming they're telling some version of the truth, it seems the gang last headed that way soon after leaving the fort. They might have smelled something in the air and decided to lay low for a while."

"It's a definite possibility," she said, adding, "God, I'm hungry. I'd kill for a candy bar."

Gunn just looked back at her—maybe for a few seconds longer than he should have. But he couldn't help it. He was feeling a bit, well . . . elevated too, due to the secondhand smoke. And it only made her look even more beautiful, if that was possible.

"So, you think this is something we should do?" he asked her.

She nodded, her blond curls going in a million different directions.

"We're down to one day and change," she said. "We tried flying all over Africa without a hit. Maybe it was too obvious to look for these guys at uranium sites. They must know about things like GIR, and they must know people are looking for them. So maybe they're experts in hiding out. It was just dumb luck we found them at that fort. No one would normally look for them way out there. They pick their spots well."

"So?"

"So maybe if we sail down this River of No Return, we'll get dumb lucky again, find this path these guys keep hacking out, and then it would be a case of follow the Yellow Brick Road."

"Please don't tell me that you just said, 'we,'" he told her. "Because maybe I go, but you certainly aren't."

She started to give him the same attitude as she had when he tried to prevent her from going down into the bunker—but she couldn't. Her defenses suddenly crumbled. She became emotional.

"I have to go," she told him directly.

"'Have to'? Why?" he asked.

Tears were forming in the corners of her eyes. She started sniffling. Gunn was startled to see her like this. He never imagined she got upset about anything.

Suddenly she grabbed his shirt cuffs and looked him straight in the eye.

"Why? Because, I want to go home, Tommy," she said, trying to hold it together. "I want to go back to America and I want it so bad, I dream about it, every night. Now, we've got less than two days left—and if it means sailing down some River of No Return with a million-in-one chance that it might pay off, well then, I've just got to do it."

Gunn was paralyzed. Did she just call him by his first name?

"Besides, it's important that I go," she said, wiping her eyes and feeling embarrassed. "Because if you go and I don't, then I'll be sick worrying about you. And I don't like being sick."

With that, she squeezed his hands once, then walked back to the smoky Truth Hut.

Gunn was on his cell phone to Wum Bakim two seconds later. Bing answered his call.

"We're going the haunted river route," Gunn told him. "And this is what we'll need."

FIVE minutes later, Gunn, Moon, Amanda and Umu were jammed into the minicopter again, flying west.

Umu had a cousin who ran a sport safari business on the upper Ingus River. He had a boat that sounded like just what the Americans needed—large enough to carry them, some supplies and the minicopter, which was important. The problem was, the boat usually went north, up the river, to its more tranquil parts. It took some cell phone negotiations and the promise of a substantial fee before Umu's cousin agreed to allow his vessel to go south, into the really haunted part of the haunted river.

They flew to the tiny fishing village of Kumpo. As usual, a crowd of villagers appeared as soon as they set down, fascinated as much by Amanda's beauty as they were by the strange-looking flying machine.

Umu's cousin greeted them warmly and led them to the riverbank. That's when they saw the boat for the first time.

To Gunn's bloodshot eyes, it looked like a nightmarish version of a Mississippi riverboat. It had three levels: a main deck; a middle deck, where a dozen or so cabins were located; and an open-air top deck. Its flat-bottomed hull was painted bloodred. Most of the rest of the vessel was patched up with pieces of vinyl siding, like one would find on a typical house in the U.S. Much of it appeared to have been adhered to the boat with duct tape. The paddle in the rear seemed too big for a vessel that was only about a hundred feet long. In the front, the wheelhouse was located on a raised tower, maybe fifteen feet high, giving the boat the appearance of a praying mantis.

Strangest of all, a series of electrical wires ran from the topmast to many parts of the boat below. Looking like clotheslines, these wires held hundreds of tiny white light-bulbs, not unlike those imbedded in the 201st's invisible aircraft.

"Those are to ward off bad spirits at night," Umu explained.

THE para-drop came twenty minutes later.

Nine of the 201st's paratroopers floated down next to the river after being dropped by the Jump Plane. The big C-17 had come in so low, in full view, the air above the tiny fishing village actually shook from the sheer power of the huge aircraft, bringing a cheer from the villagers.

The paratroopers brought a lot of supplies with them, including water, fuel and ammunition. They also brought one of the gunship's miniguns. It was air-dropped inside a metal crate that contained the weapon, its battery-driven power source and its ammo. An off-the-cuff invention of the unit's ground techs, the self-contained gun box could be easily carried and set up by two men.

Thirteen of them climbed aboard the big fishing boat: Gunn, Amanda, Moon, the nine paratroopers and Umu. Each had an individual M4, ammo, sidearm and jungle knife. They also had several of their own sat phones with them, though Gunn was sure the phones wouldn't work where they were going.

The paratroopers were put into berths at the rear of the first deck; they would share these with the crew of five.

Moon, Amanda, Umu and Gunn would have their choice of berths on the second deck. The gun box was put at the front of the top deck, where it would have its widest field of fire.

Last to go on was the minicopter. The boat had a flattened off area just aft of the second deck that was reinforced with steel sheets. By pure luck, it was large enough to serve as a helipad. They were able to lift three barrels of aviation fuel up to the pad, and rigged a foot-powered pump to get it into the small aircraft whenever needed. Once Moon piloted the small copter on board, and it was secured to the pad, they were ready to go.

Umu gave the signal to the ship's captain and the villagers cast them off. The boat crew seemed extremely nervous about the voyage that awaited him. The captain too looked very concerned. Suddenly the bonuses that Umu's cousin had promised them didn't seem so promising.

The riverboat moved away from the dock with no problem. But no sooner were the engines engaged than the vessel became caught in the swiftly moving current. Black smoke began belching from its stacks. The engines started backfiring, sounding not unlike the artillery pieces aboard the great AC-17. The entire vessel shook from stem to stern as the perilous journey began by going sideways down the river.

Clinging to the railing on the second deck, Gunn just looked at Moon, who said: "Disneyland, this ain't . . ."

PART THREE

DOWN THE
HAUNTED RIVER

CHAPTER TEN

The Ingus River

The lower Ingus River wound its way through eight hundred miles of the deepest part of Africa.

For thousands of years the southern end of this waterway had been considered unholy because, according to lore, this was where the souls of the condemned floated down into hell. Legend also said that the farther one traveled toward its source, the crazier things on the river became.

This seemed true from the start for the 201st contingent. For the first five minutes of their journey, the riverboat's captain battled the steering wheel mightily, just trying to get the boat heading in the right direction. At one point, the vessel was doing 360s out in the middle of the muddy river, and several times came close to capsizing. Only when two of the biggest paratroopers were rushed to the wheelhouse to help the captain wrestle the steering controls did the boat finally get positioned in the center of the current, bow pointing south. Only then did the journey begin in earnest.

The river was about a thousand feet wide off the village dock. But not ten minutes into the trip, the jungle on either side of the boat began to close in rapidly. By the time the sun started to set a half hour into the journey, the winding river was barely a hundred feet wide. As the riverboat was forty feet wide, very quickly it seemed like they were squeezing their way through the waterway as opposed to sailing on it. It became especially claustrophobic anytime they came to one of the many twists and turns in the serpentine river.

Then there was the overgrowth. It was so heavy above them, it was nearly impossible to see the sky. Soon enough, it seemed like they were already sailing in the darkest part of the night.

GUNN and Amanda were topside, on the helicopter pad, watching the eerie transformation take place. Moon was below, working on his laptop, still studying intelligence results from the 201st missions earlier in the long week, looking for anything, a scrap, that might help them now. The nine paratroopers on board, having been awake now for nearly forty-eight hours, took the opportunity to catch some sleep. A lot of the boat's crew were doing the same thing—either that, or they were hiding belowdecks.

Gunn sat on the edge of the makeshift helipad, weapon at the ready, his legs hanging over the side. Amanda was sitting close to him. They were both listening to the absolutely weird animal calls coming from the jungle, which sometimes was just an arm's length away. If they'd thought the noise level around the base at Wum Bakim was bad, it was nothing compared to this cacophony. The roars, the squawks, the ungodly screams—it was unnerving, even though they were both armed.

"Maybe we should be loaded with silver bullets," Amanda said at one point. "Isn't that what you use when you're shooting at monsters or ghosts?"

"I think that's for vampires," Gunn told her. "Though I

wouldn't be surprised if there were a few of them around here too."

Another sharp bend came up, and they passed so close to shore while rounding it that the screams and squawks became twice as loud, twice as scary. It got so weird that Gunn felt Amanda's hand on his wrist, digging her nails into his skin. A rush of electricity went through him, even though her nails seemed to be going right through to his bones. As soon as they cleared the bend, she quickly took her hand away. But Gunn's body was still buzzing long afterward.

An hour into the journey, the river became even narrower and the overhanging trees so thick and tall, they began intertwining about two hundred feet above the waterway. This created a canopy so dense that all parts of the sky were completely blotted out. The Wumbu elders had been right: Even the 201st's ground-imaging radar would have had trouble seeing through all this.

At one point, the captain snapped on the boat's network of tiny lights. He also began piping hip-hop music over the intercom system. It was a case of whistling in the dark, though, as the captain now seemed to be the most nervous member of all the crew. Still, the music and lights gave the impression they were passengers on a bizarre African booze cruise to nowhere.

"Is he trying to tell us hip-hop keeps the monsters away?" Amanda asked.

JUST before 2100 hours, Umu climbed up to the helipad to announce that a meal would soon to be served in the galley. Nothing exotic, he told them. Deviled ham sandwiches and tomato soup. This was the perfect medicine for Amanda, who still had a bad case of the munchies. But Gunn chose to stay topside.

"You're not starving?" she asked him, a bit surprised.

"Someone has to watch the gear," he said, secretly pulling two bennies from his pocket and rolling them between his fingers. "Enjoy your comfort food. Just save some for me."

Amanda gave him a curious look as she headed down the ladder to the galley. For once he was glad to see her go. The last thing he wanted was for her to know he was popping pills.

He swallowed the two bennies dry, then moved forward, relocating himself on the upper deck just outside the elevated bridge and next to the gun box. The captain gave him an uneasy wave. He looked like he'd rather be anywhere else but here.

Gunn happened to look down at the dark water streaming off the bow and saw an amazing, if disturbing, sight. Riding alongside the riverboat was a large pod of alligators. They were keeping pace with the vessel much as dolphins sometimes rode alongside ships at sea. These creatures looked huge, some were at least fifteen feet long, with a weird translucent glow to them. Gunn had never see anything like them.

He yelled over to the captain: "Why are they doing this?"

The captain shook his head nervously and yelled back: "I don't know. Maybe they are waiting for one of us to fall overboard?"

The night became even darker and the river more narrow and twisting as they motored along. The noise coming from the nearby riverbanks had reached almost earsplitting levels.

The boat had not gone more than a quarter mile before they came to yet another extreme bend in the river, forcing them to slow down and navigate a perilous turn. In the process they were coming so close to the shore that Gunn imagined that just about anything could come flying out of the overgrowth and attack them. He kept his M4 at the ready, safety off, even as he was shoving more bennies into his mouth.

It was during one of these turns that two creatures did jump out of the jungle and glide right over Gunn's head. It happened so quickly, he didn't have time to duck or react in any way.

These things were about three feet long, with furry arms and legs and heads with beady eyes. They weren't monkeys, or birds, even though they had wings of some sort. It was almost like they were little flying humans, in a small, monstrous way. They began diving on the boat, landing on tree branches, jumping back and forth, buzzing the lights and disappearing again. Gunn could only see them as shadows before they would streak by, scaring the crap out of him.

Finally he yelled to the captain and pointed to the creatures.

"What are those things?" Gunn asked him.

Again, the anxious captain could only shrug. "African flying squirrels," he replied. "The lights attract them . . ."

A few seconds later, one of the creatures buzzed the boat again. But this time, as it was passing over the mast, a long paw came out of the top of a nearby tree and caught the flying animal in mid flight. There was an ungodly screech, some rustling of bushes and then the sound of sharp teeth chomping into raw bone and skin. Then everything got quiet again.

Bon appetit, Gunn thought grimly.

ANOTHER thirty minutes went by.

Gunn took up a new position on the bow, this one close to a chopping block where crewmembers had skinned and filleted some fish they'd caught prior to embarking.

Left on the block now were just the heads and bones of

these fish. Gunn thought it odd that they weren't giving off any odor, when suddenly something swooped down from a nearby tree and landed on the pile of fish remains.

Gunn had his M4 up in a snap. He found himself eye to eye with an enormous owl-like bird not six feet away. It was bigger than an eagle, bigger than a buzzard; at least five feet from head to claw. Its eyes were disturbingly yellow. It didn't seem frightened of him at all as it sniffed around the fish heads for a few moments, picking over them with claws bigger than a man's fist. Then it bent down, took the largest fish head in its mouth and flew away with a great flapping of its wings.

Gunn was frozen to the spot, barely able to breathe. This thing really had been right out of a monster movie. He popped two more bennies and returned to his seat on the starboard side of the boat, far away from the fish table.

The river straightened out for a rare stretch and became a bit wider too. But if anything the water under the boat was darker and more dangerous-looking. The boat itself was moving slowly, maybe five knots or so, as the captain knew another wide bend was coming up. The lights were flickering all around Gunn. He could feel the last two bennies start to interact with all the ones he'd taken before. At that moment, he felt like he could stay awake for a week, even though his eyes were seriously drooping.

That's when he heard an odd splashing sound behind him. He turned to see that a snake-like creature had come up out of the water and was almost right beside him. Gunn stared back at this thing, so startled he almost dropped his M4. The creature's head was about the size of a cow's and it was attached to a neck as long as a giraffe's. It had strange Shrek-like ears and a tongue that was going in and out like a snake's.

Gunn couldn't believe he was seeing this—and that it was so close, keeping pace with the boat and just staring back at him, as if contemplating what it would do next.

Buzzing mightily now, Gunn didn't yell over to the captain, because he assumed it was just one of the many creatures in this very weird waterway. Still he'd never seen anything that looked so Jurassic Park.

He watched as the creature dipped its head slightly, looking at the water flowing off the bow. Then it made a sudden, violent dive, plunged its long neck into the river and came up with a huge alligator in its mouth. It thrashed the giant creature several times before finally plunging below the water again and disappearing for good. The violence and quickness of the attack was astonishing.

Gunn just shook his head, for a second wondering where he was.

I've got to stop popping so many bennies, he thought.

THAT was enough for him.

He went down to the second deck and found a small cubbyhole-like berth with a mattress atop an ancient steel spring. He lay down on the bunk and let the sheer exhaustion wash over him, counteracting all the chemicals coursing through his bloodstream.

Just how long he lay there before drifting off to sleep, he wasn't sure. But when a slight rocking of the boat interrupted his dream of swimming in a cool pool of water with sea monsters nipping at his toes, it stirred him back awake. He lay there frozen for a moment, wondering if he had dreamed all that stuff about weird animals following the boat, or whether if it had actually happened. At that moment, he really didn't know.

Then something else strange happened. He heard someone breathing, right next to him. He turned his head slowly and that's when he got the surprise of his life: Curled up on the bunk with him, just inches away, was Amanda. Eyes closed, snoring softly, her long blond curls tossed back— she was sound asleep.

Gunn was shocked. He had to make sure he was really awake, so he purposely bit down on his tongue. It hurt, so awake he was. But what was this? He was smart enough not to move an iota; there was no way he wanted this to end. But why was she here? There were plenty of other places on the boat to sleep. He didn't know—and it wasn't like he was going to wake her and ask.

So he just moved himself a bit closer to her and closed his eyes again, a smile coming to his weary face, the first real one since they'd left Nevada, so long ago.

HE eventually went to sleep again—but this time it was not for very long, as he was suddenly shaken awake by someone yelling: "Get up! Get your weapon . . ."

Next thing he knew he was looking up at Moon's ratlike face.

"Something strange is happening!" he was saying, "Hurry!"

It took Gunn a few seconds to realize this was not a dream. Amanda was gone and there was a lot of commotion all over the boat. He grabbed his M4, and he and Moon ran up on the top deck.

Here they found the paratroopers, Amanda, Umu and the boat's crew. They were all looking at something farther down the river. The formerly dark sky was now lit up with brilliant yellows, blues and reds. The night air was full of explosions reverberating like gusts of wind. Gunn looked at the ship's clock. It was 1 A.M.

He edged his way through the crowd, until he found himself standing next to Amanda. "What's going on?"

She pointed downriver and said: "You tell us."

Through bleary eyes Gunn could see a very rickety drawbridge about a quarter mile away, spanning from one side of the river to the other. It was festooned with hundreds of multicolored Christmas lights, Chinese lanterns and other kitschy illumination. There were explosions going off above, below and on both sides of this bridge, so many that at first Gunn thought they'd come upon a celebration—a fireworks party, with lights, and firecrackers exploding everywhere.

He couldn't have been more wrong. The fireworks were actually shell blasts going off, and the noise of firecrackers was actually the chatter of machine guns. A little war was going on, right in front of them. A small army on the western side of the bridge was battling another on the eastern side. They were obviously fighting for control of the bamboo bridge, which in reality looked no more than a hundred feet long, twenty-five feet high, and held together with miles of old telephone wire.

Gunn took it all in and said, dumbly: "Well, we've got to get under that bridge, don't we?"

Umu the guide was beside him. "These must be the Yikyaks and Tomtoms," he explained. "And that must be the Jo-jumbi Bridge. The stories say that these two groups have been fighting for it for years. Back and forth—day and night. They get high on qat and simba weed and alcohol and then go and they have their little war."

"But where does the bridge lead to?" Amanda asked. "Why is it so important?"

Umu just shook his head. "That's just it," he said. "The bridge is meaningless. It's a bridge to nowhere. It simply links one bank to the other. Yet both sides want to control it, so hundreds have died here over the years for that and nothing more."

But Gunn was wondering something else: How did the Yellowcake Gang make it through here? Or Kaiser, if he was also in pursuit of them? Maybe they snuck their way under it? Or went around it somehow?

He didn't know, and at the moment, he didn't care. They had a real problem here.

He studied the explosions and the racket going on all over the bridge. The explosions sounded like 122mm mortars. And there were 50-caliber machines guns firing as well. And amid all this, the unmistakable clacking of AK-47s.

Translation: Little, insane war or not, there was a lot of firepower going back and forth. Steering the riverboat through it would be impossible.

Gunn looked at the clock again. They had to get down-river as quickly as possible. Yet how were they going to get beyond this point?

Then he got an idea. It was irrational, and impulsive, but he was just too tightly wound to think of anything else.

He told the captain to bring the riverboat to within one hundred yards of the bridge and then stop.

Once the boat was in position, Gunn climbed up to where the gun box was located. Positioning himself behind it, he did a quick sighting to make sure no one was actually on the bridge and then let off a long stream of vicious can-non fire. The five-second fusillade hit the bridge dead-on, blowing it to a mass of burning smithereens.

Immediately all weapons on either side of the riverbank stopped firing. A sudden calm came to the surrounding jun-gle. Gunn signaled the captain to get the riverboat moving again. The captain did so quickly, ordering his engines full speed ahead.

They passed between the smoldering remains just sec-onds later, everyone on deck with their weapons ready. But no one fired on them from either side of the river. Instead the people on the boat just saw battle-weary soldiers from both sides looking down at them as they cruised by at high speed. The grimy fighters seemed in shock that their con-tested bridge was so suddenly gone.

Then, unexpectedly, the soldiers on both sides started cheering—some even threw hastily picked flowers onto the riverboat as it passed by. Their war was finally over, thanks to the strangers in the strange boat. There was nothing left to kill for. They cheered until the vessel was out of sight.

Then they all melted back into the jungle and it was quiet again.

With the problem solved, Gunn took the back stairs down to the little cubbyhole berth where he'd woken to find Amanda.

She was not there, at least not yet.

So he lay down and waited and waited—and waited.

But she never returned that night.

CHAPTER ELEVEN

The Ingus River

Gunn was woken by the noise of the boat's engines slowing down.

The sun was up, though he could barely tell, as the jungle canopy was still in place. He rolled off the bunk, not surprised that he was alone, and stepped out into the passageway. Next to the small berth was an ancient, all-wooden shower. Someone was in it; he could hear the water splashing around. He froze in place and listened intently. He knew the chances were not good that it was Amanda in there, naked and soapy on the other side of the shower's flimsy bamboo door. If he played the odds, though, then maybe . . .

But a sudden jolt of the riverboat snapped him back to reality. He looked out a nearby porthole and saw they were coming up on a fishing village. The boat was slowing to a stop.

"Show's over," he thought.

He went forward to the top deck; Umu was already up here. He pointed out the village on the west bank of the river.

"We are about forty miles down the Ingus," the guide told Gunn. "Which means this is the village of Nkimo."

As the riverboat approached, a crowd of villagers ran from their huts to look at them. They were barely dressed, and what they wore looked like rags. But the natives seemed authentically excited to see them.

Umu walked out to the bow as the captain guided the riverboat close to the village's small pier. Gunn noticed that the dock had been damaged recently. Some of the wood was freshly cracked and a few of the rubber tire bumpers had been torn from the mooring.

The captain stopped the boat about twenty feet off the dock. Umu yelled across to the villagers, asking if they had seen any large vessels pass this way lately.

The crowd became even more excited. Many began yelling back, but it was impossible for Umu to know what they were saying. Finally a village leader broke through the throng; his voice rose above everyone else's.

In deep, stuttering Tutsu, he told Umu that a vessel full of strangers had come down the river a few days before. This vessel was square and wide, like a barge, and was carrying two trucks on it. The people steering this vessel misjudged the river's width and crashed into the village dock as they passed by. When villagers rushed to the scene, the men on the boat fired guns into the air, scaring them.

Umu yelled back that they were the police and they were in pursuit of these men. Hearing this, the villagers cheered loudly. But the leader yelled back a warning: "These people are not Africans like us, my friend. They are from the sand."

Umu knew exactly what he meant. Gunn asked him to inquire if the villagers had seen anyone else who was looking for the people who hit their dock. To Gunn it was just as important to know if people working for Kaiser were also pursuing the Yellowcake Gang.

But the village leader said they had not seen anyone else

in the last few days. Still, that didn't mean someone hadn't passed by in the middle of the night.

"We will capture these people and punish them for what they did to your dock," Umu yelled to the villagers as the captain engaged the engines and started them moving downriver again. "This I promise you, my brothers!"

The villagers cheered again and waved until the riverboat rounded the next bend. Then Umu turned to Gunn and said: "At least we are sure of one thing—the people we are chasing have been here recently. It seems we are on the right track."

To which Gunn replied: "Lucky us."

THE rain began about mid-morning.

Even though the canopy of overgrowth covering the river was as thick as ever, torrents of raindrops still leaked through, soaking the riverboat and everything around it.

At first the cool rain was a welcome relief from the morning heat. The boat's crew and the paratroopers took advantage of the downpour, climbing to the top deck to wash themselves and their uniforms.

Gunn just stood in the pouring rain, however, clothes still on, waiting. If Amanda was going to take advantage of nature's shower, he wanted to be on hand and not distracted.

Unless that had been her in the boat's shower earlier . . .

The minutes passed, and the paratroopers finished up and went back below. Eventually Gunn was the only one on the top deck, standing alone in the deluge, now soaked to the skin. Suddenly it became even darker overhead. The rain got heavier and the wind picked up ferociously. In seconds the riverboat was being rocked back and forth. Water began splashing up over the sides and the bow. They started twisting around again, spinning in circles, even though the river was still very narrow. Gunn had visions of the vessel slamming into one of the riverbanks and becoming crippled. Then what would they do?

At that point, his concern went directly to the minicopter, tied up with bungee cords on their makeshift helipad on the stern. If it went over the side, then they truly would be lost. The wind increased again just in these few seconds, and turning aft, to his horror Gunn saw two of the bungee cords snap from the strain. The little copter was about to topple into the river. He rushed to the back of the boat, cursing himself that he hadn't been thinking about their aircraft instead of getting a free show from the beauty queen.

What was the matter with him?

He jumped down to the helipad just in time to catch the minicopter's landing strut and prevent the tiny craft from going over the side. He held on to the strut with all his might, but between the wind and the vicious rocking, he knew it was just a matter of time before his muscles snapped and the helicopter would fall overboard, bringing him down with it.

Then suddenly someone appeared beside him. It was raining so hard Gunn couldn't tell who it was, and at the moment, he didn't care. Together they pulled the minicopter back up onto the pad.

Only then did Gunn see who his helper was: Lieutenant Moon.

Gunn was astonished how strong the little guy was.

"Damn, someone's been eating their Wheaties," he said, gasping for air.

Moon just wiped the rain off his brow and began resecuring the copter with the remaining bungee cords.

"I'm more of a Sugar Pops man myself," he said.

THE wind died down and the riverboat was soon heading in the right direction again. But the rain did not let up.

Gunn went below again, returning to the cubbyhole and finally giving in and taking a shower in the boat's minuscule washroom. He was surprised how good the warm water felt, washing away the last two days of sweat and grime. He was also surprised to find a towel inside the cramped water box. Strategically wrapping it around his waste, he stepped back out into the passageway . . . to find Amanda waiting for him on the bunk.

This time he really did freeze. She was dressed in a T-shirt and her combat pants, with no shoes. It was hard to tell, but he was sure he saw no bra straps through her T-shirt either. Her hair was partially tied up, partially cascading onto her face and shoulders.

The first thought that came to Gunn's head: This is what an angel looks like.

She stood up and looked at him plainly. He saw no indication that she wanted to talk about last night.

She said instead: "We'll be coming up on another village in about thirty minutes. Umu thinks we should be prepared . . . for anything."

Gunn had started to reply when suddenly the boat and everything around them shook with the sound of a massive bang.

It was so violent Amanda fell into his arms. He held her, awkwardly, not wanting his towel to become unhitched. The whole world shook for another ten seconds before it just stopped.

"My God," she gasped. "What was that?"

"Earthquake?" Gunn replied. "Or an atom bomb?"

She disentangled herself from him. "It sounded like an airplane crash," she said.

With that, she ran down the passageway toward the bow. Halfway down the hall, though, she stopped, turned around and yelled back to him: "Well? Come on! Get dressed—hurry!"

Gunn was up on the deck in less than a minute, fully dressed, M4 in hand. The paratroopers were up there too, along with Moon and Umu.

Everyone was looking in all directions at once, trying to determine the cause of the massive bang.

Amanda was the first to spot a huge column of smoke rising above the jungle canopy to their southwest. She pulled Gunn over and pointed to it.

"God, I knew it—a plane crash," she said.

Gunn studied the column of smoke. It was pure white, going straight up, as if the wind and rain had no effect on it.

"Do you think it could be one of ours?" she asked him, her nails digging into his arm.

That thought ran a chill down to Gunn's bones. The 201st were the only ones flying big planes around this part of Africa. Of that they were sure. That their planes were in dire need of maintenance was no secret either. But would the 201st really be flying in the daytime if they didn't have to?

Moon was right beside them and immediately started pushing buttons on his sat-phone. But after two minutes, he knew it was no use. There was no way they could get a good reading on any satellite in order to get a connection back to Wum Bakim.

A helpless feeling came over all of them.

"That smoke is about ten miles away," Gunn said. "Let's see what happens when we get to the next village."

THE rain had let up a little by the time they came around the bend and saw the next fishing hamlet.

Umu had told them that this place, called Lumuba, after its inhabitants, was right on the edge of what was still rumored to be cannibal country. Thus, everyone on the boat would have to maintain a friendly manner, but with some caution.

There were a dozen villagers waist-deep in the water, throwing out fishing nets as the riverboat approached. They stopped what they were doing and started crying out as soon as they saw the vessel. Umu suggested the boat hold off the narrow dock that ran fifty feet into the river.

As was usually the case, the village's leader was quickly on the scene. He walked to the end of the dock and had a shouted conversation with Umu and Gunn across twenty feet of water.

The chief could speak no English, but he knew bits of several dialects that Umu could understand. Umu explained they were looking for another vessel that might have passed by days earlier. This vessel would be flat with two trucks on it. The chief replied that yes, such a vessel went by about three days ago, but the chief, being the smartest man in the village, urged his people to stay in their shanty houses until the strangers had moved on. A wise decision.

Was there anyone else following these people? Umu asked him. The chief thought a moment and then said no— but again, there was the possibility that someone had gone by in the night, unnoticed.

Then the chief added something quite unexpected: He asked Umu if he knew about the plane crash.

Plane crash?

The two words went through the 201st contingent in a flash. Umu asked the chief to explain—but the lack of one common language allowed the guide to get only the sparest of details. It seemed that an airplane bearing a similar symbol to the one that the 201st troopers were wearing on their shoulders—that being the U.S. flag—had crashed in the jungle near the village.

Acute apprehension gripped Gunn and the others. Again, they realized they were in a very remote part of Africa. Not many aircraft ventured over this region, simply because it was not near anyplace else.

Could Amanda's intuition be right? Gunn wondered. Could this crash have been one of the unit's planes?

"Tell him we have to see the crash site," Gunn said to Umu. "And I mean right now."

The guide looked back at Gunn in horror. "But it is in cannibal country—very dangerous."

Gunn had already loaded his weapon and was putting on his Fritz helmet.

"I know," he said. "That's why we have to go."

NOT a minute later, Gunn, Amanda and six paratroopers were running headlong through the jungle, following three of the village's scouts who were taking them to the crash site. These three men ran like the wind, and it was all the 201st could do to keep up with them. The jungle was very thick, yet the three villagers were able to run over, around and through most of the vegetation.

They ran like this for more than twenty minutes. Over streams, over rocky hills. Around swamps and into deep crevices. At times Amanda would point straight up, yelling to Gunn that she could see the column of smoke again. But each time he found the vines and overgrowth so thick, he could barely see the sky, never mind any white smoke.

Finally they descended into a deep hollow thick with creepy, crawly vines. And at the far end of this depression, there was indeed a crashed U.S. airplane.

But it certainly didn't belong to the 201st.

"Am I really seeing that?" Amanda gasped.

"If you are, I am," Gunn replied.

It was a B-24 Liberator, a heavy bomber from World War II. It lay crumpled near the base of a huge tree, its wings hanging off, its nose smashed in.

The Americans walked up to it slowly. Most of its fuselage was resting against some rocks making up the edge of
the hollow, but an entire forest of trees and bushes and
vines had grown up around it. The hot jungle and years of
heat and rain had rusted a lot of it, yet its basic structure
was remarkably intact. It still had its green camouflage
paint job and its four propellers; even its tires were still
partially inflated.

"The Allies had loads of B-24 bases across North Africa
for striking Nazi targets in southern Europe," Gunn said
upon reaching the wreckage. "But those bases were way up
in Libya, places like that."

Amanda reached out and touched the plane, as if she had
to make sure it was real. "It certainly was a long way from
home," she said.

Gunn climbed into the cockpit to find the pilot and copilot still strapped in their seats. They were skeletons, their
uniforms long ago rotted away. Their dog tags were long
gone too. But in the pilot's hand he spotted a small shiny
object. He carefully removed it and scraped off sixty-five
years of dirt and crud.

It was a compass. A small kid's compass.

And amazingly, it still worked.

"I'm guessing this belonged to his son," Gunn said, turning it over in his hands. "And he was holding on to it when
they crashed and he died."

A rare silence came over the jungle. It was a very eerie
moment for them all. Even the native guides seemed
affected.

The moment passed and the jungle came alive again.
Relieved this was not one of their own planes, the small
group had to return to the village quickly. They took a few
pictures and were ready to leave, when Amanda's eye
caught something else: It was a plastic bag stuffed under
the engineer's station that had somehow weathered the environment here for years. Inside this bag was an American

flag—forty-eight stars. It was made of thin cloth, so it was good sized, yet small enough to fold and carry in one's pocket.

Amanda took the flag and ran her fingers over it.

"Another reason for us to get back home," she said.

CHAPTER TWELVE

The Ingus River

By dusk, everyone was back on the riverboat and they were heading downriver again.

They never found out what had caused the large booming noise; never found out what the column of smoke was about either. Like Mdosi had told them, things were different in Africa. Not everything had an explanation. Or needed one.

Rounding another bend just after sunset, they came upon yet another fishing village. Lit up by dozens of torches, it looked much like the others: shanty shacks, dirt-poor conditions, a few skiffs that served as fishing boats.

According to Umu, these people were called the Djangas.

But there was something different here. The usual crowd of villagers had come down to the riverbank to see the boat approach, but this time, every one of them was armed to the teeth.

The 201st paratroopers were called to battle stations; the gun box was manned and ready; Gunn and Amanda were on the bow, their M4s out, expecting anything.

As before, Umu had the captain stop about fifty feet

from shore. He called into the villagers; at least a hundred were lined along the shallow shoreline, machetes and long knives in hand. Someone on the shore spoke one of the dialects Umu understood. A conversation was begun.

As it turned out, the villagers were not intending to attack the riverboat. Instead, they were on guard because of a problem in the next village over.

A very interesting problem . . .

As the people on the shoreline told it, a gang of troublemakers squatting in a neighboring village had gotten high on qat and homemade alcohol and had captured some "foreigners" who'd been navigating down the river, having entered it earlier by one of its several tributaries. The troublemakers were now holding these foreigners captive—and the people of this fishing village were afraid they were next. That's why they were all carrying weapons.

The members of the 201st couldn't believe what they were hearing.

Gunn prodded Umu to ask the next, fateful question: "What kind of vessel were these foreigners using when they were captured?"

The answer was startling: "The vessel was a flat-bottom boat. Huge. And it was carrying two trucks on it."

Gunn and Amanda just looked at each other.

Could it be?

Had these troublemakers somehow captured the Yellowcake Gang?

Gunn asked the captain to anchor the boat. Then with a load of MREs in hand, the entire 201st contingent plus Umu waded ashore. They distributed the food packs to the villagers as a sign that they came in peace, then they sat down with the Djanga chief, next to a roaring fire; this as several dozen armed villagers surrounded them.

"The troublemakers are Tutsis," Umu told the Americans, translating for the village chief. "They are savages. Their weapon of choice is the machete, and once they are done with you or need to be amused they simply hack you to death. They've also been known to eat the body parts of those they've slaughtered. They're psychotic, drug-addled, and without mercy. Utterly ruthless."

Moon clapped his hands together on hearing all this.

"Well, that's that," he said. "Someone has done our work for us. It sure sounds like these troublemakers got to the gang, before the gang ever got to their hideout this time. And the troublemakers probably got irradiated in the process."

Gunn laughed darkly. "If it was only that easy," he said. He knew that even if the troublemakers killed the Yellow-cake Gang, that didn't solve the problem of the yellowcake itself, or Kaiser's pursuit of it.

On the other hand, if the 201st was able to capture the Yellowcake Gang before the troublemakers killed them, they could interrogate them, find other stashes of yellow-cake and God knows what else.

"Damn, I can't believe I'm going to say this," Gunn told the rest of the unit once they were through talking to the chief. "But I think we've got to rescue those guys."

A man named Daniel Infootu was the leader of the trouble-makers.

He was a drug abuser, a former member of the notorious Tutsi militias who had personally murdered hundreds of rival tribe members, most of them defenseless women, children and the elderly.

These days he was terrorizing this part of the Ingus Swamp. He and his followers made their living raiding local villages, kidnapping elders and children and asking for large ransoms, though they frequently killed their victims anyway, even if they got paid.

The more booty they'd acquired, the bolder they'd become. A few weeks before, they'd taken over the nearly abandoned village, killed the few people who still lived there and simply moved in. A week of alcohol and drugs followed, but when it was time to look for more money and victims, the troublemakers had headed down to the nearby river.

That's where they spotted the foreigners and managed to get the jump on them by sheer numbers alone. There were fifty troublemakers—and only twenty-three foreigners.

They were able to pull their captives' boat in to the shoreline and push their two trucks through the jungle all the way to their village.

These captives were now inside the village's largest hut, still alive, but tightly bound and gagged with plastic trash bags. Their trucks were hidden in the underbrush on the edge of the clearing. The foreigners had a load of cocaine with them when captured; the troublemakers had been snorting it nonstop ever since.

Once all the dope was gone, the plan was to find out who might pay a ransom for the foreigners, and then Daniel would get word to these people somehow. The foreigners appeared rich and certainly better off than the skells he and his gang had been kidnapping recently. Daniel was confident that this might prove to be a big payday for him and his murderous associates.

He and his men had just lit a fire and started to discuss all this when suddenly a huge flying thing came out of the sky and dove on them. They were familiar with the large flying squirrels and the monster owls that inhabited this part of the jungle. Yet this thing was neither; it was a flying machine, a very tiny helicopter that appeared over the top of the trees and was now buzzing around them like some huge gnat.

They had no idea who this was. There were no police or army in this part of the jungle. Not that it would have made any difference. Daniel stood up with his AK-47, took aim at the small flying machine, and . . .

The next thing Daniel knew he was looking down at a gaping hole in his chest. The last thought he had was that this hole cut all the way to his back because he could actually feel a breeze going right through him.

He fell over, landing directly in the fire, and died instantly. In the next second, the village was filled with gunfire. Tracer streaks were screaming everywhere, troublemakers being hit with one and two head shots, all fatal. Huge cannon shells were taking out three and four gunmen at a time.

The attack was so swift, none of the troublemakers even had time to go for his machete. It lasted but ten seconds. When it was over, all the troublemakers were dead.

THE paratroopers moved into the village a half minute later, emerging from their hidden firing posts and checking to make sure all of the murderous bandits were indeed dead.

Gunn and Amanda were with them. Moon's job had been to distract the criminals in the minicopter. The plan had worked to perfection. Now it was time to see the people they'd rescued.

The paratroopers split up—Amanda led one team and went off to find the vehicles the captives had had with them when they were abducted. Gunn took the rest of the 82nd soldiers and broke into the large shack at the middle of the village.

That's when they got their first surprise.

Instead of finding a group of trussed-up al Qaeda types inside the shack, they found instead a gang of terrified European white people—yuppie types—wearing designer ghetto wear. They were not the Yellowcake Gang. Instead, Gunn learned, they were customers of an extreme adventure tour company, which had sent them to the darkest part of the continent so they could take a coke-filled joyride out.

And their vehicles? As Amanda was just finding out: Both were specially equipped long-range Land Rovers.

As Amanda said once she returned and helped untie the very lucky captives: "Who would pay to come to this part of the world?"

CHAPTER THIRTEEN

The Ingus River

The riverboat was heading south again. All hands were on board, fed and asleep by midnight.

Except Gunn.

He was lying on his bunk, praying something resembling a peaceful sleep would come to him. But as the minutes turned to hours, he knew it was a hopeless cause.

They'd left the yuppie adventurers in the care of the Djangas. Once they were healthy enough to travel, they would drive out of the Ingus Swamp in their SUVs, most likely never to return again.

In some ways, Gunn wished he were going with them.

He was beginning to believe what they said about the Ingus River. The farther one traveled down it, the weirder things became. Huge alligators and something from a monster movie were just the beginning of it. It seemed the cosmos was playing games with them. Seeing the futility of war played out in a battle for a bridge that led to nowhere? Hearing the sound of a plane crashing sixty-five years ago? Tantalizing clues that they were close to finding the Yellowcake Gang only to have them evaporate before their eyes?

Moon had been right on the money: This was no Disneyland ride.

He shifted uncomfortably on his cot. The same words kept coming back to him. Sometimes in his voice, sometime in someone else's. But always saying the same thing: "What the hell are you doing here?"

It was a good question.

Just a couple months ago, he'd been one of America's top test pilots. He had a great career going, and a nice life living in the desert near Edwards Air Force Base. Now he was on the lam from his own government, floating down a haunted river, trying to squeeze through the eye of a needle in hopes of beating a massive national security rap.

Yet this mission seemed to have been doomed from the start. He'd gone from flying one of the most sophisticated airplanes possible to riding on a riverboat that made the *African Queen* look like a luxury liner. And it was becoming doubtful that this idea to search for the Yellowcake Gang on the river would work out as they had planned. The gang might have come this way, or maybe the vessel the natives had seen was really the yuppie extreme excursion package passing by. Or maybe both. Or maybe neither.

There was no way to know what had gotten lost in the rash of translations going on, no way to even know if they were heading in the right direction, on the right tributary. Or maybe they'd even gone *too* far down the river already.

All of it was just too painful to think about. All too weird, made worse by the fact that Downes's deal was up in less than two hours.

There was only one saving grace: He was lucky he didn't have any family to speak of. No one to embarrass when all this crap eventually hit the fan.

He closed his eyes and again prayed for sleep to come.

Instead, he heard soft padding in the passageway outside his berth. Or at least he thought he did. He knew his mind could be playing tricks on him—again. Amphetamines did that to you. But if that wasn't the case, then the gods really were playing dirty this time, because this sounded just like . . .

He opened his eyes, slowly, and looked out into the passageway.

And there she was.

Amanda. Standing at the foot of his bunk. Wearing just a short white T-shirt—and nothing else. He knew this because a lantern behind her was shining right through the soft cloth. Her hair was down; she was looking at him in such a way, he knew his life would never be the same.

Or at least he hoped so.

"Are you still awake?" she asked in a whisper.

Gunn, once again, was speechless.

"Sure," he finally managed to croak out.

She squeezed into the tiny space and then knelt on the edge of the bunk. Her bare legs touched his.

"Do you mind?" she asked him.

"Of course not . . ."

"My quarters aren't this luxurious," she said, joking, looking around the cramped space. "And I'm just so tired, and . . ."

She stopped talking and just lay down next to him. He put his arm around her and thought his heart was going to burst right out of his chest. He'd known many women in his life. Some he'd really cared for, many he'd had really good times with.

But this?

Nothing was like this . . .

He had to say something. But what?

Finally, he commanded his mouth to open and ordered his tongue to start forming a word—any word.

And that word was about to come out . . .

When suddenly . . . there was a huge *crash!*

Gunn just rolled eyes. "Jesus—*again?"* he cried.

The boat came to a sudden halt, and anything not tied down went flying through the air. The engines were screaming—the crew was shouting. Gunn and Amanda could smell smoke and heard the sound of many feet suddenly running at once.

They were both off the bunk in a flash, Gunn silently shaking his fist at the sky.

"What the fuck now?" he said under his breath.

They ran topside, to see Umu and the boat's captain looking over the starboard side.

As the alerted paratroopers took up defensive positions all over the boat, Gunn and Amanda rushed to the railing and looked down into the murky black water.

Only then did they realize that the boat had hit something, something submerged.

But what was it?

Moon joined them at the rail, carrying a huge spotlight. He pointed it down at the sunken object, illuminating it for all.

But at that moment, none of them believed what they were seeing.

"No freaking way," Moon exclaimed.

"Could it be?" Amanda asked, trying to wrap her skimpy T-shirt around her.

"It is," Gunn said. "It's the real McCoy."

Incredibly the submerged object was a truck. A very familiar-looking truck.

Gunn pulled out his cell phone and went through its photos. He stopped at the one he'd taken inside the religious fort a million years ago.

He compared it to what he was now looking at in fifteen feet of water off the starboard side. Same color. Same tires. Same heavy armor all-around.

There was no doubt about it. It was one of the Yellow-cake Gang's trucks.

"Damn," he whispered. "We actually found one."

TWO things happened next.

The boat's captain managed to back his vessel off the truck. The damage to the riverboat was extensive, though. Its starboard side anchor and chain were gone, as were part of the railing and a half dozen of its tire bumpers. It was taking on water, but by some miracle, the impact had not cracked the vessel's hull wide open. The captain immediately dispatched two of his crew into the water to lather some kind of sealant on the boat's wound—this while the other crewmembers stood by with rifles, looking for alligators. But it was clear the sealant was just a temporary solution, and a poor one at that.

At the same time, the two paratroopers also went into the water. They probed around the submerged truck, looking in its cab and its cargo bay. Though they made repeated dives, they found nothing of any consequence: There were no bodies in the cab, and nothing at all in the cargo bay.

So, yes, they had found one of the Yellowcake Gang's trucks.

But it was empty.

AMANDA disappeared for a few minutes but soon returned to the deck, fully dressed and ready for business.

Obviously something unplanned had happened here. Had the truck rolled off the gang's barge, maybe in a rainstorm? Or had it happened when they were trying to unload it?

As the swimmers studied every part of the submerged vehicle, Amanda turned her flashlight on the shore nearby. She'd spotted a pile of trees and brush that had been dragged from one part of the riverbank to another, a spot about ten feet away from where the truck lay underwater.

She pulled Gunn with her, and together they went over the side of the boat and swam to the shore. They reached the spot where the vegetation had been gathered and pushed it away with their hands and feet.

On the other side of this camouflage barrier, they found a road hacked out of the jungle with two lines of fresh tire tracks on top of it.

They looked at it, but for some reason it didn't seem real.

Then suddenly Amanda hugged him.

"It's the Yellow Brick Road," she said, laughing.

And he hugged her back.

But then he said: "Now comes the hard part."

PART FOUR

"LEGENDS SAY YOU ARE NOW IN HELL"

CHAPTER FOURTEEN

GUNN checked his equipment.

Survival pack. Sidearm. Fritz helmet. RIF goggles. M4 and six ammo clips. Five bennies.

He zipped up his flight suit. He was ready.

Standing in the passageway close by his berth was Amanda, checking her own gear.

She turned to him and asked: "By the way, who's driving?"

Gunn put his helmet on and slung his M4 over his shoulder.

"How many hours do you have in rotary aircraft?" he asked her back.

She laughed that laugh as she struggled to put her helmet over her hastily assembled hair bun.

"None," she replied.

Gunn said: "Well, unless you want to start now, I think I should drive."

She finally got her helmet on, but her bun didn't take. Some of her blond locks fell out of the Fritz and rested on her shoulders. Gunn had never seen anything so sexy.

They climbed up to the top deck, where Moon and Umu were waiting by the minicopter. Moon had the diminutive aircraft nearly ready to go.

This was the plan: There was a good chance the road they'd discovered cut out of the thick jungle led to the Yellowcake Gang's hideout. But walking it made no sense; the Wumbu who survived his trip to this Hell said the gang's hideout was quite a ways in from the river. Luckily the 201st's RIF goggles were so sensitive, they could key in on both the road—because recently hacked vegetation gave off a different amount of heat than vegetation that was still growing—and the tire tracks made by the second gang truck, which gave off a heat signature of their own. If the second truck stayed on the hacked-out road, then, in theory, just flying where the RIFs took them would bring them to the gang's hideout. And if they were lucky, they would reach it before the time ran out on Downes's deadline.

The trick was, they'd have to fly most of this mission *under* the jungle canopy; it was just too thick to fly above it and hope to see anything below. In a sense, it would be like flying through a tunnel. A long, twisting, turning tunnel.

"You've got twelve feet clearance with the rotor," Moon started telling Gunn, as he strapped into the pilot's seat of the minicopter. "Most of the canopy is at least forty feet high. That huge truck had to fit through the road they hacked out, so you should be able to fit through too. But you're really going to have to pay attention to every little move you make."

Gunn was taking it all in, even though he already knew everything Moon was telling him. If they'd been able to track the hacked-out road from above, they could have followed it with one of the C-17s, had they been able to get ahold of Wum Bakim that is.

"Second," Moon went on. "Please remember, this is an

intelligence mission. Strictly reconnaissance. Just find this place. That's all you've got to do and our part of the deal will be fulfilled. No need for any heroics. No need for gun-play. Is that clear?"

"Loud and clear, Lieutenant," Gunn told him.

Moon went on: "Third: You shouldn't have any fuel is-sues. You're full in both tanks, and if the Wumbus were right, your objective is just under an hour's flying time from here. You've got to get over two sets of mountains somehow, but you should be OK. By those calculations, you'll have one hour of extra fuel to play with."

Gunn acknowledged him again and then helped Amanda get strapped in.

Moon said: "One last thing: Can we please go over the phone again?"

Now this was a potential sticking point. Their own sat-phones were not working; they were just too deep in the jungle for that. Downes's sat-phone, though, was a different animal. He claimed it would work anywhere, anytime. So Gunn was bringing it with him. If the recon mission was a success, then Gunn would activate Downes's sat-phone and give the location of the gang's hideout, both by voice and by text message. Even if the message didn't get through right away, it would be time stamped, proof that the 201st had fulfilled their end of the bargain before the seven-day deadline was up.

Gunn discussed all this with Moon, adding; "I just hope Downes paid his phone bill this month."

Umu now had a few words for them. "Where you are going is really uncharted territory. There are places back in that jungle that few people have ventured to—which is why, I'm sure, the gang decided to camp out there in the first place. Whatever you do, please try to stay airborne at all costs. A lot of heavy terrain lies between here and there—to get lost somewhere in the middle would not be a pleasant experience."

Gunn went over the copter's controls as Amanda checked out the camera Moon had given her. It looked like a typical Nikon, but it had infrared and night-vision lenses attached. Because they would also be time-stamped, photos would be important if the unit needed later on to show proof of finding the hideout.

"Just point and click," Moon told her.

Finally all was in readiness.

Gunn indicated he wanted one last word with Moon. The intelligence officer came close enough for Gunn to tell him in a whisper: "If we're not back in three hours, I want you guys to get out of here."

Moon just shook his head. "That ain't going to happen," he said. "We're not leaving you out here."

"Lieutenant," Gunn said in his best superior officer voice, "if we're not back in three hours, then something has gone wrong and that means we're probably not coming back. Now, this boat is heavily damaged. That sealant isn't going to last forever, and we know it. If you sink out here, that's too many people dying needlessly. So, three hours. That's an order. Understand?"

Moon didn't reply. He simply gave Gunn a quick salute.

With that, Gunn started the copter's engine, forcing Moon and Umu to retreat. The tiny aircraft's rotor started spinning, sounding more like a toy than an actual flying machine. Gunn rechecked his most important readouts and found everything was looking green. He turned to Amanda and asked: "Ready to rumble?"

She rechecked her seat belt then replied: "Bring it on."

With that, Gunn pulled up on the collective. They lifted off the boat and turned inland, disappearing down the hacked-out road, flying no more than three feet above the ground.

It was now 4:30 A.M.

Downes's deadline was up in one hour.

* * *

GUNN was used to being invisible—they all were. But now, riding in the tiny chopper, arm to arm with his beauty queen, just a few feet off the ground, he suddenly felt vulnerable, as if he were going into battle without his armor.

It was an odd feeling for him; dangerous missions had never bothered him in the past, because as a fighter pilot he was fearless by nature. But he liked having some air underneath him, ten thousand feet of it or so usually did fine. But even more than that, he was anxious because Amanda was with him and they were so exposed, flying down the enclosed trail in something no bigger that a Smart car. If anything happened to him it would happen to her too, and deep inside he knew he couldn't take that. He knew he had to protect her, no matter what.

Oddly she put him to rest with one simple gesture. They were zipping along, constantly checking their clearances against the jungle all around them, when off to the right, they passed a particularly high waterfall. It looked spectacular against the cool blue RIF-induced contours of the African topography. He felt a tap on his knee—Amanda was pointing it out to him.

It was such a small thing, just a simple tap on the knee. But after that, all the anxiety drained right out of him. Suddenly, he felt like Superman and she was his Lois Lane. They would get through this with no problem. And even if any trouble did arise, he would step in front of any bullets meant for her, and laugh as they bounced off. So let the adventure begin.

Though it was winding and crude, the hacked-out road stood out like a freshly laid highway when viewed through their RIFs. Although they were still just three feet off the ground, they were able to follow it with no problem. They flew through vast forests, skirted deep, dark swamps and cruised along winding, twisting streams, all while staying under the thick jungle canopy. The landscape they traversed was both forbidding and fantastic. They would see exotic animals on occasion, diving into the bush or flying through the trees as they approached. Things splashing around in water holes they zipped by. Herds of antelopes running through the jungle and across the road like four-legged ghosts in the night, startled by the purring of the minicopter as they approached.

They reached the first mountain range about fifteen minutes into the flight. They had seen glimpses of this monster off in the distance during their trip down the Ingus. Now they had to go up and over it. Gunn went up in height just a little bit as the hacked-out road slowly rose in elevation. It got colder the higher they went, and the wind whipping through the jungle became rough and brisk. The minicopter had no side doors; it was not an enclosed cockpit, just a half bubble protecting them from the front. Amanda moved closer to him for warmth, though. And again, Gunn felt electricity running through his body.

They reached the top of the mountain, and in a rare moment when they were not under the thick jungle canopy, they were amazed to see scatterings of snow on the peak.

"Not exactly Bora Kurd," Amanda yelled over to him, referring to the huge forbidding mountain where they'd fought the al Qaeda–linked terrorist group months before, the battle that got them in such hot water.

"Nothing could be," he replied.

They went down the other side of the mountain with no problems, picking up the hacked-out trail again and relishing the warmth as they descended. Once more they found themselves surrounded by some astonishingly dark and forbidding African terrain—beautiful and barren at the same time. It almost seemed like a crime that the Yellowcake Gang had cut through it.

They flew along for another fifteen minutes, Amanda becoming very wary of the time; it was important that they reach the end of the road before Downes's time limit was up. Gunn, though, just concentrated on the flying. The minicopter had two small headlights on its nose, but he didn't dare turn them on. He didn't need them as long as his RIFs were working, plus he didn't want to tip anyone off that they were coming, should the hacked-out road suddenly end in the middle of the jungle.

He was just hoping that they didn't meet the Yellowcake Brinks truck coming in the opposite direction.

THEY finally came to the second set of mountains: If their calculations were right, the Yellowcake Gang had set up shop somewhere on the other side of this range.

They easily went up and over this peak too. It wasn't as high as the previous one and there was no snow to be seen this time. In fact, the top of this mountain looked like something from a travel brochure: lush greenery and more waterfalls. Frighteningly beautiful, especially through the RIFs.

Once on the other side, Gunn quickly brought them back down to ground level. This valley's terrain was incredibly thick and almost emerald; its trees and bush seemed to sparkle all around them. The valley itself was about twenty miles long, and half that wide, with a long, narrow stream snaking its way through and gigantic steep cliffs leading off some of the mountains. The Wumbu survivor had said he'd crossed over two mountain ranges to get to the gang's hideout. If he was right, then this had to be the place.

They entered the valley at its northern end and started heading south, continually following the hacked out road. Amanda activated the zoom/search function on her RIFs and started scanning the terrain in front of them up close.

Moon had speculated earlier that the Yellowcake Gang's hideout might be in the side of a tall hill or a cliff. A cave would be the best place to store the Yellowcake 212, keeping it from prying eyes and aerial radiation detection equipment. Because this mountain range's western face was fairly sheer, and with a lot of descending cliffs, Gunn believed there could be many places where such a hideout could be built.

The mountain's western face was on their left, so for Amanda to get a better look, she had to lean over in that direction, engaging in significant body contact with him. Where he was jolted with sparks of electricity before whenever she touched him, now it felt like a lightning bolt was going through him. She was all business, of course, but suddenly Gunn had to doubly concentrate on keeping the copter airborne while following the hacked-out road.

They had flown like this for just a minute—when suddenly she started punching his arm.

"There . . . look," she said urgently. "What's that?"

Gunn followed where she was pointing, but didn't see anything but jungle at first.

"What? Where?" he wound up saying.

She flipped down his RIF zoom function and that's when everything changed. Now, through the cool blue zoomed-in hue of the reverse infrared, he could clearly see what she'd found.

A couple hundred feet ahead of them was a small clearing. In this clearing were six wooden crosses, a mutilated, dead body hanging off each one.

Gunn reduced speed and approached the clearing cautiously. But it was soon clear what this was: These were the six Wumbu slaves the Yellowcake Gang had taken on their most recent voyage down the river. Their usefulness at an end once the road had been re-hacked, they'd simply been tied up out here by the gang members and left for the animals.

"Bastards," Amanda sputtered angrily. "Inhuman bastards . . ."

"Don't worry," Gunn told her. "They'll get theirs real soon."

They flew by the bodies and sped up a little. As disturbing as it was, they knew seeing the dead Wumbus meant the hacked-out road would soon be nearing its end.

Sure enough, thirty seconds later, they spotted a slight rise in the jungle floor near the foot of the closest mountain, about a half mile from a steep, sheer cliff. This was where the hacked-out road took a sharp left-hand turn, went on for another hundred feet or so and then suddenly ended.

Gunn pulled back on the copter's controls like he was rearing up a horse. They were close now; they could both feel it.

Gunn slowly started turning the minicopter in circles, allowing Amanda to scour the immediate area with her zoomed-in RIFs.

Not ten seconds into this, he felt her nails digging into his arm again.

She was pointing at something through the trees off to their left. That's when he saw it: an encampment, located right next to the sheer mountainside, under a particularly thick canopy of vines and jungle vegetation. Thanks to the RIFs, he could clearly see holes cut into this mountainside— artificial caves. He could also see scores of armed men walking around, reflected in the pinkish glow of several campfires.

And sitting in the middle of all this was one very large, weird-looking Brinks truck.

"Bingo," Gunn said.

She grabbed his arm and squeezed it. He could feel her joy run right through his bones.

"God help us," she said excitedly. "We're actually going home."

But now it was very important that they keep their heads. Gunn immediately brought the copter to a hover, reducing its slight whirring sound to just a whisper.

They were about a thousand feet west of the encampment and well hidden in the bush. Gunn took another long look at the target, just to make sure what he'd seen was real. But it didn't take more than a few seconds to become convinced. The heavily armored truck stood out like a beacon in the night. There was just no mistaking it.

He looked over at Amanda, who nodded eagerly. Then he reached into his pocket and took out Downes's sat-phone. It was a simple device, just an activate button, a rudimentary keyboard and a stunted antenna. Gunn pressed the activate button and imagined he felt a slight electrical shock go through his thumb. Then he put the device up to his ear and, after a few gut-wrenching moments, actually heard a faint ringing sound on the other end.

He gave Amanda a thumbs-up. Then he started counting the rings.

Two, three, four, five . . .

No answer.

Ten . . . twelve . . . fifteen . . .

No answer

Twenty . . . thirty . . . thirty-five.

Still nothing.

He looked at Amanda and shrugged. He passed her the sat-phone, and after activating the tiny keyboard, she started typing out their coordinates, describing it as "the place Colonel Downes was looking for." She ended the brief message with the time and date, reinforcing the time stamp she knew would also accompany the text message. After she'd sent the message, she double-checked her watch and put it up to Gunn's eyes so he could see the time. They had made the seven-day deadline with just five minutes to spare.

She handed the phone back to him; he put it in his boot. As she got the Nikon camera out and ready, Gunn turned in his hover so she could take pictures more easily. While he kept his eyes glued on his gauges, making sure everything was kosher with the flight controls, he could hear the camera's image advance clicking away like mad. He knew that each picture she took would help them further prove their case that they had found the Yellowcake Gang before the deadline.

"Can we get closer?" she whispered to him urgently.

Gunn complied—he moved the minicopter to within five hundred feet of the camp. Amanda never stopped taking pictures. She was getting it all: the camp's power station, its fuel tank, its armory, and where the ammunition was kept, the line of tents nearby. There was also a crude helicopter pad. Just from what Gunn could see, there were at least one hundred fighters at the camp, and that was only counting those on the outside. There might be at least another hundred or so inside the handful of hollowed-out caves.

They stayed hovering like this for about two minutes. Finally Gunn sensed they'd got enough and it was time to make their silent escape. Amanda agreed—and that's exactly what they were about to do.

Until . . .

Amanda was about to stop taking pictures when they both saw a group of men emerge from one of the caves. Gunn suddenly felt ice water rush through his veins. There were six men, all carrying heavy weapons, surrounding a seventh man, who was moving toward one of the tents located close to the hidden site. But this seventh man—he didn't look like any of the others at the base. He was tall. Very tall. Taller than most people. And he was dressed differently. The others were in rags and pieces of combat suits. This man was in white robes, with an Arabic headdress. He also had a long beard and he walked with a cane.

Gunn and Amanda had the exact same thought: *Could it be?*

She was so shocked to actually see this person, she began stumbling over her words: "But . . . but I thought, he was . . . What would *he* be doing here?"

Gunn checked his RIF's zoom and made sure everything was working as it should be. It was—and that meant there was no doubt in his mind who this was.

The super terrorist. The mass murderer. The bloody hand behind 9/11.

And suddenly it all made some kind of crazy sense. If you were the world's most notorious fugitive, you'd want to hide in the world's most isolated, unlikely place. For this killer, what would be more isolated, more unlikely than a place called Lost Valley in the middle of darkest Africa?

It didn't seem real—yet it was.

"We've got him," Gunn said suddenly, his body shaking. "He's right there . . ."

"We've got to do something," she said to him. "We've just *got* to . . ."

Gunn's mind was racing. Moon's last words to them were spinning around his head: Just do the recon, no heroics. But something else was happening here. It was the old conundrum: If you had a chance to kill Hitler—would you do it above all else?

Do something?

"Yes—we've got to . . ." he replied.

She grabbed his shoulder and gave it a mighty squeeze of approval. Then she put the camera aside and picked up her M4. They were both suddenly in combat mode.

Gunn took the copter out of hover and began moving toward the hidden camp. All thoughts of a simple intelligence mission were gone now.

The situation had changed. This was something they *had* to do . . .

But what happened next was total insanity.

They checked their ammo clips; both M4s were locked and loaded. Gunn also had his sidearm—a Glock 9. Amanda was carrying her Navy issue .45.

Gunn turned the small copter directly toward the base, hit the throttle and just swooped right in. No recon pass, no double-checking, no nothing. One moment they were hanging in the air a few hundred feet away, the next they were boring in, guns blazing.

It was strange because Gunn had never flown and fired a weapon at the same time—at least not like this. He had his M4 across his lap, pointing left and downward, firing with his right hand while trying to fly the copter via the collective with his crossed over left hand. He was all tangled up. Amanda on the other hand was practically hanging outside the tiny aircraft, fearlessly firing away as they tore through the hideout, not six feet off the ground.

They caught the people at the camp totally by surprise. The several dozen who were out in the open froze at the sight of the strange little copter coming right at them. The first strafing run killed ten of them in no more than three seconds. They went down like bowling pins—and not a shot was fired in return.

Gunn pulled the copter up, back and around all in one smooth motion, missing the protective jungle canopy overhead by just a few feet. In a heartbeat, they were zooming back down again. He was trying his best to steer the copter right at their main target—the tall guy in the white robes with the long beard. At the moment, he was still frozen in place, just as his security detail was, as if they couldn't quite believe what was happening. On this second run, Gunn and Amanda mowed down another dozen or so of the armed men; those not in shock were ducking the low-flying copter as if it were some huge bug, and dying for their efforts. But the angle of attack was still not right to get a good shot at their prime target—if it was who they thought it was, that is.

Gunn was trying to get a good close-up look at him, but things were moving so fast, with the RIFs turned up to full power, he was seeing mostly streaks of colors running past his retinas. It was like a psychedelic light show—emphasized by the residue effect of all the amphetamine pills he'd taken in the past few days.

On their third pass, he sped right by their target, not five feet off the ground—and in one of those moments when it seemed everything stood still, Gunn found himself eyeball to eyeball with him. He *was* tall, and he was wearing white robes and a headdress. And he had a long dirty beard.

It *was* him.

Wasn't it?

The strange thing was that even after the third pass, just about everyone in the camp still seemed frozen in place. A few were taking cover, or hitting the dirt, but there was no return fire, no opposition at all. Gunn was puzzled by this—was he flying so fast, and so brilliantly, that no one was able to take a shot at them?

At the moment, he didn't know and he really didn't care. He went up, over and back again for the fourth time. Amanda never stopped firing; she was hitting everything and everybody who got in the way of her M4. Some of her rounds must have hit the camp's ammo supply, because small secondary explosions were now going off throughout the camp. Gunn steered clear of one of these blasts, and in doing so found himself once again face-to-face with their main target. The mass murderer. But why was he just standing there?

It was as if he was waiting for something.

Up and around a fifth time—and in this sweep Gunn vowed he would get a bullet right between this guy's eyes.

Between him and Amanda, they'd managed to tear up the encampment as well as any helicopter gunship. There were bodies strewn all over, fires burning; even the heavily armored truck was smoking a bit. Amanda was out of ammo by now, so in their fifth pass she fired off six quick rounds from her .45, emptying it, and then not missing a beat, she grabbed the copter's flare gun and started firing it at anything she could.

"This is nuts!" Gunn heard himself scream.

But throughout it all, their number one target was still

just standing there. Not out of defiance, maybe out of fear, yet managing not to fall into either one of their gun sights as they dashed by.

He was waiting for something . . . but what?

The answer came just as Gunn was pulling out of the fifth strafing run. Out of the corner of his eye he saw a man emerge from one of the caves. He was holding not a rifle but a long tube with a large trigger on it.

A missile launcher.

A SAM . . .

He saw the rocket's fire next—grossly enlarged by the flaring of the RIF goggles. He even heard the noise as the SAM left its launcher and headed right for them, a distance of only about 150 feet. In that long, long, terrifying moment, Gunn was able to contemplate just how foolish he'd been—hitting this target, convinced there was a high-profile enemy there, going for the glory, and as a result getting himself shot down and killed and killing this gorgeous, brilliant girl along with him. It was an SA-7 Strela heading their way, a huge explosive charge on its tip. This Russian-made missile was designed to shoot down large military aircraft. It would vaporize the minicopter in a microsecond.

Damn . . .

It was Gunn's test pilot skills that came to the fore now—in these moments before a fiery death, he had to try something. The SA-7 homed in on heat. That meant he had to get the heat of the minicopter's engine out of its sights. Where some pilots might have tried to climb, climb, climb to escape, Gunn dropped, pushing the controls down and slamming the copter into the tree cover. The missile blew up an instant later—not on the copter's hot engine, but on the top of a tree nearby.

The explosion ripped through the back of the copter, but the foliage took a lot of the blow. The problem was that the copter's rotor was chopping through the trees, and for a long few moments, they were halfway between flying and crashing.

Once again an ordinary pilot would have tried to climb at this point, but Gunn knew the copter was in no shape for that. He spotted a clearing below the tree line somehow and fought to get the copter to go through it. By some miracle, he was successful, and then they were flying again, not more than three feet off the ground, the copter's engine smoking crazily, but somehow still airborne.

But the problem was they were on fire—and their fuel tank was about to explode.

Gunn took a moment to look over at Amanda. She was hanging on tight, watching as low-hanging branches slapped into them, trying her best to shift her weight with the way the copter was going, helping it stay airborne. Gunn was astonished—she didn't look one bit afraid. She looked determined, almost put out—as if she was thinking: Can we get this thing over with quickly, please?

They made it out from under the canopy, and now he hoped he could spot a flat place to crash land and save them both.

But instead, they found themselves suddenly out over a cliff and looking into the very dark valley three hundred feet below.

And that's when their fuel tank exploded.

CHAPTER FIFTEEN

HENRY Amootu was the chief of the Oobu tribe, a clan that had lived in the *Dashi-dagumba* region for more than eight hundred years.

His village, spread out over six acres, was hard by a bend in the Zoogu River, a shallow, meandering waterway that ran off the massive Ingus Swamp twenty miles to the north. Hidden under a dark canopy of gum trees, the village was bordered on three sides by extremely thick vegetation. It had stood here so long because the nearby jungle supplied ample fruit and greens for the tribe, as well as monkeys, which the Oobus also ate on a regular basis.

Henry had been to the city of Yaounde twice in his fifty-five years. No one else from his tribe had been more than three miles from its outskirts, so to them he was the possessor of all great knowledge in the world. He'd seen huge air machines fly over and knew what they were. But most of the people in his tribe simply couldn't comprehend what an airplane was or how someone could fly all over creation in one.

The village did have a shortwave radio, but it was the Oobus' tradition to keep to themselves, so the device was used very infrequently.

That's why it was so frightening when the jungle suddenly started moving in the middle of the night, causing the birds and animals to put up a very loud screech. Henry was the first one to wake. His sons and grandsons were roused too. They ran to the center of the village to find a woman's body, collapsed near the cooking fire.

They turned her over and were shocked to see she was white and very, very blond.

Her clothes were almost burned away. She was covered in scrapes and bug bites. Her hands were dirty and red from burns.

She could hardly speak she was crying so much.

But she was able to tell them: "My friend is dead. He saved my life—but now he's dead."

THE Oobu search party left just minutes later.

They trooped into the jungle, sixteen of them, following the path that the white woman had used to get to the village. She was in shock and could not tell them much. But she smelled so much of oily smoke, the tribesmen knew that if they just followed their noses, they would find the woman's deceased friend.

That was, unless some jungle cat had already dragged him away.

They found the wreckage ten minutes later. It was strewn all over a small clearing about a half mile from the edge of Umbamba, the "Devil's Cliff."

It was still smoldering—which had probably kept the cats and hyenas away. But there were some big birds circling overhead, night buzzards eyeing whatever lay crumpled in the bushes as their next meal.

The searchers found the woman's friend under a part of

the wreckage. His clothes were almost entirely burned away, as was a lot of his skin. He looked as black as they were. He was bleeding from many places as well.

Chief Amootu's eldest son was the leader of the search party. He took one look at the body and said: "He's dead. Let's bring him back so at least he can be with his friend one more time."

They walked back to the village, carrying the body, singing a song of mourning as they made their way through the jungle. When they arrived, they found the woman wrapped in a blanket, sitting by the fire, rocking back and forth.

She began crying again at the first sight of her friend. The tribesmen laid him down next to her and finished their sad song.

"Say good-bye to him," Amootu's son told her.

"He saved my life," she kept saying over and over. "He saved my life . . . and now he's gone."

It was at this point that they heard more crashing through jungle. It was not an animal; rather a vehicle was coming along the path to the village.

It was a battered old truck, with a man named Soungi Nelson at the wheel. He climbed out and was quietly greeted by the chief. Nelson was a park ranger for the huge Fwawi National Preserve nearby, an educated man from the Sudan. He'd heard the crash, seen the smoke and come to investigate.

Now he saw the blond woman and the lifeless body and knew immediately it was some kind of airplane mishap. Bush pilots plowing into the jungle were not all that unusual in this part of the world. Nelson recognized the burns as being typical injuries of an airplane crash.

He looked at the man's body—he'd seen a lot in his twenty-five years of patrolling the Park Reserve, fighting off poachers mostly. But these injuries nearly sickened him.

He turned to the woman, who was injured not as severely but seemed to be in shock.

"Are you scientists?" Nelson asked her.

She started to say something but just shook her head instead. He picked up a piece of her burned clothing lying beside her and saw the remains of her shoulder patch. It displayed the silhouette of the C-17 and had the number "201" emblazoned on it. Nelson looked at this emblem for a very long time—then he began crying too.

"Was he there?" he asked her, pointing to the body. "Were you there as well?"

"Where?" she asked though tears.

"At Aylala," Nelson said. "The village that was saved by the '201' ghost soldiers. Americans. This patch—this drawing. It is now very famous in that part of the continent."

"Yes—I was there—or above it," she said softly. "And so was he. Why?"

"Because my relatives live there," Nelson told her, wiping his tears away. "You saved them—my cousins—uncles—aunts. You saved them all."

Nelson knelt down and embraced her and they cried together. Then Nelson composed himself, stood up and walked over to the chief. They had a conversation, animated in spots, which went on for five minutes. Finally, it ended with the chief nodding and soberly agreeing with whatever Nelson was proposing.

The chief ordered his sons to carry the body into the sweat hut. Nelson retrieved Amanda, helped her to her feet and led her into the hut as well.

The sweat hut was well named. It was a very small shack located on the edge of the village not far from the bend in the river. Inside was a fire capped by dozens of perfectly round rocks. The fire heated the rocks to a white-hot temperature, and anytime water was spilled onto them, the steam was immediate and unbelievably hot.

Gunn's body was laid on a mat next to the steaming heat. Still in shock, still in tears, Amanda reached over and pinched his right wrist. There was no pulse.

The chief and another tribesman crawled in after her and Nelson. The other man was the village's witch doctor. He had a bucket of mud with him and a large wicker basket. The entire village was awake by now, and many of them were gathered outside the sweat hut, adding to the drama.

The doctor reached into the basket and came out with a huge yellow snake. Its skin was so bright, it was almost luminous. It started squirming and hissing immediately.

The doctor produced a knife and proceeded to cut the snake's throat. The resulting spray of blood and fluid was incredible. The snake was about five feet long, and a couple inches around, yet it began gushing like a garden hose. The doctor directed the blood and gore into the bucket of mud and started mixing it with one hand while still holding the snake in the other. Amazingly, the snake was still squirming and hissing even though most of its insides were now dripping into the mud bucket.

In fact the snake looked just about empty when the doctor let it go. To Amanda's horror, it slithered right past her, out the door and into the jungle beyond. The crowd outside cheered, but the sight of this made her nauseous.

Her attention was drawn back to the doctor. He'd mixed the mud and snake guts into a thick paste. The smell was awful, but there was also a weird phosphorescent glow to it.

The doctor tested the consistency by tasting it, another retching sight, but he somehow declared it was good. Then, with the care of a great surgeon, he began applying the bloody paste to Gunn's limp body.

Nelson was kneeling beside Amanda, his hand on her shoulder, watching the process intently. He whispered to her: "If anyone can do this, these people can."

But Amanda wasn't really listening.

Applying the paste took ten minutes; the doctor worked very methodically, with the onlookers being absolutely silent. When he was done, he put his hands over Gunn's eyes and did a few chants. Then he looked at Amanda and motioned her forward.

Nelson whispered to her: "He sees you're injured as well."

Before she could move, the doctor took the leftover paste and put it on her arms and hands where she'd been burned in the crash.

But she was puzzled. Why was he doing this? This was just some kind of body preserving ceremony and she was just going along with it because there was nothing else she could do. So why was he rubbing this stuff on her?

The doctor smiled, displaying what few teeth he had left in his head, and had a short conversation with Nelson. Then he and the chief departed to a round of positive hoots and chants from the tribe's people gathered outside.

Nelson turned to her and said: "Stay here with your friend. He will need you through the rest of the night. Give him love. Give him support. Think good thoughts. If this is to happen, you'll know when morning comes."

Amanda was horribly confused.

"What is going to happen?" she asked Nelson.

But he just smiled, threw some water on the rocks and then put a finger to her lips.

"Give him love," he repeated. "That's all he needs."

Then he left the hut.

NOW the time moved very slowly for Amanda.

She kept reliving the crash over and over in her mind. Not wanting to, but she couldn't stop herself.

Gunn had saved her life—that much was certain.

After dodging the brunt of the SAM missile, due to a display of flying she knew that 99.99 percent of pilots could not have done, the copter was on fire and they were suddenly falling off a three-hundred-foot sheer cliff and plummeting to the hard jungle floor below.

She could still see Gunn fighting the controls—his uniform on fire, his plastic helmet lining melting from the heat. Amanda was able to beat out the flames and keep them from scorching her body, but Gunn kept his hands on the copter's controls and let the flames engulf him. He somehow held it together long enough to pull the copter to fairly level flight, using the last energy of what was left of the spinning rotor blades to half crash it, half land it on top of a willowlike tree, cushioning the blow. This allowed Amanda to fall just a few feet to safety, while Gunn was still trapped in the burning wreckage.

She hit the ground, stunned, but was able to get back on her feet and drag Gunn out of the tree, both of them falling back to the ground, smoldering. Gunn's skin was especially crackling away.

He was not moving, not breathing. She tried mouth-to-mouth, but all she got in return was a cloud of smoke puffing out of his lungs. She tried heart massage, but again, to no avail. That's when she knew she had to get help. Even though her clothes and her skin were burned, she somehow made it through the jungle and into the tribe's village.

And now she was sitting with Gunn, holding his hand, looking at him encased in the strange paste not unlike a mummy. She broke down more than once. She tried feeling for his pulse many, many times, not believing he was really gone.

But finally, she succumbed to the exhaustion. She laid her head on his chest and went to sleep, not noticing that a few minutes later, the ground began shaking again and did not stop for a long time.

IT was the sound of a beating heart that woke her a couple hours later.

It was morning. Her eyes opened—and the first thing she saw was Gunn looking back at her.

She fell away from him—she thought it was some kind of terrible dream. "My God," she screamed. "You're alive?"

He blinked a couple times unable to move because of his plaster cast. "Am I?" he asked.

She scrambled back over to him, took his hand again and locked it with hers. The fire had gone out and it was not as hot in the hut as it was before. She asked him: "Where did you go? You didn't have a pulse. You weren't breathing."

He looked her in the eye and said: "I don't know where I went, but I do know I dreamed we were married."

She was so startled by that, she couldn't reply.

He tried to move—but the paste had hardened like cement.

"Please get this stuff off me," he said.

She didn't know what to do. It was a miracle that Gunn was alive—or had come back to life or whatever had happened to him. But she knew how badly burned his body was, and at the very least he had a long, hard, painful recovery ahead of him. Fighting off infection. Skin grafts. Plastic surgery . . . and that would be under the best of circumstances. Maybe it was best that he stay inside the cast.

But he was moving around so much, the plaster started cracking on its own. So she helped him peel away some of it, expecting to see a lot of foul, burned skin beneath it. But again, she was dumbfounded. His skin underneath the plaster looked like it had healed completely.

She peeled some more away, especially around his shoulders and chest, areas that had been burned severely. And again, the skin looked no worse for the wear. Not even any scrapes or cuts.

"I don't believe this," she said. She started crying again, this time in pure unbelieving joy. Inside a minute she had all the plaster off him, and she could not find one burn, one cut, anything, on him.

He was still a bit out of it—but whatever the witch doctor had put on him certainly did have magical, miraculous properties. Even her own arms, which had been badly burned, looked completely healed when she pulled the plaster off.

"I've just never seen anything like this," she said, studying him all over. "Do you know what this means? Whatever this concoction was made from will be a godsend for burn victims, crash victims. It's an amazing thing we've come upon here."

To her surprise, Gunn actually sat up and shook the dust from the plaster off him. "I'd really like a drink of water," he said. "Cold ice water—with maybe a shot of bourbon?"

She stared back at him for a long moment—then put her arms around him and hugged him tightly.

Then she recovered a bit—let him loose from her grasp and said: "You wait here. I'll be right back."

She hurried outside—all she wanted was to talk to the chief and thank him and the doctor and explain how they must have the formula for the plaster he'd put Gunn in.

But she was shocked to see that the village was gone. All the huts had been taken up; the fire was out. Everything. It was like the tribe had never even been there. Had never existed.

She was looking around, again thinking she'd gone mad—when she saw Nelson's truck. He was asleep behind the wheel. She ran over to him and shook him awake.

"A miracle!" she screamed at him. "He's alive! My friend is alive."

Nelson hugged her through the window. "I knew it," he said. "I knew they could do it."

Amanda spread her arms out and asked: "But where is everybody?"

Nelson got out of the truck and looked around.

"They're gone," he said. "That was the hard part for

them. We intruded on their world, so their world now has to be someplace else. They did me that favor because you saved my family back in Aylala."

She stood there, stunned, as Nelson went into the sweat hut. In a few seconds, he emerged with Gunn, who, save for his seared and ripped flight suit, really didn't look any different than if he had just spent an uncomfortable night on a lumpy mattress.

Nelson helped him over to the truck, leaned him against the back and gave him a bottle of warm water. Gunn was a little more with it at this point, remembering what had happened before the crash—but Amanda still looked bewildered.

She studied his hands again, his legs, in amazement. There were no burns, no scars—nothing at all to indicate that just a few hours before, he'd looked like he'd fallen into Hell.

"Do you feel any pain? Any discomfort?" she asked, checking his back and neck.

"None," Gunn replied truthfully. If anything he felt full of energy and vigor.

"We've just got to somehow get whatever that stuff is out to civilization," Amanda said to Nelson. "I know they have their customs, but imagine the burn victims it could help."

But Nelson just shook his head.

"I'm sorry, but that's impossible," he said, knowing that the tribe had already disappeared deeper into one of the most remote, unexplored parts of darkest Africa. "These people have no desire to help anyone in the outside world. They believe any secret they give up loses them a bit of their souls."

He checked Gunn over himself and just shook his head. "So just be grateful you ran into them when you did. Had you crashed a half mile in any other direction, my friend, you wouldn't be here today, alive with this beautiful lady."

That's when Nelson noticed something off to the north-east that Amanda and Gunn didn't see. A gigantic pall of smoke was rising above the tree line, close to where the sheer cliffs of the mountain range were located. He thought he had heard more explosions during the night, but he had forgotten about them in his sleep. Now he just shrugged.

Just another day in Africa, he thought.

He opened the truck's side door for them and indicated they should get in.

"You want to return to your base as quickly as possible?" he asked them.

Gunn and Amanda both nodded.

"Then we must get you first to Karumba," he said.

Gunn looked at her and said: "Let's go to Karumba, then."

They both climbed inside the truck. Before Nelson could join them, Gunn said to her: "And I'm really sorry."

"For what?" she asked. "Saving my life?"

"No—for embarrassing you. You know—about my dream?"

She just smiled and wiped a bit of dust from his cheek. It was like waking from a long nightmare. "No problem, Major," she said. "No problem at all."

CHAPTER SIXTEEN

KARUMBA was 150 miles to the south.

Luckily Nelson got them there in less than two hours, traveling at high speed in his old truck on a straight-as-an-arrow road that cut first through the jungle and then through a wide-open savannah.

Though the trip started with her talking nonstop about the uncanny events in the village during the night, Amanda quickly fell asleep and stayed that way, using Gunn's shoulder as a pillow.

Nelson sang native songs of thanks throughout the early morning journey, giving props to the heavenly spirits for bringing Gunn back.

For his part, Gunn just looked out the window and watched the landscape fly by, wondering how it was that he'd been brought back from . . . well, from where exactly?

His last memory was of the copter soft-crashing into the trees and Amanda falling safely to the ground below. Then there were the flames—and nothing else until he dreamed his dream and then woke up to see Amanda staring down at him, a mix of horror and joy in her eyes. He'd never forget that look.

But where did he go? What happened to him?

"Don't think about it," Nelson told him finally. "It is a never-ending circle. Just be one with the fact that you are still here and that God has made it that way because there is something important that you still have to do."

Gunn looked over at him as if to say: Really?

"Either that," Nelson went on, "or you're just the luckiest bastard in the whole wide world."

Karumba turned out to be little more than a crossroads in the middle of the wild. From here the road split off in two directions, one being a glorified footpath that led back toward the jungle.

Nelson stopped the truck. As Gunn gently woke Amanda, the park ranger walked to the back of his battered vehicle and took out two ancient-looking bicycles.

Gunn looked at them and almost laughed. "And these are for?"

"For you to use to get out of here," Nelson replied. "You must now get to Lmono. It is twenty miles, in that direction. It is a river town, and from there you can get a boat to Umbango. There you will find a phone with which to contact your friends. But the only way to Lmono is this path—nowhere wide enough for me to drive you. If we went by road, it would take us almost an entire day."

Gunn looked west, the direction of the trail. It looked like deep jungle for about ten miles, after which two large mountains blocked just about everything else from view.

"Even a horse would have a hard time getting through there," Nelson said, handing them a bag containing some water and food.

"Because of the terrain?" Amanda asked innocently, with a yawn.

Nelson displayed his gigantic smile. "No," he said,

giving them the bikes. "Because of the snakes—if it stays still long enough, they can eat a horse whole."

Gunn and Amanda laughed—until they realized Nelson wasn't kidding.

Before they could say anything, the park ranger hugged both of them. Then he bowed in respect and said: "Thank you again for saving my family. Things like that are never forgotten."

With that, he climbed into his truck, blew them a kiss and was gone, bouncing back down the dusty roadway from whence they'd come.

Amanda studied the two bikes. They were as battered and old as Nelson's truck.

"You do know how to ride a bike, right?" she asked Gunn.

"Sure," he replied. "Back when I was seven years old."

"Do you feel up to it? Or do you want to ride on my crossbar?"

Gunn checked his body for the umpteenth time. He felt good, no aches, no pains. Nothing.

"I'm sure I can handle it," he told her.

They checked the bag Nelson had given them. It contained two bottles of water, plus two energy bars.

"Twenty miles," she said. "And a lot of big snakes."

"Just don't stop for anything," he replied.

She climbed onto her bike, adjusted the seat and looked back at Gunn.

"Any chance you want a race?" she asked him. "I'll bet you."

He just started pedaling. "Why bother?" he said. "I'd just let you win anyway."

THE trail was even more rugged than it looked. It was full of twists and turns, and low-hanging vines and tree limbs. At some point the jungle canopy over their heads became so thick, it blocked out the light and it was almost as if they were traveling at night. It was a little bit too much like flying the minicopter the night before, but it also served to keep them cool.

They were able to ride side by side some of the time, and would have quick, out-of-breath conversations whenever they came to a long flat stretch.

These were devoted to talking about the events earlier, not in the village but in their attack on the Yellowcake Gang's hideout. In the cold light of day, neither was sure now if the man they'd seen there had actually been the authentic item. Yet despite nearly getting killed, and destroying the minicopter, they did not regret what they'd done.

As Amanda put it: "If we hadn't tried what we did, that would have bothered me."

Somehow the bikes' tires held up to the strain of all the bumps and holes on the trail. And because they both had incentive to keep pedaling and not stop, the first half of the trip took just two hours.

It was mid-morning then by the time they reached the area of the two mountains. Thankfully the trail brought them between the two peaks and not over them.

The terrain changed dramatically on the other side of the mountains. Awaiting them now was an open valley covered with tall elephant grass. There were only a few scattered patches of jungle and no overhanging canopy—which meant fewer hiding places for any voracious snakes. The trail also looked wider and less bumpy, meaning it would be easier on their rumps.

They stopped for a breather just beyond the highest point of the path between the two mountains. Amanda broke out the energy bars and Gunn opened one of the water bottles. The combination tasted like a feast, so much so Gunn didn't miss his bennies, which had been lost in the crash.

Once the short break was over, they climbed back on their bikes and prepared to set out again. That's when they saw a stream of people heading their way.

Hundreds of Africans were coming up the trail, walking single-file among the tall elephant grass and coming from the direction Gunn and Amanda were heading toward. They were carrying bundles on their heads and bags slung over their shoulders, their life's possessions. Men, women, kids, old people.

"What the hell is this?" Gunn wondered out loud.

The line of people soon reached the top of the rise and started going by them, Gunn and Amanda moving off the trail so the river of humanity could pass. These people were in a hurry and looked scared. So much so, they barely noticed the two white people in the burned military uniforms watching them pass by.

Finally Gunn spotted a non-African in the stream. He was an elderly man, a priest of some sort with a huge crucifix dangling around his neck. He was carrying a young African child and a huge knapsack.

Gunn managed to delay him a moment.

"What's happening here?" he asked the priest. "Where is everyone going?"

The holy man just shrugged. "It is where they are coming from," he replied. "Bad things are going to happen in this area. They are all leaving before they get caught up in it."

"What kinds of 'bad things'?" Amanda asked.

"The same old African bad things," the man said, readjusting the young child in his arms. "War, shooting, killing."

He started on his way again, swept up in the deluge of people fleeing what seemed to be the very peaceful valley beyond.

"But how do they know?" Gunn tried to call after him.

The priest turned halfway and yelled over his shoulder: "This is Africa," he said. "They just know."

* * *

IT took almost a half hour for the line of people to pass by.

Finally the trail was clear and Gunn and Amanda could resume their journey, though now with a bit more apprehension than before. The last thing they wanted was to get caught up in whatever trouble the refugees "just knew" was coming.

They pedaled for another thirty minutes, acutely aware of any movement on either side of the trail, but finding nothing more than birds flying off or some small creatures scurrying away from the sound of their bike tires.

They came to another rise and, reaching the top, stopped again.

Before them now was a true savannah—an immense, flat grassy plain, with only a few clutches of trees and scrub bushes. In the distance, maybe five miles away, they could see a wide river bending its way around another mountain. Smoke rising from several locations told them this was their destination: the village of Lmono

But right away, Gunn knew something was wrong.

He directed Amanda's attention to an area off to their right, a place beyond a line of mopane trees, maybe half a square mile in all. The landscape here seemed different; the flora didn't match the rest of the flat, open plain. The gold and green colors were slightly skewed, and though there was a brisk wind running west to east, nothing seemed to be moving very much in this particular spot. To the untrained eye, all this would probably not register. But Gunn and Amanda knew differently.

"See anything familiar?" he asked her.

Their old base in the middle of Nevada, the place where the 201st was born, was a masterpiece in the art of hiding in plain sight. More than a dozen buildings, some of them immense, oversized hangars, had been covered with the revolutionary camouflaged netting that used billions of tiny, overlapping electromagnetic images to perfectly mimic the surrounding terrain. The result was an optical illusion that was not apparent unless one walked right up to it and saw that what appeared to be a small, sandy, brush-covered hill was really an enormous aircraft barn, draped in the futuristic covering. The same kind of netting covered the unit's planes back at Wum Bakim.

And the same sort of thing was happening here.

They could just tell.

"Who would bother hiding out here?" she asked. "This whole place is hidden from the rest of the world. They don't call this part of Africa the 'Lost Valley' for nothing."

"Our base in Nevada was out in the middle of nowhere too," Gunn replied. "And still, they felt the need to spend millions of dollars to hide it."

She had to agree. But the question was, what should they do about it?

"We have to take a closer look," he said.

MOTHER Nature chose to help them out at this point.

Gunn had spent time in the Midwest and had seen thunderstorms start out on the horizon in early morning and build and gain strength for hours before finally sweeping through with torrents of rain and winds by mid-afternoon. It took a while for the big storms to form and start moving.

Here, on the edge of the Lost Valley, though, that process looked to run in fast-motion. Just in the time he and Amanda had stopped to study the strange piece of landscape to their east, a wave of massive thunderheads had darkened the sky to their west—the direction the wind was blowing. From their slightly elevated position, they could see that wind was now charging across the savannah, bending trees and bush in its wake. Birds were scattering, animals running to avoid the oncoming tempest. This had all happened in less than five minutes—and it was coming right at them.

Gunn just looked at Amanda, who shrugged and said: "Let's go."

They started riding toward the suspect area, and were about two thirds of the way when the rain finally caught up with them.

No amount of mad pedaling could spare them. When the rain came, it came in sheets. It was so heavy, Gunn actually lost sight of Amanda every few moments, even though she was just a few feet in front of him.

The last few minutes were like riding a bike on the bottom of the ocean, but eventually they made it to the area in question. And sure enough, out here on the fringe of the Lost Valley, there was a thin electrical fence strung around an area encompassing several dozen acres. Not pleasant for any animals wandering through.

They got off their bikes and hunkered down in a pepper stick bush, just outside the wire. They were drenched but well hidden.

From this position they could see that yes, the area was heavily draped in camouflage netting. Maybe not as elaborate as what the 201st used back in Nevada or at Wum Bakim, but good enough to do the job out here.

What they saw underneath was a somewhat typical air base: three big hangars, a scattering of support buildings and one good-sized runway, about six thousand feet long. There was a crude blast pad at the beginning of this runway, indicating that large jet aircraft were used here. At the far end of the runway they saw two cranes, their towers currently retracted, but obviously used to pull back enough of the camouflage netting to allow planes to take off and/or land.

It was all pretty rudimentary as far as hidden bases go. But apparently it worked for someone.

The question was: Who?

"I don't see any guard posts," Gunn whispered to Amanda. "No flags. No indications who this place belongs to. Not even a main gate. I'm not sure anyone is even here at the moment."

"It looks to be not so much an active airstrip as it is a place to store things," she agreed. "Or better put, hide them. I mean I see tire marks on the runway; and that's a helicopter pad next to the middle hangar. But this seems to be a place that people mostly fly to, as opposed to legging it out here. That's my guess."

"Well, either way, something smells here," he said. "I'm getting a bad vibe from this place."

"Me too," she said.

They hid the bikes and moved along the wire toward the rear of the base. At the back of the first hangar they saw two vehicles hidden under what looked to be more typical camouflage netting. They were trucks with machine guns sticking out of them. Technicals . . . the weapon of choice for murderous groups like the Janjaweeds.

"What you smelled is bad guys," Amanda said, noting the notorious trucks. "Why did I think we were through with these Janjaweed types?"

"They're everywhere," Gunn said. Then he asked: "So what should we do, Admiral?"

She took it all in one more time, then replied: "I think if there is anybody here, they are probably taking their lunch break or maybe they just don't want to get wet."

"So?"

"So—I say, let's go in and take a look around."

GETTING over the juiced wire was not a problem. It was meant to zap animals not humans.

And the rain was coming down even harder by the time

they stole their way over to the first building, one of the hangars. It was located off the north end of the wired-in area. It was made of aluminum with a crude wooden base and a ring of bumpy macadam. There was only one window in the place; it was on the side access door. Gunn stood watch while Amanda peeked in. She pronounced the place empty of guards or anyone else. Gunn stopped for a moment, thought about whether they were really wise or foolish to do this, and decided it didn't matter. Amanda had already jimmied open the door lock and was going in. He had no choice but to follow.

There was a plane inside the hangar—but because there were no lights on within, and it was pitch black without them, it was hard to determine just what kind of aircraft it was at first. It was huge, though; there was no doubt about that. Four big engines, a long fuselage, immense swept-back wings. They felt their way around it, almost as if they were reading Braille, feeling around for any clues. Gunn's first thought was that it was an airliner—an old one in fact. But the nose felt extremely distorted and heavy and the engines smelled somewhat new.

"I'm sorry," Amanda finally said. "But it has to be done."

Gunn just shook his head. "OK—but only for a half second. This could be some guy's company jet that he's hiding from his auditors or something. Not everything is out of a Tom Clancy book."

She laughed a little and stared back at him in the dark. "We are," she said definitively.

Then she was gone, over to the wall, looking for a light switch. Gunn followed her, walking backward, trying his best to squint enough to make out the overall shape of the airplane.

Finally she found the electrical box. It held not one but a dozen switches. This was good, or so it seemed. Turning on one switch would probably illuminate just one lonely lightbulb somewhere, reducing the chances of anyone noticing, if anyone were even here at the hidden base.

"Ready?" she asked. "It might be pretty dim."

"Please just for a half second, no longer, OK?" he replied.

But she'd already thrown the switch. And it was weird because it took a moment or two for anything to happen. But when it did . . .

It turned out the switch she'd hit was not just for one light—it turned on every light in the hangar. One would have been sufficient, though, because what they saw shocked them—so much so that she didn't switch off the lights for about five seconds.

Finally, Amanda got her head about her and turned the lights off. But what they'd seen in front of them had already burned an image on to their retinas.

"Did I just see that?" they both asked at once.

"It's a . . . a . . ." Gunn began stuttering.

"Yes," she said. "One of those . . . what do they call them?"

It was a Boeing 747—that much they knew. But this was no typical airliner.

Its nose was crooked and lowered. Its engines were indeed new. There was a large canoe-shaped attachment hanging under the fuselage and a second bulbous protrusion sitting atop the plane just aft of the cockpit. And the markings? Unmistakably those of the U.S. Air Force.

"It's an E-4B Nightwatch," Amanda finally said. "A survivable command airplane—you know in case anything goes wrong."

Her description was right on the money. This plane was a very specially adapted Boeing 747, something along the lines of an E-7 or E-8 electronic warfare plane. It was stuffed with command and control, and ultra high-tech communications and surveillance equipment. Painted more like Air Force One than a military plane, its purpose was to get airborne in times of dire national emergency and function as a flying command post should Washington or some key U.S. military facility be knocked out.

It was a bit chilling to see one, up close and personal, because under most conditions, if a Nightwatch plane was flying around, it meant something catastrophic had happened to the United States. Gunn recalled that on that dark day, September 11, 2001, when all planes everywhere were grounded across the U.S., he looked to the sky above his home in the desert and saw one of these planes eerily flying over.

They were among the most highly classified, and expensive, airplanes ever built. So what the hell was one doing way out here, in the middle of remotest Africa, locked up like this?

"The question is," Amanda whispered, before Gunn could even ask it, "not what it's doing out here, but is it real?"

She ran her hand alongside the fuselage for a couple feet and then stopped. "There's a lot of dust on it," she said. "This plane's been sitting here for a while."

The next thing Gunn knew she was pulling him under the wing and toward the front of the aircraft. Once there, she began tapping on the bulbous nose, the place where a real Nightwatch plane contained a lot of high-tech communications and spying equipment.

Her tapping came back hollow—just as she had suspected.

"It's empty," she told him.

Then she pulled down the emergency access panel located directly under the cockpit. Before he could stop her, she had already boosted herself up into the plane. Again, he had little choice but to follow.

They were both struck by the stink of jet fuel as soon

as they climbed into the plane. No surprise, they discovered the interior contained several large fuel bladders, flexible containers meant to hold extra gas.

"There's enough fuel in here to go around the world," Gunn said.

"Or to blow it up," Amanda replied. She was pointing to canisters at the back of the aircraft, almost hidden among the fuel bladders. They were clearly marked: *High Explosives*. They guesstimated there was at least several tons of the stuff. More ominous were the six empty barrels located in the midst of the high explosives. Their tops were off and neatly placed beside them, indicating that something else was going to be loaded aboard the plane.

"I hope no one within a mile lights up a smoke," Gunn said wryly. "This place is just one spark away from blowing up half of Africa."

They climbed up inside the cockpit, and Amanda found the trouble light—a very low illumination that bathed the cockpit in green once she switched it on.

And here it got weirder still.

"This is not the cockpit of a Nightwatch plane," she declared after scanning the instrument panel. "The primary flight controls look legit—but all this other stuff—the screens and such? They're not hooked up to anything. In fact, I'm guessing there's nothing they can hook into. This is just a typical 747 cockpit, stripped down to the bare essentials. Except this . . ."

She pointed to the pilot's seat. It wasn't typical of a 747—it was actually an ejection seat, something more commonly seen in a fighter aircraft. Above it was a blow-out panel, a covered-up hole in the flight deck ceiling so the ejected pilot could get out of the aircraft cleanly.

"Wouldn't want to be the copilot in this plane," she remarked dryly, noting that there was only one ejection seat. "It's like not having a passenger-side air bag in a car."

A sudden and particularly loud clap of thunder shook both of them.

"Let's go," he told her.

And this time, she agreed.

THEY retreated from the hangar to find the storm had become worse.

The rain was coming down so hard now, it sounded like one continuous rumble of thunder. This was good, at least from Amanda's point of view, because there were two more buildings she felt they had to explore.

But though the storm had grown in intensity, off on the western horizon they could tell the end was in sight. It would be over in a matter of five minutes—maybe less.

"Split up?" he suggested, yelling over the sound of the pounding rain.

She pointed to the hangar behind the one they'd just visited. "I'll take that one," she yelled back. "Meet back here in four minutes, OK?"

Gunn nodded; she gave him a squeeze on the shoulder and was gone, vanishing into the downpour.

Gunn scrambled across the tarmac and reached the third hangar. It was smaller than the one that held the bogus U.S. plane, smaller than the one Amanda was reconning.

Like the other hangar, it had a single door with a flimsy lock. He looked inside and again couldn't see any signs of life. He pushed on the door and it opened easily.

He didn't need to switch on the lights to see what this hangar contained. It was filled to the rafters with weapons and ammunition: assault rifles, mortars and plenty of anti-personnel mines. And technicals, several dozen of them, enough to supply a good-sized militia army. Gunn checked the weapons storage boxes. All of them had *Made in China* stamped on their sides. All of them were dusty as well, indicating they'd been there for a while.

There were also two planes in there, both weird and out of place.

The first one, the closest to the door, was a Russian-built Su-34—a very unusual aircraft. Originally designed to be both a fighter and a medium bomber, Moscow had built the airplane strictly for export sales. Its purpose was to give countries that might not have the luxury of in-flight refueling the ability to fly very long distances. So its fuel capacity was huge. But also, because long range missions meant long flying times for pilots, the cockpit of this plane was built extraordinarily large, to include not just roomy side-by-side seats and an expansive control panel, but a small galley, a small sleeping area, even a toilet. It was like the RV of fighter-bombers.

Gunn wasn't even sure what African country he was presently in, but he supposed that it wasn't too out of the ordinary that the Russians would find a few customers in this part of the world for their unusual aircraft.

But again, why was it here with the fake U.S. command plane?

The second aircraft was even more unusual. It was a U.S. Navy F-18—or what was left of one. It was in pieces: The wings, the fuselage and the cockpit were more or less intact and laid out on the floor as if someone was putting it back together. The myriad of other components—the landing gear, the engines, the weapons—were scattered about in oddly camouflaged wooden boxes, again, as if they had been shipped there with the intent of some kind of rebuilding project. Where did the plane come from? Gunn didn't have a clue.

Using a finger squished in an oil puddle, Gunn wrote the serial number on his flight boot, and then, hearing a clap of thunder, and sensing that the rain was finally letting up, he headed out the door.

Amanda was waiting for him when he arrived at their predetermined spot—but immediately he knew all was not right with her. She was almost pale and her pretty features were twisted with worry.

"What's wrong?" he asked her.

She shook the rain out of her eyes. "Let's get out of here first," she said. "Then I'll tell you everything."

THEY found their bikes and were about to make their escape when they spotted a white Land Rover heading for the hidden base.

Taking cover back in the pepper stick bush, they watched as the truck entered the air base through an opening in the electrical wire and stopped near a small building they assumed was the administration hut.

Six African men got out; they were soldiers, or at least they were dressed in military clothes. They too were soaking wet, and they also had a long pole that was holding a number of recently killed animals such as rabbits, moles and even a couple monkeys.

"They just made a lunch run—that's why this place was empty," Gunn said. "Good thing the Lost Valley McDonald's is far away. We would have been uninvited guests if we hadn't got out when we did."

"Roger that," she replied. "And I'm not so much in the mood for a monkey burger."

They waited until the six men disappeared into the admin hut. Then they jumped on their bikes and rode as fast as they could, using the dwindling rainstorm as the last of their cover.

They made it back to the main trail in an amazingly short amount of time.

Finally out of the line of sight from the hidden base, they stopped and Amanda told Gunn what she'd discovered inside the third hangar.

"It was an airplane," she began, her voice still a bit shaky, uncharacteristic for her. "Russian design. But I'm not positive what type it is."

"Draw it," Gunn told her.

She took a stick and drew an outline in the dust. What it depicted was an aircraft of massive size. Bigger certainly than their C-17s—bigger even than a C-5 Galaxy, the largest aircraft in the U.S. military and the second largest operational aircraft ever built. And which one was the first?

"It had six engines," she said, adding detail to her drawing, "a very long fuselage and winglets on the tail. It was huge."

Gunn looked at the drawing and then blurted out: "It might be an Antonov of some kind. Maybe a 225—or a knockoff of that design. The Russians have a plane bigger than the C-5. It's a huge cargo plane."

She nodded worriedly. "Yes—it probably is a variation of an Antonov design."

Gunn quickly told her about the Russian Su-34 he'd found, plus the remains of the Navy jet. "What the hell are they doing out here?" he said. "Building an air museum?"

But the worried look never left Amanda's usually bright features. "I didn't tell you everything. That big plane—it wasn't empty. Nor was it a fake like the first one we saw."

"What do you mean?" he asked.

"It was full of weapons," she replied.

"So was the hangar I went into," he told her, revealing the combat weapons he'd seen.

"No, this was different . . ."

"Bombs, you mean? Or stuff being delivered somewhere?"

But she was shaking her head. "No—I mean it had

weapons on it. Installed. Machine guns. Cannons. Artillery. It was armed."

Gunn almost laughed. "A big plane like that? They don't put stuff like that on . . ."

And that's where he stopped—because that's when the message finally reached his brain. Yes, normally such weapons are not installed on large cargo planes, unless that plane has been turned into a gunship—like one of the 201st's planes.

"Damn . . ." he just muttered. "Are you sure?"

She nodded. "It's a Russian gunship—a big one—bigger than ours. It must have had at least two dozen weapons sticking out its port side—it looked like they were on two levels, like some old Man-of-War with wings. And it wasn't dusty. In fact, its engines were hot. I think it just came back from somewhere."

"Damn . . ." was all Gunn could say again.

"But it gets even weirder," she told him.

"How so?"

She pulled a document from her pocket. "I stole this. It was tacked up on the hangar wall."

Gunn looked at the single piece of paper. It was somewhat weathered and crumpled. It contained a crude drawing that seemed to illustrate an air attack on a facility of some kind with an airplane in the background that looked a lot like the Nightwatch plane they'd found in the first hangar. It was hard to make out any more than that, except for a bizarre notation scrawled at the bottom that read: "When looking on map for target, this U.S. Air Force base does not have a runway. Easy to spot from the air."

Gunn just looked up at her. The rain had stopped, the sun was back out and it was illuminating the water drops on her skin.

"What does it all mean?" she asked him, sweet and innocent, a switch from the tough chick who'd run wild through the rain, and had stolen through the hidden base.

He took the paper, folded it and put it in his pocket. Then he got back on his bike and she got on hers.

"What it means," he said, "is that we have to catch the next boat out of Lmono."

CHAPTER SEVENTEEN

THEY reached the river town of Lmono twenty minutes later; it was about four miles across the plain from the hidden base.

It was just as Nelson had described it. A small village located on a bend of a winding river, a place where passage could be booked on riverboats going downstream to the larger settlement of Umbango, where a phone could be found.

The problem was Lmono was deserted. There were a couple dozen buildings there, all having to do with the commerce on the river: waterside eating places, fishing shacks, boat repair shops, and a pier where the riverboats docked and departed.

But all of these places were empty. Gunn and Amanda pedaled down the dusty main street, seeing not a soul. The doors of the businesses were open; in one case they saw two plates of fish and rice sitting on a table outside a saloon, untouched. It was as if the customers had simply vanished just after their food arrived.

It was a ghost town, one that had been hastily abandoned.

"Now we know where all those people we ran into were coming from," Amanda said as they finally came to a stop near the town square. "They thought something bad was coming this way. So they picked up and left."

Gunn just shook his head. "They sure must know something we don't."

They dismounted their bikes and checked each open building they came to, but they could not find anything resembling a phone. Nor were there any boats tied up along the river or even in any of the boat repair shops.

There was another strange thing about the little town: Attached near the front door of just about every building was a sign that read: *Legends say you are now in hell.*

Gunn and Amanda found at least two dozen of these signs. Most were old and battered; all were written in English. They contemplated the signs' meaning for a long time, but were baffled. Just another thing in Africa that made no sense. At least to them.

THEY found a couple cans of peaches in one of the open stores and appropriated them.

Sitting on the abandoned dock, they shared the fruit and drank their second bottle of water and pondered their situation. The biggest problem was they had no idea where they were. They weren't even sure what country they were in, never mind where the next town or city was. So it wasn't like they could just set out down the nearest road on their bikes. They might be pedaling for days before they reached the next point of civilization. Yet they felt it was crucial that they get word of the sinister hidden base back to the main unit at Wum Bakim as quickly as possible.

So they had to go to Plan B.

Gunn pulled out just about the only thing that had survived with him during the minicopter crash: Downes's satphone. He'd put it in his boot before they commenced their wild minicopter attack, and the good old USA shoe leather had protected it through his ordeal.

Now he held it up for Amanda to see, and just shrugged.

"Worth a try," she said. "I mean, this guy owes us now, instead of the other way around. So why wait anymore?"

Gunn pressed the activate button again, feeling no jolt of electricity this time. There was a burst of static and then he heard ringing on the other end.

"Maybe he's home this time," Gunn said.

But in a replay of the first time he'd used the phone, he let it ring and ring—and ring. And again, there was no answer.

He activated the keyboard and started to type a message but stopped himself. "What am I going to say?" he asked Amanda. "That we're stuck in hell? Can you give us a lift?"

He turned off the phone and returned it to his boot. That's when they heard a strange noise off in the distance. A chugging sound, oddly familiar.

"What is that?" Gunn asked, looking upriver, where the racket seemed to be coming from.

Amanda cocked her head in that direction too, trying to identify the sound.

"I've heard it before," she said. "I know that much."

A few seconds later they saw a dark shape coming around the bend in the river. And the chugging noise got louder. And was that hip-hop music?

They were both immediately on their feet.

"I don't believe this . . ." Gunn said.

"Not in a million years," Amanda agreed. "This can't be real."

It was their riverboat, coming around the bend.

That's when it all fell into place for Gunn. This was the

Ingus River and the riverboat had made it through to the other side of the *Dashi-dagumba*.

And all those signs reading *Legends say you are now in hell*?

They were part of an inside African joke. This was the other end of the haunted waterway. This was where all the condemned souls were supposed to reside. This little fishing village. Hell . . .

They flagged the boat down, laughing and waving madly from the dock. It was listing mightily to starboard; the wound it had suffered the night before now ran just about the length of the hull. It seemed a miracle the vessel was still afloat.

Gunn also noticed right away that the boat was now covered with many heavily armed paratroopers, about three times the number that had been there when they first began the journey.

The riverboat came up to the dock. The people on board felt just like Gunn and Amanda did: astonished to see them both alive and in one piece. Gunn and Amanda happily jumped aboard, leaving their trusty bicycles behind.

They were warmly greeted by Moon, Umu and the captain. It was clear that everyone on the boat had given them up for dead. They went down to the galley and Moon set them up with some coffee. They gave him a very abbreviated version of what had happened to them after they'd left the riverboat the night before: finding the Yellowcake Gang's hideout, calling Downes but getting no answer, attacking the encampment after they thought they'd spotted the world's most "high-profile target," crashing and Gunn's virtual resurrection.

"Now, before we go on, please tell us," Gunn said. "What happened on your end after we left?"

Instead of replying, Moon just handed him a small stack of photos. They all showed the same thing: an aerial view of a huge burning hole in the ground. Neither Gunn nor

Amanda recognized what it was at first. But then some of the surrounding terrain started to look familiar. Thick jungle, a long sheer mountainside, a twisting, turning stream nearby.

"Is that the Yellowcake Gang's hideout?" Amanda asked excitedly.

"That's what's left of it," Moon replied. "Which, as you can see, isn't very much. I mean, you can't even see the wreckage of the two yellowcake trucks down there, never mind any bodies. That place was hit *very* hard."

Amanda and Gunn were stunned.

"No way we did all that," Amanda said. "Where did you get these pictures?"

"They came aboard with the second group of paratroopers," Moon explained. "After you two left, we stayed anchored off the entrance to the hacked-out road, for three hours, just as you said. We had no way of knowing whether you found the hideout or not. But shortly before daybreak, we saw a flight of six unmarked, all-black helicopters go overhead. They looked to us like they were heading toward where we assumed the Yellowcake Gang's hideout would be. Shortly after that, we heard sounds of fighting on the wind. It lasted maybe ten minutes, then it all ended with one long, sustained sound of thunderous heavy weapons fire. After that, there was nothing.

"It turns out Bing had been flying over the *Dashidagumba* area all along, in hopes of spotting us and the riverboat. He saw the huge pall of smoke and took pictures of it—and put two and two together. He figured you'd found the hideout, had contacted Downes and Downes had someone go in and destroy the place.

"We hated to do it, but again, like you said, we moved on when you didn't come back. When we broke out of the heavy jungle, we finally got our sat-phone to work. We called Bada and he dropped us more guys and these pictures."

It took Gunn and Amanda a few moments to digest it all. Then Gunn said: "So there's no doubt that Downes actually got the call. But he hasn't been in touch with us since?"

Moon shook his head no. "He hasn't contacted the base. Nothing. Maybe the idea is, we're not under arrest, but we have to make it home on our own."

Gunn shrugged. It wasn't anything he'd even contemplated, because he'd never really thought the 201st would be able to actually fulfill their end the bargain. So, did this now mean they were free, out from under any threat of being arrested and brought back to stand trial—just back to being ordinary expatriates?

He didn't know. None of them did.

In any case, they had more pressing things to do now.

That's when they told Moon about the secret base they'd found on their way to Lmono.

Moon couldn't believe it. "It sounds like it's the armory for every Janjaweed type on the continent," he said.

"It's at least that," Gunn replied. "They've got this Russian fighter-bomber out there, this fake Nightwatch plane and this enormous *gunshipski.*"

Then they showed him the document Amanda had found, the one containing the reference to doing something involving an Air Force base that had no runway.

"I'm not going to pretend I know how all this connects," Gunn concluded. "But I'm sure of one thing: We have to flatten that base out there, before the people who run it do some real damage."

AS it turned out, Umbango was just ten miles downriver. It was abandoned too. But it had a huge, dry lakebed close by, and this was where Bing landed the Jump Plane after dark and picked up the river contingent of the 201st.

They bid good-bye to the boat's captain and crew, giving each man a gold ingot for his trouble, and another few to buy enough gas for the vessel to take the long way around in returning to its home village. There was no way the Americans wanted the boat to go back up the Ingus, after what they'd all been through.

When they landed back at Wum Bakim, Gunn felt like he'd been away for a million years and not just less than forty-eight hours. He climbed off the Jump Plane and took a long look around. Everything seemed different. Not as gloomy, not as dim. The air smelled fresh and clean. The heat felt good on his skin. The place had a new sort of beauty to it.

Maybe it was because he was free now, now that he didn't have the weight of the U.S. government hanging over his head.

Maybe that's why Wum Bakim appeared so different to him now.

Or maybe it was something else.

CHAPTER EIGHTEEN

Five hours later

It was midnight when Bing took off.

He and the Tank Plane's copilot Lieutenant Stanley were the only crew on board the Jump Plane at the moment.

With the loss of the incredibly versatile minicopter, the Jump Plane had been pressed into service as a pre-strike reconnaissance platform.

Its target: the hidden base Gunn and Amanda had found on the plains at the edge of the *Dashi-dagumba.*

While the other 201st principals were gathered in the Ops room, planning the unit's next bolt from the blue, Bing and Stanley were in charge of snapping IR and heat-sensitive pre-attack photos of the objective, which everyone was now calling the "X Base," as in *The X-Files*, because of all the strange things that were found there.

Though nothing was ever easy in the world of special ops, the 201st's upcoming air assault seemed mercifully low on potential complications. The X Base was easy to find (once you knew its location); was situated on a flat, open plain, which was perfect for targeting; was far enough away from any civilian population, so there would be no collateral damage; and with only a handful of monkey-eating mooks in residence, had few people to shoot back at them.

True, this was a bombing mission, and the 201st had no conventional bombs to speak of. But that was not a problem, because the unit excelled at improvising. Tonight's plan called for them to put to use those dozen or so barrels of untreated, watered-down aviation fuel that had come out of their elderly in-flight refueler. The barrels were being filled with sand, rags and fertilizer at the moment. These materials would soak up the flammable liquid, causing them to expand within the sealed barrels themselves, which, when equipped with impact fuses, would create an explosive device equivalent to a standard issue five-hundred-pound aerial bomb.

The task for Bing and Stanley was to capture pre-attack images that would indicate the best place to drop these barrel bombs, which would be delivered low and slow by no more elaborate means than rolling them out of the back of the Marine armor plane at one thousand feet. The hope was that the fuel-filled barrels would build up enough velocity in their fall that they would easily break through the hidden base's camouflage canopy and go splat when impacting the buildings below. It was estimated that three bombs per hangar would be enough to do the job, especially with the large amount of explosives already present in at least one of those hangars. If everything went right, the secondary explosions as a result of their bombing promised to be especially spectacular.

So everything seemed set, save for this one last recon of the X Base. There was no doubt the weapons and explosives the 201st would destroy during the mission would deal a serious blow to the many Janjaweed-like groups operating in this part of Africa, especially in the Darfur region, not to mention whatever havoc the people who'd assembled the fake Nightwatch airplane and the *gunshipski* were looking to do. Just as important, though, the entire unit knew this would probably be their last mission to help the people of their strange but endearing adopted home, and to a person, they wanted to go out with a bang.

The X Base was about a twenty-two-minute flight from Wum Bakim. The short trip would take the unit's planes over the darkest, deepest parts the Lost Valley. A mountain range separated the jungled part of the *Dashi-dagumba* from the savannah where the target was located. Though they would be silent and invisible, this range would even further mask the 201st's approach in the last few seconds before the attack.

Bing and Stanley flew this route now, routinely making note of the atmospheric conditions along the way. They were cruising at one thousand feet, just as the unit's Tank Plane/converted bomber and its two escorts would be. As Bing prepared for the overflight, Stanley began monitoring data from the digital camera pod that had been installed in the nose of the big C-17. They would also sweep the target area with their ground-imaging radar/RIF combination, hoping to pick up anything that Gunn and Amanda might have missed during their abbreviated visit to the hidden base the day before.

All systems were go, and all devices were working when Bing floated the big plane over the top of the mountain. Using his crash helmet's RIFs, he easily spotted the hidden base below.

And that's when things started to go wrong.

As soon as Bing activated his RIF's zoom function, he knew all was not as it should be. Instead of finding a lifeless, deserted weapons storage facility beneath the camouflage netting, what he saw instead was a full-blown, up-and-running military base, filled with hundreds of armed troops and bustling with activity. Even worse, the place was now ringed with Russian-made mobile SAM launchers and

Chinese-made antiaircraft guns. At least a dozen of them combined.

"Damn," Bing swore upon seeing all this. "I think things just got very complicated."

TWENTY-TWO minutes later, the Jump Plane was back at Wum Bakim and Bing was in the Ops building delivering the bad news to the rest of the 201st officers.

No one liked what they heard.

"Damn, we are off by twenty-four hours," Gunn said, looking at the images of the suddenly active, heavily defended base. "It would have been a milk run if we were just a day ahead of ourselves."

"Why should we expect anything to go easy now?" Moon said dryly.

"But who are they?" Amanda asked, voicing the number one question. "And where did they come from all of a sudden?"

They didn't have a clue. The best guess came from Colonel Mdosi. He theorized that the couple hundred or so fighters now inhabiting the base were probably mercenaries or rogue army elements hired by someone to create havoc in central Africa. But there was no way of the 201st knowing for certain.

Which led to a second question: Why now? Their thinking had been that the X Base's dusty weapons were sitting there to be used sometime in the future—weeks, months, maybe even years away. So why had the place suddenly come to life literally overnight?

Again, they had no idea.

Then there was the mystery *behind* the mystery: the crude document Amanda had found when she and Gunn stole into the base the day before, the one that spoke of attacking a U.S. Air Force base that had no runway. With all the controlled pandemonium in planning the big strike, no one had been able to figure out what that meant exactly. Their only guess was that it was a reference to an attack on an Air Force base not yet built or under construction that didn't have its runways installed yet. But that threat seemed a little more immediate now too.

So the unit's problem was almost too simple. Had this been the slam dunk they'd been hoping for, they wouldn't have been burdened with trying to figure out what the mysterious no-runway target was or who was planning to attack it. Just as long as they'd destroyed the camouflaged facility, including the fake Nightwatch airplane and the *gunshipski* while they were still on the ground, they could have left it to the African Union or the UN or someone else to sort it all out afterward.

But now that the outcome of the 201st's pending attack was not so certain, due to the presence of the AA weapons and the sudden appearance of so many enemy gunmen, they'd been brought back to the biggest question of all: Who the hell built this base and what were they intending on doing with the exotic weapons they'd stored there?

The change in the situation meant that the 201st would have to find out the hard way.

From a tactical point of view, the unexpected presence of all the armed men and the AA weapons at the X Base dramatically changed the dynamic of the upcoming mission. First, there was no doubt the 201st would now face some kind of opposition once those on the ground realized they were under attack.

Second, stomping the small army of gunmen was now just as important as destroying the base itself. Even if the 201st was successful in destroying the hundreds of weapons, explosives and the two large airplanes stored inside the hidden facility, letting hundreds of armed potential terrorists flee into the wilderness just meant they would live to terrorize another day. They couldn't let that happen.

Third, as the reality of the suddenly active base meant whoever owned the place probably planned to use everything stored away on it soon, the 201st felt they had to find out exactly what was going on—and the only way to do that was to capture at least one person at the base and make him talk.

All this meant that while Gunn's AC-17 would be able to do its thing, and try to take a heavy toll on the base's defenders, the 201st would have to drop the 82nd's paratroopers on the base too. That was the only way of making sure that while the couple hundred mysterious gunmen were taken care of, a few could be found who were willing to flip.

But this brought up *another* problem: What to do about the X Base's camouflage covering? The paratroopers couldn't jump through it—it might be too strong for that. And to get caught up in it would invite a slaughter. Yet the 201st couldn't use their makeshift fuel bombs on it either, as originally planned, as that would mean the paratroopers would be dropping onto a burning target. The other alternative, having the paratroopers land somewhere outside the base and then attack it horizontally, was definitely a poor option. Their forte was surprise and shock from above. All that was lost if the outnumbered 82nd had to engage the base defenders on foot.

So the job of destroying the camouflage net would fall to Gunn's Fireship. Most of the sixteen weapons he carried aboard could fire some kind of incendiary projectile, and spraying them around would have a far greater effect than trying to fuel-bomb the enormous camo net in a few places and hoping the whole thing would quickly burn. The thinking was that one pass from the huge gunship using incendiary ammunition might be enough to set the covering on fire all at once. If Gunn hit all the right spots and it burned rapidly, then the paratroopers would have a big hole to jump through—and then the gunship would be free to start hitting other targets.

But in order to further support the paratroopers, the Tank Plane would now have to be directly involved as well, which meant Amanda was going on the mission in more than just a backup role. She would land the Marines somewhere near the base, dropping off their tanks in the most advantageous position possible. In fact, she would have to do her part first. Because only once the M-1s were in position, and the paratroopers ready to drop, could the AC-17 come in and try to quickly burn up the camo netting.

And as if they didn't have enough to worry about, there was also the question of fuel. Anything could go wrong in a mission like this—that was exactly the problem. So, on top of everything else, the broken-down old refueling plane would also have to show up at some time over the hidden base, to be on hand for aerial hookups should any of the 201st's planes need gas to get back to Wum Bakim.

The worst part of all this, though, was the time it took to revamp their original plan. Three precious hours drained away trying to come up with something they thought might have a shot of working. It was now 4 A.M., and they still had to get the planes ready and the personnel briefed. This meant they would have to attack after the sun came up, in the daytime, just after dawn. Not good for three big planes that made their living flying invisible at night.

So from a simple plan now had come an enormous, dangerous undertaking with tons of machinery and hundreds of people having to move through time and space at precise moments for it to have any chance of success.

And what if none of it worked?

The 201st officers didn't want to think about that—because there was no Plan B.

*   *   *

THE crews finished getting the three huge planes out onto the runway by 0500 hours. The sun would be up in less than thirty minutes.

As always, Gunn, Amanda and Bing checked over the exteriors of their aircraft before climbing in. All was in order with their Star Skins, even though they would not be of much use today. Bing's Jump Plane was already prepped from his recent recon mission. He was the first to take off, his cargo bay filled with paratroopers.

Amanda was due to leave next; her Marine tanks were already loaded on board. Again, Gunn tried to arrange it so he would see her just before she climbed into her plane.

He caught up with her as she was completing her walk around. They met at the front of her aircraft, once again by the illumination of the nosewheel light.

But this time, it was different. This time it seemed like they'd been to the end of the world and back together, which was not far from the truth. So the old bromide of "Be careful out there" just wasn't going to work.

She began the conversation with: "Are you sure you're OK to fly this mission? You were at the Pearly Gates this time yesterday."

"I'm fine," he said. "But thanks for reminding me."

He smiled, she smiled—but an awkward moment arose. He couldn't think of anything appropriate to say, and neither could she. If they'd been in a movie, it was always this time in the script when they would have kissed.

And to his great surprise, that's exactly what they did.

She just leaned over and, by the light of her plane's nosewheel, kissed him right on the lips. It lasted three, four, five full heartbeats before she finally pulled away.

Then she straightened out his collar, put her helmet on and climbed up into her plane without another word.

Gunn just stood there, unable to move, barely able to breathe.

"Talk about seeing the Pearly Gates," he whispered to himself.

HE finally got himself moving and climbed up into his airplane.

After fist-bumping his copilot, Lieutenant Mike Robinson, he checked with his gun crew in back. All was OK with them. They taxied the plane out to their spot on the runway and watched Amanda take off. Then, right before he ran up his own engines, Gunn took out Downes's satphone again and pushed the activate button. He thought it was important that the SOF superstar be aware of what the 201st was doing, maybe even provide some last-minute help of some kind.

But as before, all he heard at the other end was the phone ringing and ringing, with no answer.

Twenty minutes later

The AC-17 gunship came over the top of the mountain and immediately went into a steep, left-hand bank. They were flying at just five hundred feet, very low for such a large airplane, but necessary if they wanted to start a fire quick.

Gunn had activated his Star Skin shortly after takeoff, and he kept it on now, even though the sun was up and the vast savannah before him was brightening by the second. It was still a little murky around the hidden base itself, however. An early morning fog was helping to keep the dawn's early light to a minimum. The Star Skin had the ability to record any atmospherics above the plane and project them on its bottom, be they stars or clouds, or early morning haze. It wasn't the same as being invisible, far from it. But between this ability, the plane's stealth technology and the fact that the camo covering also hindered people below it from getting a clear look at the sky, Gunn hoped they would get over the hidden base at least once without getting their asses shot off by a SAM missile.

He was quickly lined up on the base, and using his RIFs to pierce the camouflage netting, he instantly saw what Bing and Stanley had first discovered: The place was ringed with AA weapons and populated with at least a couple hundred gunmen. He could see many of them lolling about the place, eating their morning meal.

There was no reason to hesitate. Gunn clicked on his weapons sight, which was a HUD display attached to his left-hand window, and pushed the screen on his weapons control panel to standby. They were directly over the base a moment later. Sighting a large swath of the camo screen at the northeast corner of the base, Gunn pushed the screen icons for his Vulcan cannons and his mini-guns and let loose with seven long, frightening streams of sizzling incendiary rounds. He was hoping to ignite the camo covering at the north end of the base and watch the fire spread out from there.

But there was a problem. The wind was blowing in from the savannah, toward the mountains. So the fire did indeed spread quickly, but only to the far edge of the covering, the opposite direction to what he wanted, where it promptly went out.

Gunn couldn't believe it. All that firing, and only a fraction of the covering had burned.

He had no choice. If he wanted to get rid of the camo covering, they would have to go around again.

By this time the people on the ground, while not noticing the gunship, became aware that something had just ignited part of their camouflage screen. Within seconds the base's alarms were going off. Gunn could hear them all the way up inside the AC-17's cockpit.

"So much for the goddamn element of surprise," he cursed.

They started going around a second time. Gunn was pushing the huge plane all over the sky now, but it was not in love with the thick predawn humid air, especially at this low altitude. Still he was turning as fast as the airframe would allow him. He could see people scrambling below, rushing to investigate the short-lived fire. All it would take was for one to look up through the small hole he'd created, and the jig would be up.

Back over the base again, Gunn fired the Vulcans and the mini-guns once more, this time at the southern edge of the camo covering. The people below saw the fusillade this time, and to most of them, the long streams of shells must have looked like they'd materialized right out of the morning mist. But they were not so dumb that they didn't realize they were under some kind of attack.

The incendiary ammo did its work this time. The southern edge of the camo cover caught fire, and thanks to the prevailing wind, the flames spread quickly. Gunn could see the gunmen below running about, trying to grab fire extinguishers and fire hoses, but they'd be of no use. Because it was essentially a thin layer of fibers and fiberglass, the camo screen burned so rapidly that by the time Gunn went around a third time, the fire he'd started had engulfed the entire camouflage covering.

"Finally," he muttered.

Now he *really* had to go to work.

He pushed the screen icons for the rest of his weaponry—the Bushmasters, the M102 artillery pieces, the Bofors and the mighty Phoenix CIWS—and hit the engage button. A deluge of fire and lead washed over the base, catching many of the gunmen out in the open and causing dozens of secondary explosions. Gunn was able to take out the line of SAM launchers located near the front of the facility, which made everyone on board breathe a little easier. He stayed in his turn and swept across the rear of the base too, hitting smaller support buildings, a water tank and the base's generator.

Then he went over one of the three big hangars, the one containing the fake Nightwatch plane. He reengaged his Bofors and the M102s for this one, intent on taking out the air barn and the weird airplane within. But even though the resulting barrage was tremendous, his shells simply bounced off the top of the building.

He couldn't believe it—and neither could Robinson. In his brief time inside the hangar, Gunn never thought to look up to the ceiling. Was it so heavily reinforced with armor plating that bombs or gunfire couldn't get through?

"It's just like those weird yellowcake trucks all over again," Robinson said as they both watched their explosions having little effect on the hangar's structure. "Our stuff is pinging right off! What's with that?"

Gunn could only shake his head. "I got no idea," he said.

LIEUTENANT Bing's headphones came alive two seconds later.

He clicked on his secure radio and heard Gunn's words: "It's your show now . . ."

Bing acknowledged the call. Then he yelled back to the eighty-four paratroopers and one ground observer loaded into his cargo bay: "Get ready—we're going in!"

He was an expert at doing this by now—that is, putting nearly a hundred paratroopers down in an area the size of a baseball diamond. It took timing and it took skill. It also took the ability to make the huge C-17 stand still in the air. Or at least appear to.

They called it "doing an Elvis." It was a maneuver he'd first seen performed by the guy who used to fly the Jump

Plane, a pilot everyone called Elvis. What he did was pull the engines back to nearly stalling speed, lower the landing flaps, lower the C-17's movable forward wing, lower the landing gear, and then head directly into the wind. When it was time for the paratroopers to go, he would open the rear door, pull back on the controls and lift the big plane's nose skyward. It gave the illusion that the C-17 was frozen in air, and in a manner of speaking it was—at least long enough for the paratroopers to go out the back like a bunch of carnival chutists, pulling their rip cords and hitting the ground just a few seconds later. Doing an Elvis was the ultimate in delivering shock troops, because the manner itself was rather shocking.

Bing called the ten-second warning back to Vogel, the paratrooper's CO. Vogel yelled the go sign back. They came over the top of the mountain at a crawl, Star Skin turned on, even though the sun was fully up by now. Bing started pushing buttons and throwing levers. His flaps went down, his wing went down, and his gear went down—and it was like slamming on the brakes of a race car. Reducing throttle further completed the preliminaries. They were exactly one thousand feet high, flying level, and the back was open. Then the green light came on. That was Bing's cue. He pulled back mightily on the C-17's controls and the next thing he knew he was looking up at the half moon hanging in the morning sky. The paratroopers started going out the back in twos and threes.

His copilot, Lieutenant Jackson, slapped Bing on the knee as soon as the last guy went out the back. Now came the hard part—trying not to fall out of the sky.

Bing pulled the nose down at the same time he slammed the throttles forward. They hung there for a long moment, as if the airplane were making up its mind whether to keep flying or just quit then and there. But slowly they started moving forward again, increasing their speed incrementally. Bing raised the gear and the flaps and straightened out the movable forward wing section. They were quickly clean again. And behind him, the seven dozen paratroopers were landing just where Bing wanted them to.

He let out a long whistle in relief and did a fist bump with Jackson.

That's when the AA shells came crashing into the cockpit.

They came in a flash of fire and smoke—blinding Bing. The next thing he knew, the flight deck was in flames. There were explosions going off all around him, so many he couldn't see the controls. His hands were still on the stick, but he could see that the rubber in his flight gloves was starting to melt off. There was fire everywhere.

It took a few long seconds, but the AA fire finally stopped hitting the flight compartment. But Bing could still hear shells impacting all along his fuselage, on the wing, on the engine cowlings and back toward the end of the gigantic plane. Extremely visible and going extremely slow, they'd flown right into the sights of at least two very powerful AA cannons, maybe more, and the cannons were ripping his big plane to shreds.

He reached over for Jackson. They were the only two left in the plane. Luckily he felt Jackson's hand coming over to reach for him at the same instant. In a weird moment they fist-bumped again.

"Are you still in one piece?" Bing yelled to him. The windshield had been blown away and now the wind was tremendous.

"I think I am!" Jackson yelled back.

Bing checked himself over, even though between the smoke and the wind and the flames, the plane could have been heading straight into the ground for all he knew. His face and scalp were cut—and he'd taken a piece of something in his right leg. He was bleeding, but nothing was gushing out of him like a garden hose, so he took that as a good sign. In a fit of brilliance, Jackson had blindly reached out in front of Bing and pushed the plane's autopilot to on. They both felt a mighty shudder—but then the computer got the message and started flying the plane straight and true on its own. This gave Bing time to reach behind his seat and grab the fire extinguisher. He pulled the pin and just started spraying everywhere, dampening the flames a little, but not nearly enough to put them out.

Tossing the fire extinguisher aside, Bing stole a glance out his cracked side window and saw that yes, they were flying, but they were just barely above the savannah, not even two hundred feet high. He could actually see gazelles bouncing and running away from them, scared to death at what they were seeing above.

The autopilot was doing its thing, but it was wounded too. At least a few of the explosive AA shells had imbedded themselves in the flight control panel, and it was lit up like a Christmas tree. Bing waved away the smoke and saw that while two of his engines were running at 80 percent, the two others were down to 30 percent and failing fast. The array was his inboard port wing engine and his outward starboard engine. Stability-wise it was a wash, but it would be a rough ride at the very least.

He grabbed a second fire extinguisher, and this one doused most of the larger flames. They were still smoldering just about everywhere, but at least now he and Jackson had some visibility.

Bing somehow was able to look at his flight clock—though it seemed like an eternity had gone by, barely thirty seconds had passed since they'd been hit. The longest half minute of his life.

He began to turn the big plane to the left. He had to try to get back to Wum Bakim, though at the rate they were losing fuel, it was going to be a close-run thing.

That's when he got some really bad news.

"Damn" was all he heard Jackson say.

Bing instinctively turned to the left and looked back at his wing.

It was completely engulfed in flames.

CAPTAIN Vogel saw Bing's C-17 get hit. Now he watched as it caught on fire and began faltering.

This was not good. Like a flash back to a newsreel of D-Day, he expected the big C-17 would flip over at any second and slam into the ground, killing the crew and plane that had just so perfectly dropped him and his paratroopers here.

But Vogel couldn't think about that at the moment. Other things were happening. No sooner had he and his men hit the ground than they started taking fire from the army of gunmen that had so suddenly appeared at the X Base. Within seconds, they were shooting at the paratroopers from behind concrete barriers, under vehicles, even from inside the big hangars themselves.

Vogel immediately split his force of eighty-plus paratroopers into three groups. Each group had the responsibility of securing one of the three hangars, neutralizing most of the opposing force defending it and destroying the hangar itself, if necessary. It was important as well to destroy any weaponry they could find on the base, but they also needed to capture a few of the gunmen alive.

Once his men were linked up with their squads, Vogel sent them on their way. First Squad started making its way around the back of the base, heading for the hangar containing the fake Nightwatch plane—they too realized by now that this structure was heavily reinforced. Second Squad was tasked with securing the hangar containing the Chinese weapons and the Russian- and American-built jet fighters.

Vogel and his 3rd Squad were responsible for attacking the air barn Amanda had scouted, the one that contained the huge Russian version of a gunship, so he quickly got his men moving in that direction. Running in a sort of flying wedge, they went right after the small army of gunmen who were obviously charged with defending the *gunshipski's* hangar. The ferocity of Vogel's attack pushed these men back on their heels, and they were soon retreating toward the big building itself. But just as quickly, the gunmen managed to line up several vehicles about fifty feet in front of the hangar, stopping the flying wedge in its tracks. The problem with fighting on the tarmac of the wide-open base was there was precious little cover for the paratroopers. With most of his men suddenly lying flat-out and under sustained fire from the gunmen, Vogel knew he needed help.

So he took out his sat-phone and made a call.

AMANDA had never been inside a tank before—but she was in one now.

She was standing in the second open turret of Cardillo's lead M1 Abrams. They were parked about five hundred feet from the front of the hidden base, situated on a slight rise, with a clear view of the action. Their role here was to provide a sort of mobile artillery support for the 82nd's three-prong attack.

Amanda was subbing for the tank's radioman, who was helping the M1's loader because the automatic load system on this particular tank was not working. She had delivered the pair of tanks to this spot with no problems, landing on the flat, grassy savannah just as if she were landing on a typical unprepared combat airstrip. They had deployed quickly and silently just seconds before Gunn made his first pass over the hidden base, the first attempt to get its camouflage netting ablaze.

She had watched with growing anxiousness as the big AC-17 was forced to go around twice in order to get the net to catch fire. That finally done, it successfully laid down a wave of ordnance allowing the paratroopers to jump in. But then, Bing's plane was hit with AA fire, causing it to burst into flames. And all this had happened in less than a minute.

Now the firing from the base was getting louder and louder, and the smoke and flames thicker and thicker. Amanda had lost sight of Bing's airplane just seconds after it went right over them, smoking heavily, flying not even two hundred feet above the ground. She couldn't imagine it staying airborne very much longer, and her heart ached at the thought that Bing and Jackson and one of the unit's three big aircraft would not survive this crazy battle.

But she was also trying to spot Gunn's airplane. It had passed over the mountain to her right after laying down its last wave of fire, and she hadn't seen it since.

If anything happened to *him* . . .

There *was* a large plane circling high above the battle site—but it was not Gunn's plane. It was the on-loan air-refueling plane. The crappy refueler and its crappy crew had finally decided to join the party.

"Just stay up there out of the way," Amanda said. "We don't need any more complications . . ."

These thoughts were interrupted by her radio coming to life. It was Vogel. His men were pinned down and he needed help. That's what the tanks were there for.

Vogel gave Amanda some rough firing instructions, and she repeated them word for word to Cardillo, who started barking them down at his crew. An instant later the entire tank shook mightily as its crew fired a shell right into the heart of the base itself. It was a frightening, exciting moment. The shell reached its target even before it seemed to come out of the tank's barrel. Amanda couldn't believe the noise and violence of it.

She heard Vogel shouting back into the radio.

"Right on the money!" he was yelling. "Now we need about twenty more just like that!"

VOGEL yelled for his men to stay down and stay covered up. Seconds later, two more 122mm shells went over their heads and crashed down on the enemy trucks in front of them, blowing two of them into the air.

Right after that, another pair of tank shells came in. Then two more and two more. The enemy gunmen were being literally blown apart right in front of the paratroopers' eyes. Still, the tank fire kept coming.

Those gunmen that survived the initial bombardment retreated to a blast wall built about twenty feet from the hangar door. They did so in a controlled, professional manner, which gave Vogel pause. This indicated their enemy this day were hard-core fighters and wouldn't be pushovers, despite the presence of lots of 82nd troopers and two tanks.

Vogel led his men to the cover of the recently destroyed vehicles, dodging a wall of fire coming for the retreating gunmen. A vicious firefight ensued—the gunmen were just twenty-five feet away now. Some were armed with AK-47s loaded with armor-piercing shells, and they seemed well schooled in the art of concentrated fire.

Another call from Vogel to the Marines brought another barrage raining down on the enemy fighters. This time eight shells landed in the space of a half minute—the fusillade vaporized nearly three quarters of the remaining gunmen. Still, a determined force of a dozen or so remained behind the concrete barriers in front of the hangar.

Vogel's squad opened up on them once again, and this time the paratroopers began advancing as they were firing. The gunmen fought ferociously, emptying their weapons and even firing at the squad with handguns. It went on like this for one full minute, but when the paratroopers were close enough to hurl hand grenades at their enemy, both sides knew it was over. Though Vogel yelled to the last two gunmen to surrender—after all the idea was to take some of these guys alive—they used their remaining bullets on themselves, proving they were hard-core to the end.

Vogel and his men finally reached the front of the hangar and confirmed that all the gunmen were dead. They quickly inspected the bodies. Each gunman was wearing the same generic black camo suit with a wool cap that could be pulled down to make a ski mask. They weren't Africans, though. They might have been Europeans, mercenaries perhaps. But just *who* they were was still a mystery.

Vogel tried to open the hangar's doors, but they'd been sealed shut from the inside, as had the side access door. He called for his sappers. These guys arrived with a knapsack full of *plastique* explosive. Vogel had no idea if any gunmen were waiting inside the hangar. But if they were, he wanted to give them a shock before he and his men tried to seize the huge building from them.

The sappers set up their explosives and suggested everyone take cover. The resulting explosion was tremendous. It was so powerful it blew one of the hangar's thirty-foot-tall doors right off its hinges. It came crashing down to the hard asphalt, making such a noise it blotted out the racket of all the gunfire going on across the base.

The explosion also created a lot of smoke. Vogel and his men used it as cover to advance right up to where the door had been blown off. Vogel threw two frag grenades into the building and stepped back to avoid the blast.

When he received no return fire, he finally peeked in.

"Son of a bitch," he cursed.

This hangar was supposed to be holding the massive Russian gunship.

But it was empty.

The gunship was not there.

* * *

LIEUTENANT Stanley wasn't sure exactly how it was that he landed with the paratroopers.

It had happened so quickly, it was all a blur. Just as the strike force was leaving Wum Bakim, someone remembered that whenever there was a gunship operating with friendly troops close by, it was prudent to have an experienced pilot on the ground, to call in fire where needed, and to cut it off quickly should it get too close to its own side.

Stanley was usually the copilot of the Tank Plane and had flown many hours with Lieutenant Gorgeous. However, he'd also made a number of low-level parachute drops earlier in his career, as part of advanced special ops training. That's why he was the natural choice to go boots-on-the-ground with the 82nd.

Next thing he knew he was climbing out of the Tank Plane and climbing aboard the Jump Plane. During the twenty-two-minute flight to the target, he got a quick refresher course on how to jump shallow, then someone handed him a whistle, a sat-phone and a parachute. When the rest of the 82nd contingent went out the back of the Jump Plane, he went out with them. If it all hadn't happened so fast, he would have been scared shitless.

It had been a short trip to the ground. One moment he was going off the ramp of the Jump Plane, then he was free-falling through the air, then his rip cord was pulled, and then he was floating, somewhat fast, toward the base's tarmac.

He hit correctly, feet first, with a mild rollover, just the way he was taught. But when he tried to get up, he got tangled up in the cords, lost his balance and fell hard on the asphalt, badly hitting his forehead. He almost blacked out; his vision went double for a few terrifying seconds. He couldn't hear anything, and his legs didn't want to work. He rolled over, but this only further entangled him in his chute. Meanwhile, the 82nd paratroopers he'd jumped with were already engaging the base's gunmen in a series of fierce firefights all around him.

Stanley finally untangled himself from his cords and chute. His vision was still blurry, but at least he wasn't seeing double anymore. He unpacked his M4 and then pulled the sat-phone off his hip. A check of his weapon's magazine came next—he was locked and loaded. The sat-phone came alive with a faint buzz. He adjusted the dial and then the volume and started pressing the activate button, trying to connect with the Fireship.

Only then did he realize that those sounds whipping by his ear were not coming from the wind blowing off the savannah, but rather were fusillades of machine-gun fire going right over his head. Still he just sat there, confused, feeling a stream of blood come down his check as a result of his head gash. It was like everything was swirling around him—but none of it was real. Being a pilot, this was the closest he'd ever been to combat. He realized it was exhilarating and incredibly frightening at the same time. Paratroopers running this way, bands of enemy gunmen going that way. Grenades going off. Buildings on fire. Smoke getting very thick. He couldn't help but stare at all the excitement around him.

That's when a paratrooper ran by him, slid to a stop, retrieved Stanley's helmet and jammed it onto his head.

"It's dangerous out here, sir," the soldier said before running toward the next firefight. "You've got to keep this on."

Reality came crashing in on Lieutenant Stanley at that moment. It was like someone threw a bucket of cold water in his face. Bullets and shrapnel were flying everywhere—and he'd been sitting in the middle of it all, until just a few seconds ago, without a helmet.

Son of a bitch, he thought.

He jammed the helmet farther onto his head, then

brought his M4 up and ready, intent on shooting anything that came within ten feet of him. He was shaking from head to toe. He looked at his watch and realized that he'd been on the ground for no more than thirty seconds.

Why was he here again?

It was the sat-phone buzzing that brought him back to reality. He pushed the receive button—and heard Gunn's voice on the other end.

"We're through our turn and about thirty seconds away," the gunship pilot told him. "Can you set us up with some targets?"

Stanley looked around the enemy base. The paratroopers were engaged in at least a dozen firefights, all of them centered around the three hangars. The AC-17 specialized in pinpoint accuracy. Still, no one wanted its awesome firepower getting anywhere near friendly forces, so Stanley knew he would have to choose wisely.

He scanned from left to right. He saw a large radio tower—a means for the people here to communicate with the outside world. None of the U.S. troops were near it, so that would be the first to go. About a hundred feet from the tower was the pair of AA guns that had shot up Bing's plane. Partially hidden by some supply shacks, their barrels were depressed and firing at paratroopers in another part of the base. They were target number two. Next to the AA guns, a line of Range Rovers—a means of escape for the bad guys. They were target number three.

Stanley pressed the send button and raised Gunn. He started giving position points for the big gunship to fire at, all the while making sure the areas in question remained clear of friendly troops.

"We are ten seconds away," Gunn replied. "Get everyone's head down."

That's what the whistle in Stanley's pocket was for. He began blowing it madly—and to their good luck, it was shrill enough to be heard even over the cacophony of gunfire and explosions going on. Every 201st soldier knew what the whistle meant. The Fireship was incoming and about to do its thing. Take cover and stay down until it was done.

The huge AC-17 arrived overhead ten seconds later, just as Gunn had promised. It blotted out the brightening sky, like a huge cloud moving at the tip of a storm. It was flying very low, and slow, and was very visible, not its usual combat environment. And of course it was silent. But its sheer size moving through the air seemed to make a sound of its own.

Stanley never stopped blowing the whistle. Hard and loud and in every direction. The gunship sighted the targets he'd selected and went up on its right wing, lowering the left. Then it let off a barrage of fire from its two Bushmasters. The radio tower was gone in a flash. Next came a deluge of shells from the Phoenix CIWS gun. They tore into the AA guns and the fleet of Range Rovers parked nearby, instantly turning them all into bits of metallic dust. A nearby gas tank also received the gunship treatment. One shot from each of the plane's two artillery guns and the fuel tank was blown sky-high.

The flames and smoke were tremendous, but blew away quickly. The Fireship moved away, but not before sending another stream of fire at the hangar containing the Nightwatch plane, only to see its ordnance bounce off again. It then headed back over the mountain, turning all the time so it could quickly do another pass.

Stanley scanned the air base again. At the far northern end he spotted a concrete dugout sticking up just a few feet from the asphalt. He knew an ammo bunker when he saw one. He relayed the coordinates to Gunn and then started blowing the whistle again.

And once again, the light of the sky was blotted out as the huge airplane swept overhead. This time, the Fireship opened up with its miniguns. A stream of fire slammed into the concrete bunker, first throwing thousands of tiny concrete chunks into the air and then, a microsecond later detonating all of the ammunition that lay within. It went up all at once with an earsplitting *whomp!* The entire air base shook—Stanley could see the asphalt opening up and cracking all around his feet, like an earthquake. Such was the power of the AC-17.

The Fireship moved away again—but only after trying a third time to make a dent in the Nightwatch hangar's roof, again to no good result. The AC-17 was soon back over the mountain again, its right wing dipping, the beginning of yet another turn, heading back.

Stanley scanned the battleground a third time. The firefights started up again after the shock of the massive explosion of the ammo dump had passed. Beyond the dump's burning remains, Stanley spotted what looked like a barracks. He could see machine-gun fire coming out of its windows and correctly deduced that enemy gunmen were firing on 201st members from this shelter. Target number six, he thought.

He keyed the sat-phone again, but then, oddly, saw the huge shadow cross the asphalt in front of him. This threw him for a moment—he was surprised to see that the AC-17 was back so quickly.

He yelled into the sat-phone: "We have a barracks in northern end—see it?"

But Gunn replied: "We are still a half minute into our turn . . ."

That's when Stanley looked up and realized this was not the AC-17 Fireship going over. It was something else.

"Jesuzzz!" he heard himself yell. "Where did *that* come from?"

ACTUALLY, Amanda might have been the one who saw it first.

A dark shadow coming from behind the tank, an interruption in the sunlight off to her right.

She took her eyes off the battle for a moment and saw the gigantic plane pass overhead, moving as if it were in slow motion.

No, it wasn't the AC-17.

It was the An-225—the Russian-built gunship.

The *gunshipski* . . .

It was even bigger than she remembered it. Seeing it in the hangar the day before, it seemed as large as a USAF Galaxy C-5, or maybe even larger.

But now, seeing it in flight, it was like a battleship passing over their heads. Huge fuselage, enormous wings sporting not four but six individual engines. A tailfin so immense, it had its own vertical tail planes on it.

Cardillo saw it too, an instant after Amanda did. Even the battle-hardened Marine found himself awestruck as he watched the huge aircraft go over.

It was heading right to the center of the battle. And both Amanda and Cardillo could see that its weapons ports had slid open and it was now turning on its left wing.

Suddenly it was as if the sun exploded. The Russian gunship fired all of its guns as once, creating a tidal wave of destruction across the broad eastern expanse of the air base. That it was mostly the base's own fighters caught under its wave of fire didn't seem to bother the huge airplane's crew—or whoever was firing the weapons. It just seemed intent on killing anyone in its path.

Somehow the majority of the 201st soldiers had seen the big ship coming and were already on the move—disengaging from their firefights and watching as the cornered enemy gunmen had no other place to go when the *gunshipski* opened up on its first pass. But then the big plane was moving off to the north and beginning to turn. And this was bad news, particularly for the paratroopers' 2nd Squad.

They'd been fiercely battling a gang of enemy gunmen

protecting the third hangar, the one that held the heavy weapons, the Russian Su-34 fighter-bomber and the disassembled U.S. Navy F-18. They'd closed to within fifty feet of their objective, causing many fatalities among the black-suited gunmen. But then they were suddenly surprised by the appearance of the *gunshipski* and everything changed.

They kept their heads, though, and made a hasty but orderly withdrawal to the western corner of the base, getting out of the An-225's line of fire, if just for the moment. But their only fallback position from here was the base's wide-open runway. And with no cover out there, it was a killing ground for the big airplane if there ever was one.

Now time seemed to speed up—again bad news for the 2nd Squad. Most of them were able to find cover behind the remains of the blown-away magazine bunker—but though the pieces of concrete were large, they knew the *gunshipski's* weapons could turn them to dust with well-aimed fire.

The big Russian-built plane went over again, very low and very slow. This time 82nd troopers all over the hidden base began firing at it with their M4s, but their bullets bounced off it like they were pebbles. At that same moment, though, both of Cardillo's tanks fired their massive cannons at the gunship, raising their gun barrels as high as they could go. The first tank shell missed completely, impacting on the mountain far behind the base. But the second shell grazed the right wing of the huge plane, knocking it off center just a bit and causing its withering fire to fall mostly on the expanse of asphalt between the third hangar and where the 2nd Squad paratroopers were hiding, under cover.

It had been a lucky shot, but it was not enough to seriously affect the enemy gunship. And now it was turning again, and this time its guns would come right over where the 2nd Squad paratroopers had congregated.

Every American not engaged in a firefight turned an M4

on the huge plane again. The tanks did too. But no amount of ground fire was going to stop the flying behemoth from dispensing hell onto the doomed paratroopers below.

It was so strange then that just as the big plane was about to open up, a string of small explosions ripped along its right-hand side, the side without the weapons. The big plane shuddered—its engines bellowed out an ungodly scream. It immediately righted itself, its weapons ports closing in a flash. The Russian gunship seemed to hang in the air for a second before resuming forward travel.

The 2nd Squad paratroopers were shocked—what happened? What had saved them from certain death just moments away?

They looked behind them to find that another cloud was moving across the sky.

It was the AC-17 gunship. It had arrived at just the right moment and delivered a broadside to its rival counterpart.

The *gunshipski* increased power and accelerated toward the savannah. Meanwhile, the Fireship dipped its wing and fired off another barrage, this one at a gang of enemy gunmen who'd been trying to outflank the cornered paratroopers. Not one of the enemy survived the barrage.

This finally allowed the 2nd Squad troopers to get out of their tenuous position and seek better cover.

The relief was short-lived however, as the scream of six violent engines once again ripped across the sky. All eyes went south to see that the huge Russian plane had turned yet again and was coming back.

And over the mountain to the north, the AC-17 was doing the same thing.

It didn't take an aeronautics expert to see that the massive airplanes were heading for a near-collision right above the base. Someone yelled out what was on everyone's mind: "Is this really happening?"

It did seem unreal. Both planes were lined up with their

272

gun sides facing each other, like two Man-of-Wars, heading for a final showdown.

Even some of the enemy soldiers stopped to see what happened next. The two planes met right over the burning base. They were both at about a thousand feet high. No more than a hundred feet separated them. They seemed to take up all of the sky.

Both planes opened up at once—and again it was like two old wooden warships unleashing broadsides with all cannons firing. The sky was filled with a fearsome bright light, a storm of brilliant red and orange flashes as three dozen large weapons fired at each other from point-blank range. Both planes were hit—and both shuddered mightily from the hits they'd taken. Both were quickly on fire. But, amazingly, both stayed airborne.

And now, incredibly, both were turning again—both inside-out maneuvers—which would have them pass close again with their weapons pointing at each other.

ANOTHER important goal of the 201st's attack was to get access to the hangar that held the mysterious faux-Nightwatch plane. It was important that the 201st get a look at this aircraft and destroy it, as there was no doubt that it was meant to do no good.

The appearance of the Russian-built gunship had stalled the paratroopers' advance on the two remaining hangars, the one holding the Nightwatch plane and the one containing all the weapons and the two fighter planes. But after finding the gunship hangar empty, Vogel and his men had linked up with 1st Squad, they being the group charged with getting to the weapons hangar. Now, taking advantage of the lull caused by the spectacular encounters of the gunships above the base, Vogel instructed a dozen of his men to gather their wounded and the handful of KIAs and head for the Tank Plane outside the base. Then he took the rest of the combined squad and headed off toward the hangar containing the Nightwatch plane.

Though the fierce battle was still going on, the gunfire had quieted down a bit. A lot of the enemy gunmen had been killed by this time; many by the paratroopers, many by the AC-17, many by their own airplane. But still Vogel knew he'd have to be careful.

He and his men had made it about halfway across the base when the two mighty gunships met once again. If anything they were even closer to each other now. They passed within fifty feet of each other's wingtips and again let fly with everything they had. Though it was almost imperceptible, it seemed to Vogel that the Russian airplane took the worst of it. Gunn had fired first and had physically knocked the Russian plane up and back, causing much of its broadside to go over the top of the American gunship. Both planes had taken major hits, but the Russian airplane was the one that seemed to be faltering.

The AC-17 banked hard left and cleared the area. The Russian plane, though, kept going straight. It had taken a massive hit square on its flight deck. It became unsteady, like it was flying without anyone at the controls. Instead of climbing to get itself over the mountains to the north, it was actually losing altitude and falling off to the west. Vogel let out one loud cry to everyone who could hear him: "Hit the dirt!"

The huge Russian plane flew right overhead. The noise was incredible, and oddly, it started to gain altitude. Going up to about twenty-five hundred feet, it almost looked like it was going to survive. But then there was a string of explosions along its wings as its internal gas tanks began blowing up.

It flew on for about thirty seconds more, but then it slowly turned over and plunged straight down into the small, empty nearby town of Lmono.

AMANDA still couldn't believe what she was seeing.

The Russian-built gunship couldn't have hit the town of Lmono any more squarely had it been aiming at it. So the villagers' instinct had been right. Something bad had been coming in their direction and they'd been smart enough to get out of its way.

The crash's explosion was so violent, even though it was several miles away, it knocked the feet out from under just about everyone involved in the air-base battle. A huge mushroom cloud rose from the impact site. The ground was reverberating like an earthquake. The shock wave alone felt like a hurricane.

But while all this was going on, two other strange things were about to happen.

One was that the victorious AC-17 Fireship, heavily damaged and straining mightily to stay airborne, headed out toward the savannah belching a long stream of black smoke and flame.

Second, just as Vogel and his combined squad of paratroopers were about to advance on the hangar containing the Nightwatch plane, the doors of this air barn suddenly burst open—and the base was assaulted by yet another sound: that of four more jet engines roaring to power.

The paratroopers hit the pavement again as there was a great stirring within the hangar. Suddenly the fake Nightwatch plane emerged and rocketed right by the stunned soldiers.

As it went by Vogel, he could clearly see a pilot in the cockpit, sitting behind the controls. The man had his hand up to his face, intentionally blocking it as he went by. The big jet raced across the tarmac, to the runway, and turned into takeoff mode. Just like that, its engines screamed again; it rumbled down the runway and was off the ground in a flash. It gained altitude quickly and turned due west.

While this was happening, miraculously, the AC-17 had somehow managed to turn around and, smoke and flames and all, was heading back to the secret air base. The two planes crossed within a quarter mile of each other—but the gunship's weapons were pointing in the wrong direction. Still, for a moment it appeared that the AC-17 was trying to turn itself around, in a futile attempt to chase the fake airplane.

But then there was another loud explosion, and more smoke and fire came pouring out of the gunship. It was an unbelievable sight to see the mighty AC-17, the prime aircraft in the 201st, on fire and coming apart at the seams.

But somehow, it wobbled its way back to pointing north and started coming in for a landing at the secret base.

CARDILLO and his tank crews had the best view as the crippled AC-17 went right over their heads.

"Oh man, I don't like this," Cardillo said out loud.

The commander of the tank beside him yelled back: "If anyone can do it, Gunn can . . . I think . . ."

The flaming gunship was barely moving. Pieces of it were falling off its wings and tail section, sending burning embers to the dry grasslands below.

Cardillo had turned to say something to Amanda—when he realized that she was no longer standing in the turret next to him.

He looked forward again and saw her running full speed toward the air base, and at the same time watching the crippled AC-17 pass right over her head.

"Damn!" Cardillo cursed.

He started calling after her—ordering her to come back. Running into the battle zone was absolutely foolish. But either she didn't hear him or she didn't care. It was clear Gunn was either going to crash and die at the base or somehow land in one piece. It was also clear she wanted to be there either way.

The AC-17 finally reached the end of the base's runway, but it was swaying wildly all over the sky. Its left wing clipped the top of one of the cranes used to erect the camo net. This caused the gunship to dip crazily to the left, before righting itself again. Those watching this drama could almost feel Gunn urging the airplane to just keep it together, just for a few more seconds.

And somehow that's what happened. The big plane slammed onto the asphalt and bounced once, twice, three times before its landing gear collapsed and it finally came down for good.

It screeched madly down the runway, smoking heavily and leaving a trail of burning parts before coming to a violent ear-crunching halt.

Paratroopers from all over the base ran to the plane just as all its doors burst open. They all pitched in to help the gun crew get out; some were merely wounded; others were seriously injured.

Gunn and Robinson were forced to crawl out through the plane's smashed windshield. Vogel caught Gunn as soon as he hit the ground. The 201st's CO said one thing: "Who's flying that Nightwatch plane?"

Vogel replied: "We got no idea."

The 82nd CO waved two of his medics over to tend to both Gunn and Robinson. Considering what they had gone through, with just a few cuts and bruises, they were in remarkably good shape.

More depressing, though, was that the great AC-17 gunship lay crumpled on the runway, burning, its fuselage torn and ripped, its wings cracked and burning. Ammunition was going off inside the plane's skeleton, sinking it further into its death throes. Everyone on hand knew it was the end of an era—the plane that in many ways symbolized the 201st was in ruins. It was like watching a great ship sink at sea.

But already other things were happening.

Amanda arrived on the scene, out of breath, but over-joyed to see Gunn alive.

"Are you OK?" she asked him anxiously. "I mean, *really* OK?"

He assured her he was—and he was happy for two reasons: that she was showing great concern for him, but also that he was still breathing. Never would he have thought he could live thorough the aerial Man-of-War duel he'd just fought with the *gunshipski* or the violent crash landing that followed.

Amanda looked at some of his bigger cuts and bruises.

"If only we had some more snake mud," she said to him.

He almost laughed at that—more out of relief than anything.

The battle at the air base was suddenly just about over. There was still some scattering of gunfire, but many of the enemy gunmen were dead, mostly due to the 201st, but many also by their own hand.

Just about every small structure on the base was either burning or smoking heavily. Of the three huge hangars, the one that housed the *gunshipski,* was totally engulfed in flames. Conversely, the hangar that housed all the weapons and the two fighter jets had been virtually untouched.

The hangar closest to where the AC-17 had plowed in was the one that had held the Nightwatch plane. It was mostly unaffected, and empty too—or so they thought. For as the medics actually started working on Gunn's injuries, injecting him with a massive dose of morphine for starters, Amanda happened to look into this hangar—and got the shock of her life.

"You've got to be kidding me," she said. "This can't be. Can it?"

That's when it all came together for her—causing her to immediately grab Gunn away from the medics and start dragging him toward the hangar that housed the two fighter planes.

As she was doing this, she said to Vogel: "Call those lazy asses in the refueling plane and tell them to follow us no matter what."

"Follow you?" Vogel asked, plainly stumped. "Follow you where?"

Amanda didn't reply. It was like she'd been shot out of a cannon.

"And please give me your sat-phone," she said to him, taking the phone right out of his hand.

"What is this all about, Lieutenant?" Vogel said in such a way as to remind her who was the superior officer.

That's when she finally stopped and showed him what she had found inside the Nightwatch plane's hangar.

It was a white Range Rover with a Red Cross on its door.

"Don't you get it?" she asked him directly. "That Nightwatch plane? The yellowcake? That Range Rover? That's *Kaiser* in that Nightwatch plane! That's his MO, right? Cause a lot of havoc somewhere, while he's really going to do something somewhere else? He must have gotten some more yellowcake somehow, made a dirty bomb, and now he's on that plane with it and probably heading for the U.S. And we've got to stop him."

Vogel was trying to take it all in.

"Who's going to stop him?" he asked, baffled. "How?"

"We are," she replied.

She resumed dragging Gunn over to the weapons hangar, leading him right to the oddly designed Russian-built Su-34.

"You can fly anything, right?" she asked him.

"Sure. At least at one time I could," he replied woozily, the morphine suddenly taking effect.

"Then here's your chance for a refresher course," she told him.

That's when he finally realized what was going on.

He looked at the Russian-built fighter-plane, then back at her. "You? Me?" he said. "In that?"

She smiled impatiently. "That's right," she answered. "You and me are going after him—Kaiser. And this plane just happens to be the perfect aircraft to do it with. I used to fly against them when I was at Top Gun up in Fallon. So come on, let's go. He's getting away."

TWO frantic minutes passed. Though his head was swimming in the most pleasant way, Gunn had nevertheless figured out how to hot-start the Su-34 and soon had it taxiing out onto the runway.

He went right by Vogel and Cardillo, who looked up at him in absolute astonishment. They were yelling at him: "You don't even know where that plane is going!"

Amanda leaned across the cockpit and gave Vogel and Cardillo the pinky finger-and-thumb hand signal meaning "Call me."

Then Gunn hit the throttles, and the Su-34 rocketed down the runway and up into the smoky African sky.

The chase was on.

BY the time the Su-34 had disappeared over the horizon, the last few gunmen at the base were cornered in the burned-out ruins of the *gunshipski's* hangar.

There were six of them and they were surrounded by paratroopers. Vogel was quickly on the scene and called for the trapped gunmen to give up, hoping they would see the wisdom in not fighting on, as the paratroopers had yet to capture a single prisoner. But as before, the last holdouts used what was left of their ammunition on themselves, gruesomely committing suicide instead of being taken prisoner.

Vogel and Stanley were the first to reach their bodies. They would have the closest look at the enemy gunmen anyone had had since the attack commenced.

As they already knew, each man was dressed in a black camo combat suit and wearing a wool hat that when pulled down became a ski mask. Some were armed with AK-47s, but these particular gunmen had M16s.

And then Stanley noticed something else.

He looked at the boots on one of the dead men.

He called Vogel's attention to them. "Look at this," he told the 82nd CO. "See anything familiar?"

Vogel studied the man's footwear. Then it hit him.

"Damn," he said under his breath.

The boots were heavily waterproofed.

JUST how Lieutenant Bing was able to nurse the damaged Jump Plane back to Wum Bakim, he would never know.

When he'd flown away from the field of battle, his left wing was totally engulfed in flames. But he and Jackson did two smart things instantly. They shut down both engines on that wing, then shut off all fuel flowing to them. A couple hairy moments passed, but gradually the fire started to die down and eventually it flickered out. This meant they were flying on only one engine, the inner starboard one. It made for very rough riding, but somehow the big plane stayed airborne.

The most frightening part was flying over the edge of the Lost Valley. Bing knew way too much about that place by now, and the last thing he wanted was to crash down there, as it would take five or six decades at least for anyone to find them.

So he and Jackson pulled out every trick in the book. While Bing battled the balky controls, Jackson threw anything not tied down inside the plane out one of the many gaping holes in the fuselage. All kinds of ultrasophisticated and expensive equipment fell into the jungled depths of the *Dashi-dagumba*, including their entire GIR module and all of the spare equipment left behind by the 82nd. Dozens of spare unopened parachutes, helmets and ammo belts spun their way down to the deepest parts of the Lost Valley.

The wounded plane's bad engines might have been shut down, but they were also smoking heavily, all three of them. The result was a long, black contrail cutting across the clear blue sky. The sun was fully up by now, and Bing felt like every eye on Africa was on them.

But somehow they made it back to Wum Bakim.

It took a lot of muscle power in the last two minutes, as they had lost all their backup hydraulics, in addition to all their fly-by-wire systems being shot away. But still they were able to line up on the base's long runway and slowly bring the huge wounded bird in. It was 0705 hours—and Bing had never landed at Wum Bakim in the daylight before. It was a strange experience, because as they finally set down, still smoking and burning in spots, the first thing he noticed was that the runway lights were still on.

Bing gave his retro rockets one last goose, providing enough reverse thrust to slow the big plane down before it went off the other end of the runway and into the river beyond. It was noisy and it was ugly. But finally, they came to a halt.

He and Jackson just sat there for ten long seconds, trying to recover from the ordeal. They were both shaking and bathed in sweat. But they were both very happy to still be alive.

They did a fist bump, and then Bing finally shut down their last good engine.

Jackson told Bing he'd take care of the plane's remaining systems. Bing thanked him and climbed off the flight deck, nearly falling to the tarmac after crawling out the access hatch. He could have kissed the ground, though. That's how happy he was that they had made it back.

He wasn't sure what to do first. He had a bunch of small but bloody injuries, which needed at least some bandages put on them. But he also felt like he should report to Mdosi and Moon in the Ops building and brief them on what had happened. He decided to go to the Ops building first, but for one reason only: He was hoping Mdosi would pour him a tall drink of the scotch he always had on hand.

Or maybe even a couple.

He walked into Mdosi's office ten seconds later to find the AU officer sitting behind his desk, looking very tense. Moon was sitting nearby, also looking extremely apprehensive.

Both were sweating bullets.

Mdosi said: "I'm sorry, Lieutenant."

Bing was confused. "Sorry about what, sir?"

Mdosi nodded toward the other side of the room. Bing turned in that direction and saw a dozen gun barrels pointing back at him.

He almost laughed. "What the fuck is this?"

There were twelve men in all-black uniforms, ski masks and Fritz helmets pointing their weapons at him.

"Drop your sidearm," one of them ordered him. "And then put your hands over your head."

This time Bing did laugh. "This is a joke, right?" he asked Mdosi and Moon.

But both were shaking their heads emphatically. "I'm afraid not," Moon said.

Bing was growing angry. He'd just been to hell and back. He had no use for this bullshit.

"We've already been through all this," he told the dozen men. "Didn't you get the memo? We found what you guys were looking for. We beat the deadline and we've been waiting for you to make good on your deal."

One man stepped forward and looked at Bing like he was from outer space.

"What the hell are you talking about?" he asked. "We got the same thing from these two."

Now Bing was just plain stumped. "What the hell are *you* talking about? Who are you people?"

"We are Delta Force, Unit 66, Detachment 55," the man replied crisply. "We are here under the direct orders of the House Security Committee and the National Security Council. We are to bring you and anyone else connected to the 201st Special Operations Wing back to the U.S. for prosecution on a number of national security crimes. Here's the order—and your arrest warrant."

The guy showed Bing a swath of legal papers. Bing read what little he could understand—and then just turned to Mdosi for some kind of explanation.

But the colonel had none.

Bing pleaded with Moon. "Please explain this to me . . ."

But Moon could only shake his head.

"I wish I could," he said. "But I have no idea what's going on."

PART FIVE

THE SCIENCE
OF CONTRAILS

CHAPTER NINETEEN

DRIVING the Russian Su-34 was like driving a truck—with wings.

It was big, it was heavy. It was noisy and crudely put together.

But it was fast. Very fast.

And that was just one of the problems in this wild goose chase.

That it was most likely the mysterious Adolph Kaiser in the Nightwatch plane made perfect sense to Gunn now. The überterrorist's machinations had been riding just below the surface in everything the 201st had been involved in the last seven days, so why would it change now? It seemed their fates were entwined.

If Kaiser's MO was to cause disruption on a grand scale in order to divert attention from what his real plans were, then, yes, the 201st had got to the X Base just in time. Gunn shuddered to think what the huge *gunshipski* and all the weapons found at the hidden facility could have done to the innocent people of central Africa or even in Darfur.

But while the unit may have interrupted Kaiser's plan for diversion, the phantomlike world terrorist was apparently determined to pull off his grand scheme anyway.

But what was it?

No doubt it had something to do with the document Amanda had found at the hidden facility, the reference to a U.S. Air Force base that had no runway. But Gunn and Amanda were pretty sure there were no U.S. Air Force bases in Africa, or at least none under construction.

Add in that Kaiser's disguised 747 was packed with extra fuel, along with what they now realized were the building blocks for a massive Yellowcake 212 dirty bomb, and the indications were that he was planning to fly a long way to commit his act. And the fact that he had gone through so much trouble to disguise an old 747 jet airliner to look like one of the most secret planes owned by the U.S. government told them his target had to be somewhere in America.

But again, where?

These and other things were what Gunn and Amanda talked about in the first fifteen minutes of their flight in the huge Su-34 fighter-bomber. These things—and just how crazy what they were doing was.

And crazy was the word for it. Gunn knew it and she knew it. But this was her show. An attempt to save the country she loved from disaster. And he was determined to see it through with her.

No matter what.

He had to give her a lot of credit. She'd had this all figured out in a matter of seconds. Seeing the Red Cross truck inside the hangar was all it took for her to put the pieces together and come up with Kaiser being the mastermind behind just about everything that was happening around them.

It was also brilliant of her to think that the Su-34 was the perfect plane with which to chase the fake Nightwatch aircraft—to a point anyway. The Russian warplane was built for long-range missions: It had huge fuel tanks, ultra-long-range radar capability and advanced communications. It even had a kitchen for Christ's sake. Again, it was the RV of fighter-bombers.

But Winnebagos had to stop for gas once in a while, and that was a concern. There was no way they could pursue Kaiser's big plane all the way to the U.S. as is, even with the large amount of fuel the Su-34 had on board.

Which was why Amanda had also had the forethought to tell Vogel to order the refueling plane to follow them in the pursuit. If they could just get on Kaiser's trail, figure out where he was going exactly—and then gas up with the refueling plane—they might be able to catch him and prevent what was sure to be a monumental catastrophe.

The problem was, Kaiser had a head start.

THE first fifteen minutes of the chase had been frantic.

Besides them trying to come up with a plan, and talking about the options, Gunn was trying to learn the basics of flying the enormous Russian plane, and Amanda was using the sat-phone to relay their position to the refueling plane, hoping the crew of the aerial gas truck was listening on the other end and would eventually catch up to them. But whether her messages were getting through or not wasn't clear. At times, she thought she could hear someone on the other end of the line saying: "Yes—OK—we hear you." At other times, though, she couldn't hear any response at all.

Because of this, they didn't have a lot of faith in the refueling plane being a big part of what they were trying to do. Which was not good.

But it also might be purely academic, if they didn't find Kaiser's 747 and get on his tail for real.

* * *

THEY'D thought they'd got lucky just a few minutes after takeoff from the X Base.

On Amanda's suggestion, as soon as they were airborne, Gunn headed northwest, the straightest line to the American mainland, almost five thousand miles away. Just after passing over the coastline of Liberia, they spotted a contrail up at forty thousand feet, also heading northwest. As it turned out, contrails were a science, and Amanda had done a research project on them while at Annapolis. Judging from the deterioration rate of this one and other factors, such as Kaiser's departure time, average speed of a 747, and that no other big planes were around them at that altitude or any other, she was pretty certain this one belonged to the faux Nightwatch plane.

It seemed crazy, to pick one contrail and determine it was their madman. If this had been Bada Bing or Stanley or Robinson or any of the other pilots in the 201st, Gunn would have turned back a long time ago.

But Amanda was sure of it and he was sticking by her, even though with each mile they went west, it became all that much harder for them to return to the firm, dry ground of Africa.

We're ghosts chasing a ghost, Gunn thought, as the last of the African landmass fell away behind them. With a lot of water in between.

FLYING the Su-34 took some getting used to. Gunn's talents as a test pilot were definitely needed, just as a Ferrari owner would need a few instructions on how to drive a tractor-trailer truck.

Even more complicated was trying to get the Su-34's search radar to work. Like everything Russian, it was powerful but overly complicated. It seemed about the size of a big-screen TV and took up most of the space in front of Amanda's seat. It had too many buttons and switches, too many overlapping elements—and some controls didn't appear to do anything at all. It took Amanda nearly thirty minutes just to get it turned on—and at that point they were already two hundred fifty miles off the African coast, still following the contrail at forty thousand feet. When the search screen finally blinked to life, they both let out a whoop. But then, after a half dozen sweeps, they could see no sign of the Nightwatch plane on the screen. It was just too far ahead of them,

"Damn" Amanda said in a whisper. "Maybe this is just a wild goose chase."

Gunn told her not to worry. "Just keep working the knobs. Something will happen."

But trying to work the gigantic radarscope was like doing quantum mechanics with a screwdriver. Again, the Su-34 was built to be an ultra-long-range fighter-bomber, and it was also intended mostly for export sales. So the thought was that everything on board should be as simple as possible. But this was not the case.

"If I could just get this thing to go to its maximum search mode," Amanda said after another twenty minutes of screwing with it—and now nearly an hour into their flight. "Then we might be able to see something as far out as a hundred miles. If we were just able to get a slice of him, we could stick to him like glue. But I can't get this thing to work right . . ."

That's when Gunn just reached over and gave the radarscope a hard *whack!* Incredibly, the screen blinked once, and just like that Amanda was looking at the device's longest range possible.

She stared over at him in amazement.

"How did you know where to hit it?"

"Beats me," he said with a shrug.

She turned back to the scope and started working the

refinement knobs. But then she swore again. "Damn . . . nothing," she said. "This thing is powerful—but he still must be too far ahead of us."

She rubbed her eyes and ran her hands through her hair.

"What should we do?" she asked.

"Do you believe we are on his trail?" he asked her back.

"I really do" was her reply.

"Then we keep going," he said.

THEY flew along like this for another hour, following the contrail, but picking up nothing on the radar screen.

Gunn kept their airspeed at a constant four hundred knots. Even though he was tempted to just boot it and try to catch up to the end of the contrail, he knew that could be disastrous fuel-wise, unless they had a clear indication they were following the right aircraft. The idea now was to just keep pace and hope by some miracle the fuel plane was somewhere close behind them. Only then would they have extra fuel to work with and still have a prayer of landing when they were done.

So there was much apprehension in the cockpit, as he did the flying and she hovered over the radar, praying for something to change. The weird thing was that, though crudely built and oddly designed, the Su-34 had also been made extremely comfortable for the pilots. The flight deck was pressurized, meaning they didn't have to wear oxygen masks. They had plenty of room to move their arms and legs. Their individual zero-G ejection seats even had pulsating massages inlaid in them.

But the interior of the Su-34's cabin was also heated, and two hours into the pursuit, it had become sweltering hot. In among doing all these other things, they'd looked for some kind of air stabilization control in the cockpit, but none could be found. The problem was they were bundled in triple-layered Russian flight suits, and it was getting hotter by the minute.

Finally Amanda couldn't take it anymore. She tapped Gunn's knee and said: "Can you watch everything while I go to the powder room?"

He agreed in an instant. It was strange enough that the big fighter had a small galley and even a place for one of the crew to stretch out and sleep on an inflatable bunk contraption, but it also had a lav.

She disappeared in the back and he kept flying the plane. He'd spotted a coffeemaker in the tiny galley too, and wondered what a cup of coffee would do to him now. He was already buzzing from all the bennies he'd ingested over the past week; enough to keep him awake for a month. The morphine was like icing on the cake. He feared a cup of Russian coffee might put him right over the top. But then again, over the top might be where he wanted to be.

Amanda returned to her seat. In the past, he'd tried to keep his eyes in his head as he didn't want her to see him leering at her the way just about everyone else did. He so much wanted to be different from everyone else.

But this time—this was different. Because what she had done was remove her bulky flight suit, and she was now dressed in just a T-shirt, combat shorts and her flight boots. She had also let her hair down. The T-shirt was already moist with her sweet, clean perspiration and was clinging to her in such a way that Gunn could see she had also taken off her bra.

His heart began beating very fast. *Boom, boom, boom.* It felt like it was coming right out of his chest. She put her helmet back on and strapped back in.

Then without missing a beat she said: "Still nothing on the scope."

Gunn couldn't look away. Here he was, driving this strange plane, chasing a mystery man who was bent on disrupting nothing less than the entire world order, and still he couldn't take his eyes off her.

"He's out there, somewhere," he was barely able to blurt out. He was sure she could hear his heart beating against his rib cage.

Her eyes remained glued on the radarscope—but she said. "I'm much more comfortable now without that Siberian flight suit. So, by all means, feel free . . ."

Gunn couldn't move though.

"I don't think I can stand up at the moment," he said, a bit mysteriously.

THEY flew on.

Amanda finally figured out how to get the long-range search radar to stay on automatic, meaning she could turn her attention to other things. The first thing she did was pull out her BlackBerry and delve into its memory.

"We'd be so much more ahead of the game if we could find out where this guy was going," she said.

It took her more than a few tries and a lot of frustration, which she bled off by shaking her hair back and forth, thus jiggling the upper half of her body. But by sticking with it, pushing buttons like crazy into her keyboard, using the few clues they had about the mysterious pilot and where he might be headed, she finally hit the jackpot . . .

"Oh my God, I think I've found it," she declared.

"His target?"

"Maybe" was her reply.

Then she leaned over, and suddenly Gunn was looking at her BlackBerry screen, her long blond hair cascading all over him. The jet dropped a bit, causing her to fall further into him.

He quickly righted the plane, got it back to flying straight and true.

"See?" she said pointing to the screen. "There are actually two Air Force bases in the U.S. that don't have runways."

"Really? That doesn't seem to make sense," he replied.

He tried to read the screen. It said: "Schriever Air Force Base, Arizona."

"Schriever? Never heard of it."

"Neither have I," she said, returning to her seat. "But here it is: Schriever used to be where the Air Force controlled the Global Positioning System. It's just a bunch of buildings. No runways. Not even a helicopter pad."

Gunn was shaking his head. "But it's in Arizona," he said. "There's no way Kaiser thinks he can cross the Atlantic and then fly across the country to do what he's going to do. Even if he is flying a Nightwatch plane, they'll catch on to him before he crosses the Mississippi."

"I know—but like I said, there's another base just like it," she told him. "It's the replacement for Schriever. In fact they just shifted all controls for the GPS to this place last month.

"Where is it?"

"In Florida," she said. "Right outside Palmwater, down near the Keys. It's called McCune Air Force Base. Here's the picture. It's just like the other place. No runway—just a bunch of buildings. *That's* what Kaiser's going for. He's going to knock out the GPS system. Can you imagine the chaos that will cause?"

A real chill went through Gunn now. Just about everything flying and sailing these days relied on the GPS system to get to where it was going. Thousands of airplanes at any given moment—thousands more ships at sea. Cars, trucks, everything. If the GPS went out at its source—what would happen? Amanda had used the correct term: *chaos*. Which is just what Kaiser sought for the world.

"This really ups the ante," Gunn said. "But it also means that if we suspect that's his target, we can contact someone, anyone, and at least warn them something might be coming. Even if they think we're crazy, they still might do something about it."

Amanda agreed it was the thing to do. But how? The sat-phones were certainly unreliable. Which left only the Su-34's communications suite.

No surprise, it was crankier than the radarscope. No matter what she did to it, Amanda just couldn't get the damn thing to work properly. She *was* able to turn on the microphone and eventually the speakers, no problem. And they could hear people talking on the system. Russian voices. Eastern European voices. Polish. Czech. Some languages they didn't know, and some that didn't seem to be coming from planet Earth.

But try as she might, she couldn't get a message out to anyone who had the common sense or ability to call back. So, it really *was* up to them alone to try to stop the Nightwatch plane.

Even if it killed them both.

And once another sixty minutes had passed, that had become a distinct possibility.

THEY were running out of fuel.

It was almost four hours into their flight and their fuel gauges were sinking more rapidly by the minute. That was the inherent problem with any aircraft. It was always about fuel. Whether you were flying the top-shit fighter or the lowest cargo humper, you could only go so far, depending on how much fuel you were carrying.

Gunn and Amanda knew that if this was indeed Kaiser they were chasing, he had the advantage on them. They'd gotten a peek inside the fake Nightwatch plane; they knew it had many gallons of extra fuel on it. Plus, it was basically an empty shell except for the gas, the explosives and the dirty bomb they were certain he was carrying in its cargo hold. And in fact, the gasoline was probably there as much as part of the explosive element as it was to provide the big plane with extra range. So it became a question of math. The more fuel the Nightwatch plane used, the lighter it got, meaning the more efficient it would be.

It was almost the opposite for them in the Russian fighter. While it had huge fuel tanks and a theoretical range of twenty-five hundred miles, it was heavy and was carrying much more inside than just its fuel tanks, including tons of war-fighting technology. Its engines alone were enormous and sucked up fuel like twin black holes.

Most disheartening, though, was that although Amanda had been calling the refueling plane on the sat-phone on a regular basis, giving out their speed and heading, she'd stopped getting the phantom replies an hour ago.

Once their fuel gauges passed into the critical zone, a grim silence descended on the cockpit. They'd passed their Bingo point—the point of no return fuel-wise—a long time ago, and the ramifications of this were starting to hit home. Amanda remained at her post, quiet but working. She had her eyes glued to the long-range radar screen, while still using the sat-phone to diligently recite their position and speed in relation to their last report. That was the only way she could do it. They weren't sure where they were exactly— ironically the Su-34 was not equipped with GPS—so they could only send out information on where they'd been and hope the dopey refueler crew was able to follow the bread crumbs. So she worked hard and was in constant motion, searching mightily for anything on the radar screen, all while Gunn flew the plane and silently let her be.

But then finally, five hours into their journey, and with the fuel tanks closing in on empty, he felt her hand wrap into his. He looked over at her and found she was crying.

"This was so dumb of me," she said. "Trying to play the hero never really works, does it?"

She looked down at the vast expanse of ocean. "God—I

always wanted to be in the Navy, but never did I think I'd end up lost at sea."

They held hands. Gunn could feel her shaking. They were both exhausted, having run purely on adrenaline—or at least she had—and being caught up in it all. After all, they *were* trying to save the world. But now all the excitement was draining out of them, to be replaced by cold, hard reality.

He squeezed her hand. He knew just saying, *Well, we gave it a shot,* wouldn't be enough.

So, fueled by the last of the morphine and the bennies, he decided to tell her how he felt. How he'd been head over heels about her since the first time they met. How every time they'd talked and every time they'd done something together, he'd been on cloud nine, feet never touching the ground. The words tumbled out awkwardly, but sincerely. He'd never laid himself bare to anyone like this before, never mind the most beautiful woman in the world.

She held his hand throughout his speech. When he was done, she leaned over and kissed him. Then she said: "You believed in me, that's the most important thing. In everything I've done—the Navy, NASA, the modeling business, I never really felt anyone believed in me—until now."

"The world is full of surprises," he told her. "What I've found out is that sometimes it's the most unlikely person who comes through for you in the end."

And at that instant, suddenly, Amanda's borrowed satphone came to life. She answered it on the second beep.

A deeply accented voice on the other end said: "We come to give fuel with you."

Gunn immediately looked over his left shoulder. He couldn't believe it. The old creaky Russian-built aerial refueler was coming up behind them.

He looked back at Amanda. She was glowing. He'd never seen anyone so happy in his life.

She leapt over to his seat and hugged him tightly.

Then she drew back and said: "OK—up!"

"What do you mean?" he asked.

"The good news is that they found us," she told him. "The bad news is now we have to actually hook up with them. I've done it before and it's no job for the faint of heart."

IT was true. Amanda had been through this before and it had not been a pleasant experience.

Since that frightening night over Nigeria, for the most part, the aerial refueler had been little more than a land-based gas truck for the 201st. The unit's C-17s had fueled up plane-to-plane on the ground whenever possible, as no one wanted to go through an in-flight adventure with the old IL-76 and its barely-trained crew unless they absolutely had to. As a result of this and the bad weather, the refueling crew had spent most of the past week napping at Wum Bakim.

But now here they were.

Just in time to save the Americans.

If they could.

Gunn and Amanda switched seats, and what happened next was almost a repeat of her first encounter with the refueler. The long hose was reeled out, and Amanda activated her receptacle pod, after searching forever to find it. Then she moved the bulky fighter up to the hose, which was like trying to juggle a couple cats. A long stream of precious fuel came flowing out of the hose before she could even get close to it, fouling the Su-34's windshield, until the gas droplets froze and blew away.

It took four tries, but somehow, someway, she was able to jam her receptor into the female end of the hose. The fuel started flowing immediately and within five minutes, the Su-34's tanks were full again. Amanda broke off contact and Gunn let out a long whistle of relief. He would have killed at that moment for a glass of Mdosi's scotch.

Then the sat-phone rang again. It was the refueling crew wanting to know how much more gas they would require. Amanda explained the situation to them, calmly and concisely—and somehow they came to understand it all on just the second try. They were searching for the bad guy, she told them. They thought he was just up ahead, but there was no way of knowing for sure unless they sped up and caught him on their long-range radar. And to do that, they needed as much gas as the refueler could give them.

The reply almost brought tears back to Amanda—and Gunn.

"We stay with you," the voice from the refueler said. "We stay as long as you need."

SO they flew along like this, gradually increasing their speed, the refueler always close by. Incredibly, Amanda still had the contrail in sight—always factoring in the wind drift and so on, always feeling that the 747 was just out a little ahead of them, just off the screen.

And it turned out she was right.

Once they'd increased their speed to six hundred knots, flashing out in front of the refueler for a few minutes, they were just able to catch the phantom plane's radar signature on the long-range scope. Amanda let out a whoop when she saw the indication. It was indeed a 747-sized plane they'd been chasing, the same plane that had been leaving the telltale contrail.

By this time, they were not far from land; the U.S. Virgin Islands were just over the horizon somewhere and coming up fast. They had made the dash across the Atlantic from Africa to the Caribbean in a little over six hours.

But now it was time to make their move.

They took on fuel one last time, and for once it went smoothly, with no problems at all. But now Amanda's concern was for the refueling crew. She knew they couldn't possibly have much more gas left for themselves.

"Where will you go?" she asked them.

"Cuba," came the reply. "We will try to make it there. But do not worry. Go catch your bad guy. Save world. We will enjoy sleeping in the sun."

With that the big refueler broke off the connection, blinked its navigation lights and then turned due west. Incredibly, the people they'd discounted the most had come through for them in the end, saving their lives and making it possible to stop Kaiser.

As the big, ungainly plane faded away into the clouds, Gunn looked over at Amanda.

She was crying again.

THEY climbed back into their flight suits, tied down any loose items in the cockpit and made sure they were strapped in tight.

Gunn was back behind the flight controls. He looked over at Amanda and asked: "Ready?"

"More than you'll ever know," she replied.

He crossed his fingers and hit the plane's afterburner.

Suddenly, it was like they were on an amusement park ride or, better yet, starring in a science fiction movie where someone had just hit the button for warp drive. One moment they were gliding along at five hundred mph, the next they were rocketing through the thin air at twelve hundred mph, almost twice the speed of sound.

They didn't have to go very far to find their target. It was thirty seconds tops before they spotted the huge 747 lumbering through the clouds with no idea that it was being stalked. The forward dash had used up loads of fuel, but that didn't matter now.

They knew they had to shoot Kaiser right away. His whole plan of flying this mission in the fake secret government aircraft was obviously based on his talent for bullshit-ting people into believing he was something that he wasn't. These days most air traffic controllers would snap to attention after picking up visual and voice communications from a plane that looked and acted and sounded like a highly classified Nightwatch aircraft.

Meanwhile, here they were, piloting an Su-34, one of the top airframes from a country that was not exactly warm and cozy with the United States. There was no better way to invite a couple dozen F-15 interceptors to show up than flying an unidentified Russian-looking fighter toward the U.S.

So, yes, they had to stop Kaiser here and now.

The Su-34 was carrying two Atoll air-to-air missiles. These were the Russian version of the famous Sidewinder missile. They sought out the heat of the enemy aircraft and made a beeline for it. They also contained a huge warhead, and getting hit by one was guaranteed to ruin your day.

Again, though, Amanda had to go through a quick learning process trying to figure out how to shoot the damn things. But she finally pushed the right buttons and heard a noise, which seemed to indicate that they had a lock on the 747, now just two miles in front of them. Gunn pushed the missile activate button and the left-side Atoll went off its rail.

The missile streaked through the air, all fire and smoke—but it didn't hit the Nightwatch plane. That would have been too perfect.

However, its warhead did explode right next to the 747's starboard wing, and fragments of it penetrated the outboard engine. This started a fire, which spread down the interior of the wing itself and ignited leftover gas fumes in the big 747's empty wing tanks. This, in turn, caused a small ex-plosion, which tore a hole through the top of the wing root. In seconds there was a long stream of heavy black smoke coming from the big plane.

Gunn and Amanda high-fived each other when they saw it.

But the 747 kept on flying.

Gunn fired the second missile. They had fallen behind by now, and it looked like a long shot for the elderly Atoll missile. But the damage done by the first missile had slowed the 747 just enough for the second missile to catch up to it.

They saw a small puff of gray smoke way off in the distance—and then a flash of light. And then, finally, the unmistakable plume of red and yellow flames.

The missile had hit its mark. The big plane was on fire.

Amanda reached over and hugged Gunn again, but then it was right back to business. He goosed the throttle and they moved back to within a mile of the crippled Nightwatch plane. They had no more missiles, and there had never been any ammunition in the plane's big gun, so all they could do now was watch.

The Nightwatch 747 was definitely burning, but would it be enough to cause it to crash into the sea? And would that crash finally kill the phantom terrorist named Kaiser?

They had spotted some land up ahead; Amanda was pretty sure it was Pitts Island, a small spit of sand located off the most southeastern part of the U.S. Virgin Islands. For a moment, it appeared that the smoking 747 was starting to veer in that direction. But then suddenly there was a flash of light from the top of the big airplane. It wasn't another explosion. Rather it was the plane's ejection seat, installed so that when Kaiser was beginning his dive on the GPS facility, he could escape the plane before it hit its target.

But now, with his aircraft on fire and his plans dashed, Kaiser was punching out early.

As soon as they saw his parachute open, the big 747 just turned over on its right wing and went straight down. It hit the water with a tremendous crash about a mile off the coast of Pitts Island. There was no explosion, no huge cloud of yellowish radioactive smoke. Whether the airplane had ever contained a yellowcake dirty bomb or not, it was now headed for a watery grave at the bottom of the warm Caribbean Sea.

Meanwhile, the pilot was descending peacefully to that same warm water, heading for a spot not a half mile off the idyllic beaches of the isolated tropical island.

Gunn immediately put the big fighter into a dive, and in seconds they were circling around the spot where Kaiser was just hitting the water.

To their dismay it looked like a perfect landing. They could even see him discarding his chute and inflating a life raft.

This was not good.

If Kaiser made it to the island, they might never catch him, and he'd be free to terrorize the world again. It was, after all, his myth that was most important to him, just the fact that people would know he'd gotten so close to the U.S., with what might have been an immense dirty bomb, would prolong that legend and the fear of him for decades.

Gunn just couldn't let that happen. Kaiser had caused enough misery in the world.

So, completely on impulse, and with a little urging from the drugs in his system, he reached over and touched Amanda's arm and said to her: "Block your eyes and get ready to fly this thing—and then land as soon as you can."

She knew instantly what he was going to do—but before she could say anything, he hit the ejection button . . .

He thought he would have a second or two before it actually activated. But, as always, nothing was ever certain when it came to Russian equipment.

He began to mouth the words to her: *I love you—very much . . .*

But the ejection seat went off just about the second he hit the button, and before he could say anything, he was rocketed out of the aircraft.

* * *

THE Russian ejection seat worked just as all Russian-made things did: roughly and powerfully. Gunn was thrown up and away from the Su-34, and began tumbling immediately. His chute did open—eventually. But it took way longer than he thought it should. He found himself wondering: How do those 82nd Airborne guys do it? But soon enough he was floating down to the big blue ocean below.

He spotted Kaiser's life raft still about a quarter mile off the tip of the tropical island. He started twisting and turning his body and manipulating the chute's cords, trying to steer himself close to the raft.

He was partially successful in this, landing about a hundred yards away. But he hit the water way too hard, plunging about fifteen feet below the surface and seeing little birdies all the way down. He fought his way back up and tried to inflate his Russian-made Mae West on surfacing, but his head was spinning and, typically, the life vest was complicated. He started pulling cords and pressing buttons and twisting switches, but nothing seemed to work. Finally, the thing just inflated on its own.

He started swimming madly toward the raft, though his vision was blurry and his head felt like someone was smashing it with a hammer. He could just barely see Kaiser looking out at him, crash helmet on, sun visor pulled down, anonymous to the end. This might be easy, Gunn thought. But then he saw Kaiser's right arm rise up, and then little splashes of water were going off around Gunn's head. It took him a few seconds to realize Kaiser was shooting at him.

He ducked underwater to avoid the bullets, but his life vest began fighting to keep him afloat. This problem was solved when one of Kaiser's bullets grazed the vest, deflating it very quickly. Gunn slipped the whole thing off and went underwater again, just before two more bullets zipped by him.

He started swimming like mad—before he realized it had been a long time since he'd been swimming in anything other than a hotel pool. He was exhausted in seconds.

Bullets were still coming his way, though, and it was around this time that he remembered that he was armed too. He managed to get his Glock pistol out, but in the process it went off, his own bullet zinging so close to his ear that he nearly lost all hearing in it.

Still he swam on, trying to shoot and move his arms at the same time. Kaiser shot at him twice more, and then stopped. Gunn had made the mistake of not counting how many bullets had been fired at him, but he was sure it was at least six, and maybe eight. In any case, unless Kaiser was packing extra rounds, he was most likely out of ammunition by now.

Gunn finally reached the life raft, two bullets left in his own pistol—but he found the raft was empty. He was about to climb up into it when he felt a tug on his leg. His first thought was that a shark was pulling on him. Then he was suddenly under the surface again—and Kaiser's hands were around his throat.

Sheer anger activated all of the adrenaline, all the amphetamines and all the morphine in Gunn's body. He began fiercely pummeling his attacker underwater even as Kaiser was fiercely pummeling him back. Kaiser still had his crash helmet on and his visor pulled down; hitting him in the head made no sense. So Gunn concentrated on punching him in the stomach, elbowing him in the chest, kicking him in the groin.

Then Gunn saw the flash of a knife—Kaiser was trying to stab him. By pure luck, Gunn was able to pull the knife out of the terrorist's hand, but at the same moment, he lost his grip on his pistol and watched it sink below him.

Then Kaiser disappeared, swimming away in the now murky, churned-up water.

Gunn surfaced, sucked in as much air as he could in a short amount of time, then went back down again, knife between his teeth, looking for his assailant. Suddenly there was a huge *boom!* and the water around him began vibrating violently. The sonic disturbance was so intense, he thought his eardrums would be blown out.

He surfaced again and looked to the north, just in time to see pieces of the Su-34 hitting the water a half mile away.

He was stunned.

Did that just happen?

The Su-34 crashed?

Why? Did his ejecting cause something to go wrong?

Had it finally run out of gas?

Amanda . . . he killed her?

He started to go into a state of shock . . . and suddenly, he was slipping below the surface, arms and legs gone limp. For a moment he considered just letting go and sinking and ending it all. He couldn't live with himself if what he'd just seen was real.

But, in the next instant, he knew this was not the way to go. Not yet. He had to do one more thing before he died. He struggled back up to the surface. It took a mighty effort, but finally he broke through and started breathing again.

That's when he saw that the bright orange life raft was not more than fifty feet away from him and Kaiser was back in it.

Perfect, he thought, taking the knife from between his teeth. Now I'm really going to kill him . . .

All the anger and frustration and now the loss that Gunn felt because of this man came boiling out of him. He remembered the words of Nelson, the park ranger. He'd told Gunn that he had survived the horrendous copter crash because God or someone higher up still needed him to do something important. Now that made sense to him.

What he needed to do was to get rid of this guy, this person so dedicated to causing human misery that he was indeed the Devil himself.

But as soon as Gunn surfaced and grabbed the edge of the life raft, knife ready to strike, he saw the blur of the man, still wearing his crash helmet, his visor pulled down, pointing a pistol at him.

Gunn's pistol . . .

"It's over, Superman," the voice said.

He started to squeeze the trigger . . .

But then suddenly Kaiser was engulfed by a cloud of smoke.

He started shaking uncontrollably. He turned around and Gunn could see a hole burning its way through his back. It was getting bigger and bigger, and flames were shooting out of it. Kaiser's clothes caught on fire; now he was burning up right before Gunn's eyes. The heat was so intense, it melted the helmet to his head, and the sun visor to his face. He let out one long, ear-piercing scream and then fell backward into the water.

Gunn couldn't believe it. He was two seconds away from getting a bullet in his head—and suddenly Kaiser goes up in a puff of smoke.

That's when he saw someone hanging on to the other side of the life raft.

Someone with long, wet, blond hair.

It was Amanda, her parachute harness floating in the background.

She was holding a flare gun. It was huge—and Russian-made.

And with it, she had just shot Kaiser—and saved Gunn's life.

She yelled across to him: "Now we're even!"

They climbed into the life raft and held each other for a very long time.

"How did you get here?" he kept asking her. "How . . . ?"

Finally she replied: "Didn't you know swimsuit models actually have to know how to swim?"

He kissed her firmly on the lips. She broke away only long enough to say: "But that's the last time I want to use a Russian ejection seat. I think I'm a couple inches shorter after that experience."

THEY drifted along for at least five minutes in the gently rolling water, just holding each other, not letting go.

Then, they paddled back over to where Kaiser's still-smoldering body was floating. Gunn grabbed it and tied it to the raft using a lace from his boot.

Finally Amanda said to him: "What are we going to do now? Shouldn't we try to call somebody?"

And that's when it got *really* weird . . .

She told him she'd lost Vogel's sat-phone while bailing out of the Su-34. So basically their only link to the outside world was Downes's sat-phone, which Gunn had kept in his boot the whole time. Feeling they had nothing to lose, he pushed the activate button—and suddenly heard ringing.

But it was not so much on the other end. The ringing was also coming from another sat-phone nearby.

They both looked at each other and then at the body riding alongside the life raft. Amanda went through its pockets and fished out another sat-phone. They were both stunned.

This phone was ringing.

"No freaking way . . ." she breathed.

That's when they finally pried off the melted-on mask and saw the face of the man named "Kaiser" for the first time.

It was Colonel Downes.

THEY hand-paddled the life raft toward the island. Since they were going with the tide, it might have been the calmest, most relaxing thing either of them had done in weeks.

"It makes sense—now," Amanda said, doing her best to ride the waves into shore. "This character was famous for getting other people to do his dirty work, including us. He knew if anyone could find the Yellowcake 212 in the jungle, we could. When we found it for him—he went and took it, and then greased the place with the *gunshipski*. No wonder its engines were hot when I touched them yesterday. I just wonder if that means al Qaeda's Mr. Big is just a puddle of goo somewhere in the Lost Valley. If so, then something good came out of this."

"I hope so," Gunn said. "But I have to think about those people defending the X Base. Or the special ops guys who took over Wum Bakim. Or even the refueling crew. Maybe we were all innocent victims. Maybe he lied to us all."

They eventually reached the beach, pulling the raft and Downes's body up above the waterline. They tipped the raft over to cover the charred corpse, then they both collapsed to the wet sand.

"I'm not sure," Gunn said, finally looking around, "but I think we *could* be on U.S. soil. I mean, it might be the very farthest tip of the most eastern part of the U.S. Virgin Islands, just barely the U.S., but . . ."

"But that's good enough for me," she said, gently interrupting him. She hugged him tightly and said, "Thank you for getting me home."

Another passionate kiss followed, but par for the course, it was interrupted by Downes's sat-phone ringing.

"Who in the world could this be?" he asked, hitting the activate button.

It was Moon, calling Downes's phone.

He was more than astonished when Gunn answered.

"What the hell are you doing answering this guy's phone?" Moon asked Gunn incredulously.

"How the hell did you get this number?" Gunn asked back.

"I asked you first," Moon replied.

Gunn tried to explain what had just happened—but Moon cut him off before he could get halfway through his story. The diminutive intelligence officer was major-league pissed.

"We've all been arrested," he told Gunn. "And this time it's for real. I'm sitting in Mdosi's office right now with half of Delta Force around me—they were able to come up with this number because they don't believe our story. But I'll tell you this: Downes is a total fraud. He screwed us. In fact, I think he's connected to Kaiser somehow. We got evidence of this."

Gunn almost started laughing. "We are way ahead of you on that one."

Finally, he was able to finish his story about shooting down the fake Nightwatch plane and discovering Kaiser and Downes were one and the same.

There was a long silence at the end of the phone. Gunn knew Moon was putting it all together, just as they had. Downes being Kaiser explained everything, including the real Delta Force showing up to arrest the unit.

"So?" Moon said after the long pause. "What do we do now?"

Gunn replied: "Tell Delta to cool their jets and suggest that the colonel give them all a drink. When they hear our story, they'll be giving us medals, guaranteed. We'll explain it all when we get back to civilization."

"Back to civilization?" Moon asked. "But when will that be?"

Gunn looked around; except for the fact that there was a dead body nearby, he and Amanda were sitting on a little piece of paradise.

"Maybe tomorrow," he said. "Or the next day."

He started blowing into the phone's mouthpiece, pretending that he was losing the connection.

"Gotta go," he yelled into the phone. "Talk soon."

Then he turned the phone off and tossed it away from him.

He lay back down with Amanda. A passing rain shower went by, very quickly, dousing them. It was refreshing while it lasted.

"I wish I'd brought my beach blanket," Gunn said to her. "You look a little chilly."

Amanda thought for a moment, then said: "We don't have a blanket—but we have this."

She reached into her back pocket and came out with the plastic bag containing the American flag they'd found in the crashed B-24.

They unfolded the flag and wrapped it around themselves.

"So, how do you feel—being a rich man?" she asked him.

"What do you mean?"

"The fifty million dollars," she said. "You know, for the capture of Adolph Kaiser—dead or alive? We can split it fifty-fifty. And after taxes, it will only be about fifteen million or so each. But still, that kind of money can buy a lot of things."

Gunn smiled, then pulled her closer and tightened the flag around them.

"I've already got everything I need," he said.